Praise for *The Potrero Complex*

"A near-future, post-pandemic novel of lost lives and liberties, *The Potrero Complex* speaks directly to the challenges of contemporary life. Amy Bernstein has written a scarily prescient novel that deftly explores the fraught connections between individuality, society, public policy, and technology."

–Courtney Harler, Harler Literary LLC

THE POTRERO COMPLEX

Amy L. Bernstein

Regal House Publishing

Published by
Regal House Publishing, LLC
Raleigh, NC 27587

Printed in the United States of America

ISBN -13 (paperback): 9781646032501
ISBN -13 (epub): 9781646032518
Library of Congress Control Number: 2021943784

Interior layout by Lafayette & Greene
Cover imagesand design © by C. B. Royal

Regal House Publishing, LLC
https://regalhousepublishing.com

Printed in the United States of America

For Clifford and Hannah

“Step aside, please, while our officer inspects your bad attitude.
You have no rights that we are bound to respect.
Please remain calm, or we can’t be held responsible
for what happens to you.”

—Harryette Mullen, “We Are Not Responsible”
from *Sleeping With The Dictionary*

1

MISSING: A teenaged girl with lanky, blonde hair and a sunburst tattoo on her cheek.

The holographic posters, brighter than day itself, lit up the air on every block of Main Street. They were the first thing Rags Goldner noticed as she and her partner, Flint Sten, arrived in Canary.

The girl's name was Effie and she was sixteen.

Effie's pixelated image beamed down at Rags like a celebrity unaware that her fifteen minutes of fame were up.

Rags refused to give a damn about the missing girl who, after all, she didn't know. Nor did she know much about the town, Canary, where the driverless ShareCar she and Flint had leased for their move had brought them. But missing kids make news, and as Canary's newly imported one-and-only newspaper editor, Rags knew she'd be expected to do something about it. Which meant she wouldn't control the news hole on day one. Which meant all kinds of people would come at her to do one thing or another.

Rags hadn't been in town five minutes and already she could tell things were going to get complicated—and complicated was the very thing she and Flint were trying to get away from. Damn all the politicians and peacekeepers and their gatekeeping bullshit, she thought.

As the car made a final turn toward its programmed destination, Rags's twitch flared up: the muscles in her upper left cheek and the outer corner of her left eye performed an uncontrolled little dance. "Ah, crap," she said. "Turning Main Street into Times Square won't help them find the girl. What a waste. And all that light pollution." She stretched her face, willing the twitch to stop.

Flint held up his dataphone and aimed it at one of the digital posters as they cruised by. The static image of Effie sprang into augmented-reality motion: she turned her head, blinked, and laughed.

"Stop doing that, Flint," Rags said. "Just don't." *No way that girl, out there somewhere, is smiling.*

"Don't get spun up so fast." Flint looked over at her for the first time in hours. Their connection was like a faulty wire, fritzing on and off. "Give yourself some room to ramp up," he said, putting his hand on top of her head in a familiar gesture: simmer down. It helped. The twitching nearly stopped. "We haven't even come to a full stop yet. Pace yourself."

"Well, look," Rags said. "They've plastered her face everywhere. Probably been like that for weeks."

"You think the story about this girl has gone cold, right?" Flint said. "What do you call that?"

"Beat up. I'm guessing the story's beat up. The first thing I'm going to hear is that they want me to flog it some more. Remind me, why are we doing this?"

"Let's not," Flint said, looking back down at his screen. "Anyway, it was your idea."

As the ShareCar rolled noiselessly down Main Street, Rags saw just one person hanging around the deserted downtown: a woman standing on a corner who appeared to be waiting. For what? Rags wondered. As they slowly passed by, Rags caught a dead look in the woman's eyes. A block further on, Rags watched a man and a woman, both in shabby coats, as they appeared to argue, their faces contorted with anger. The man handed the woman a bicycle pump. She handed him in return a loaf of bread. *What kind of town is this?*

The ShareCar parked curbside at 326 Main Street. For well over a century, the little brick building, sandwiched between other little brick buildings, had housed the *Canary Courant.* A chatty little newspaper, the *Courant*, as Rags knew from her research, printed anything and everything within the bounds of what people once called 'common decency' about the town of Canary, a tiny hamlet in the northwestern corner of Maryland, not far from the Pennsylvania border. The kind of town that flew under the radar for anyone who did not live there.

The fact that the *Canary Courant* was still a going concern in 2030 was astounding, even mysterious, and a key reason that Rags was here. Though perhaps not the only reason. The paper's survival was even more of a puzzle when one considered that the town itself, which had been shriveling for decades, was now skeletal. The pandemic, which everybody called The Big One, had raged for nearly five years. It hollowed out an already hollowed-out place, killing off over two-thirds of the elderly population living out their days in Canary. Those folks never knew what hit them—their dreams of slipping into gracious idleness on their front-porch rockers, eating breakfast on the cheap at the town diner, destroyed in an agony of fever and blood.

On Canary's rural outskirts, on their way into town, Rags had seen the crematorium, a hulking cinderblock rectangle erected for one single purpose: to incinerate the infected dead into piles of decontaminated black ash. She was sure Flint missed it—though it was very hard to miss, rising up from a flat expanse of undeveloped land—just as he'd missed seeing Effie until she pointed it out. *Like I'm his goddamn tour guide.*

Now, nearly two years after The Big One had been officially declared over, Rags suspected that Canary's survivors were like a mouth full of missing teeth—families broken by a plague that took not merely the elderly but also children and their parents with a seemingly vicious and terrifyingly random determination. With an emphasis on *random.* Survivors everywhere were known as "Luckies," though Rags only ever used that term in its most ironic sense.

And yet, even in a near ghost town like Canary, in a still-brittle economy, in a world where print media was a rare novelty, the ink-on-paper edition of the *Canary Courant* lived on, as quirky and creaky as Miss Havisham in the attic, each folded issue tossed at sunrise every Wednesday and every other Sunday into doorways and onto walkways by a young father and son living on gig income.

Rags deliberately suppressed her own journalistic instincts when it came to figuring out how this newspaper managed to keep going years past its natural expiration date. Turning a blind eye to its improbable existence was both expedient and convenient for her. She knew that income from print ads—about as old-fashioned as you could get—was the sole reason the paper was able to keep going. It surely wasn't due to subscription revenue. But she didn't know why anyone would buy print ads in a tiny newspaper serving a dying community in a digital world. There'd be time, she figured, to get to the bottom of that.

The main thing was that this improbable job as the *Canary Courant*'s editor came her way at a time when she and Flint were looking for an escape hatch that would take them away from the exhausting hysteria and suffocating autocracy that made post-pandemic, big-city living unbearable in countless ways. They came to Canary in search of a simpler life—though Rags, if pressed, could not readily have defined what that would look like. *Freedom from fear? Freedom to forget?* She kept these notions to herself because she did not think Flint would admit to any of it—let alone acknowledge the possibility.

Rags had worried before they arrived that an out-of-the-way place like Canary might have borne an influx of people seeking—or imagining—that this place would prove to be some kind of oasis. But from the little she'd seen so far, there was nothing oasis-like about this town. The garish and intrusive billboards of the missing Effie radiated an anxious *thrum*, nothing like a small-town welcome.

Rags and Flint left the ShareCar with programmed instructions to continue on and wait for them at the house they were renting a few blocks from Canary's minuscule town center. The entire move, including Rags's new job, had been planned remotely, so this was their first time actually in Canary. In the grand scheme of things, given the terrifying and unpredictable upheavals they'd already lived through, moving hundreds of miles away to a new place sight unseen didn't feel at all risky.

From the outside, the newspaper office mimicked the virtual

reality images Rags had already seen online. A plate-glass window with old-fashioned gold lettering rimmed in black spelled out *Canary Courant. Since 1910*. Rags doubted there was anything very "current" about it; the very name advertised its status as a relic with a pretentious echo of French. Rags wondered who else knew that *courant* in French had more than one meaning—not just "current" but also "ordinary." Someone must have had the lettering on the window repainted many times over the years—and who even knew how to do that sort of thing, anymore?—but this was a line item Rags wasn't going to worry about. She was here on purpose yet still felt faintly ridiculous about the whole thing.

All this ye-oldy feel-good yester-year crap, she thought. Some kind of amusement park for blinkered folks. A post-apocalyptic Disneyworld? Or maybe Westworld—a place where you could trick yourself into relaxing, just for a moment.

Yet here she was, along with her IT-guru partner Flint, a software developer steeped in AI arcana, who was definitely not the ye-oldy type. Fitting in, for both of them, was beside the point. Rags figured they'd both settle for some kind of new equilibrium. She waved her dataphone in front of the digi-lock and the heavy front door swung open. The newspaper office was a step up from the threshold because, Rags learned later, the floor had been reinforced a century ago to support the heavy metal printing presses that used to take up a third of the space with their loud, clackety racket.

As Rags entered the square-shaped newsroom, the old floor creaking, a woman likely more than twice Rags's age—a surprise in and of itself, in this day and age—stood up quickly from a battered wooden desk, her chair scraping against the floor. Rags knew only her first name, Merry. She was tall with broad shoulders, like a swimmer, dressed in loose-fitting, wrinkled clothes, her hair silver-gray and so long it touched her buttocks.

"You're here," Merry said with a slightly accusatory edge that did not escape Rag's notice, as though she'd been doing something she shouldn't.

"Yup," Rags said as she scanned the room. She made a quick mental list of all the things she intended to change. Rags hated clutter the way healthy people hate cancer: it was offensive, invasive, and should be eliminated quickly and surgically. The heavy furniture would have to go, and the old-fashioned filing cabinets, and the shelf of tacky journalism awards—the fake-gold winged angels, the stupid quill pens mounted on blocks of glass. Rags guessed that most if not all of the people who'd won those awards were long dead, one way or another. She'd call someone as soon as possible to haul all this crap away. The place looked like a mausoleum, for chrissakes. And that told her all she needed to know about Merry, who radiated the territorial energy of a fox guarding its cubs.

"I've got tomorrow's front page made up on screen," Merry said, standing rigidly by her desk. "I suppose you want to see it." Rags saw Flint make a tiny, familiar gesture: flicking on his ear discs (he'd insisted on upgrading from old-school earbuds), so he could drown out the voices around him and listen to the soundtrack of his choice. With this personal sound cushion enveloping him, Flint glided around the room like a restless ghost, ignoring the two women, fingering every piece of tech there was, and there wasn't much. Rags turned her attention to Merry—watching her watching Flint, to see how much this invasion of Merry's claimed space unsettled her. Rags didn't bother to introduce them, as Flint wasn't likely to visit the newsroom again.

"Is it all about the missing girl?" Rags asked.

"Is there another big story in town I've missed?" Merry asked, her blue-gray eyes staring icily at Rags. "Because if so, be my guest. You've got two whole hours until we send the file to the printers." Merry stepped away from her desk, as if inviting Rags to step in. Rags read the gesture as it was intended: *What the fuck do you know?*

Well, this wasn't going to be pretty. In that moment, Rags had to admit to herself that while she thought she longed to live in a place where she could pursue small stories of no consequence, instead of big ones that traded in life and death, she was never going to check her personality at the door. She wouldn't look for trouble, but she wouldn't back away from a fight, either, especially if she knew going into it that she had the upper hand. She was editor-in-chief, after all, not Merry—a holdover from a previous regime with an ill-defined job, as far as Rags knew.

Rags sat down at a battered desk nearly identical to Merry's and began opening drawers, which contained random bits of long-obsolete office junk: Post-It notes, ballpoint pens, paper-clips, a box of peppermint Tic-Tacs. Rags popped a Tic-Tac in her mouth and bit down hard; it was stale and tasteless.

"That's Freddy's desk," Merry said.

"You mean it was," Rags said.

"For a long time, yeah. He was a damn good copy editor. Nothing got past Freddy. That's what everybody said."

"Except The Big One, I'm guessing," Rags said, without an ounce of sympathy. "Snuck right up on him."

"Yeah, it did," Merry said flatly, turning back to her screen. "So what's your plan, Polly?"

"Don't call me Polly. Call me Rags."

"I was told the new editor-in-chief is named Polly," Merry said, as if trying to catch Rags in a lie. "I wasn't told anything about somebody named Rags."

"Yet here I am," Rags said, rising from Freddy's chair. She stood behind Merry and looked at the screen. "How many stories on this girl, Effie, have you run this month, Merry?"

"We try to post something every week."

"Why?" Rags asked.

"Why? Because we're trying to flush out new leads, Pol—Rags."

"Are there any?" Rags asked, scrolling around the digital home page of the *Courant*. Merry hovered over her, as though she feared Rags would break something.

"Not in over a week," Merry said.

"So it's a beat-up story but you keep milking it for, what, sympathy?"

"No!" Merry said, turning red. "You don't have any children, do you? Because if you did, you'd—"

"Bury it," Rags said.

"You want me to bury the lead story? And replace it with what?" Merry's cheeks flushed. She bit her lower lip. Rags noted how little it would take to get her really and truly riled up.

By this point, Flint had found an ancient PC from 2010 sitting on a dusty windowsill and he was taking it apart, down to the motherboard and its old components. Rags knew he was going to wait her out, and this would keep him happily occupied until she was good and ready to leave. He was patient in this type of situation, which Rags appreciated; his tolerance of her own need to press on, push hard, was essential to balancing them out. Maybe here, finally, she'd find a way to press less, though the situation was not promising in that respect.

Rags touched Merry's screen to scroll through the pages of the main news well. It was only a couple of pages long before you hit sports, the crossword (unkillable), and then those unaccountably robust print ads listing everything from flying lessons to bizarre personals. She told Merry to make the lead a story she'd spotted about a leaking septic tank and to bury the Effie story right before the sports section. The need for the switch was obvious. The Effie story had had its day, and anything that remotely threatened public health, like a septic tank problem, belonged well above the fold. It was a thin fold, in any case, despite the ads.

"And when the next kid goes missing, you want us to bury that too?" Merry asked.

"What do you mean, the next kid?" Rags asked.

"It's going to happen," Merry said, biting her lip.

"You don't know that."

"You don't know *anything*," Merry said.

"Then tell me, Merry. Tell me what I don't know."

Rags could see Merry's chest rising and falling, as if she was struggling to hold something in. But Merry said nothing.

"Switch the stories," Rags said. There was no way she'd back down and let Merry have her way. And besides, if there was nothing new to report on the Effie case, then there really wasn't a compelling reason to give the story the banner headline for the week. Rags had no qualms about her decision. "Flint, let's go find our new home."

Flint had his head deep inside the guts of the old PC he'd found. She called to him again. He straightened up, dusted off his hands, and followed Rags out without a word to Merry, leaving the deconstructed computer in bits and pieces on the desk.

2

Blood is pooling around Rags's feet. It's everywhere, seeping into her shoes, coating her flesh, penetrating her bloodstream like undulating black snakes. She looks down, watching a vicious invader colonize her body. Her limbs grow cold and numb; she is paralyzed. When the toxin reaches her lungs, she cannot breathe.

Rags woke suddenly, panting and sweating. She could not remember where she was. The room was dark and unfamiliar. But Flint was there, asleep beside her. She shook him. He woke to her rapid breathing.

"The dream?" Flint asked, cradling her in his furry arms. He gently placed his wide thumb on her twitching eye. "It's been a long time."

"I thought I left it behind in the city," Rags said, forcing herself to take deep, slow breaths. "Coming here, starting over, the whole idea is to forget."

"You need time. We both do."

"Nothing fazes you," Rags said, sounding almost angry. "How do you do that? Where do you put it all?"

Flint stroked Rags's dark brown hair, thinned by stress over the last few years. "Oh, I have my demons."

"Do you? I never see them."

"Maybe you're just not looking," Flint said lightly.

Maybe I don't know where to look, Rags thought. Or maybe you've buried them so deep, you can't find them either, the lurking demons.

"Now go back to sleep," he said.

"Hold me," she said softly, fighting the sense of shame that accompanied her need. Flint curled into her; they lay quietly. They had not lain like this, entwined, for a long time. A minute later, Rags heard Flint's deeply even sleep-breaths. She lay awake until dawn revealed the opened suitcases and cardboard boxes strewn around their new bedroom.

The rented house was nothing special: two stories, weathered white wooden clapboard with black shutters, a cracked slate roof, a slightly damp basement, and no attic. The fireplaces in the living room and bedroom had been sealed up long ago, and a dank chill penetrated the house even on sunny days. Like everything else in Canary, the house was an anachronism, built in the very early twentieth century and still hanging around, the worse for wear, a third of the way into the following century. It sat a few yards back from a quiet street, flanked by nearly identical houses on either side. The entire block had obviously been built around the same time, when Canary still meant something to a fair number of people, when a small town still had a bright future and its residents wouldn't let anybody tell them otherwise.

Rags knew the only thing Flint really cared about in their new home was unfettered access to the lightening-fast satellite-based info highway that was vital to his consulting work. Back in the city, they'd had standard IoT—internet-of-things connectivity linking all their appliances, including the refrigerator, thermostat, and lights. In their Canary house, the appliances that came with the place were too old to be smart. The refrigerator emitted a hum that was anything but high tech; it was merely the unending complaint of an aging condenser motor working hard.

Exhausted and wired at the same time, Rags crept downstairs to make coffee. The coffee maker and a bag of ground beans had been the unpacking priorities the night before. Looking around, Rags realized they hadn't brought much with them, as there wasn't much they needed. Disasters have a way of forcing you to cull your possessions, to strip down to the essentials so it's easier to flee. A few boxes of kitchen basics, clothing, and linens were really all they had and all they'd brought. Everything else of importance—like reading material—was in their cloud. Apart from basic appliances, the house was already minimally furnished with a bed, two bureaus, a few tables, chairs, and lamps. Rags did not know anything about the previous occupants, and she didn't want to know. The front door bore a blinking green disk—an official certificate of sanitation—so she knew it had been thoroughly disinfected. For whatever that was worth.

Rags brought a mug of coffee into the small living room, which was more like an old-fashioned parlor where the mistress of yore would have received guests on a dull and endless Sunday afternoon, or so Rags imagined. She was supposed to take her temperature every morning, first thing—everyone was. But Rags had quit the habit over a year ago. *Enough was enough.* Flint kept it up, maintaining a meticulous chart going back years. He charted his personal data against worldwide averages—hundreds of data points forming the peaks and valleys of his graph. Rags didn't see the point, but this was vintage Flint.

She turned a heavy upholstered chair, its dim flower-printed fabric nearly worn to shreds, so that she could face the window looking out onto the quiet street. She noticed for the first time that two cherry trees stood in the small front yard—one of Maryland's natural wonders that had been impervious to disaster. They bore small clusters of tight-fisted blush-pink blossoms, nearly ready to burst in the fair spring morning.

The sight of those trees filled Rags with a rare sense of peace and hope. She felt her shoulders drop. She wished the feeling could last forever. She wished she could carry it around with her all day, into the office, out onto the streets of Canary, where the news of the day lay waiting to be discovered and explained. But this was a luxury she did not believe she could afford. Vigilance equated to survival; hard emotional armor was necessary to cope with the unknown, head-on—even if that amounted to nothing more than a leaking septic tank. A vision of the missing Effie, wide-eyed, silently imploring, obscured her view of the cherry trees. *They should not ask me or expect me to…* She pushed the thought aside.

Flint padded in to join her, bearded and hairy-chested, his

jeans unbuttoned. Rags pointed to the cherry trees and smiled. He smiled in return, and let out a long, slow breath, as if to calm them both. "You chose well," Flint said.

"We got lucky—for once."

"You know I don't believe in luck. There's only—"

"What is," Rags said. "I know."

"I'm going to set up over there." Flint gestured toward a corner of the parlor flanked by a window and the old fireplace mantel. She remembered he'd said the same thing back in the city, when they were moving in together the first time. Did he remember too? "Good light. I'll have a great view of all the parades."

"Sure thing," she said. "Marching bands, floats, kids spinning batons." They both knew there'd be no parades any time soon. Maybe not ever. Maybe that was yet another way the world had been changed.

"Maybe you can write a story about that marching band, about the girl who plays, oh, trombone." He was trying. She could see that. Not that she'd touch a story like that in a million years. She'd get somebody else to do it, keeping her powder dry for the shit that mattered.

"I should get to the office," Rags said, not moving. "I want to watch all that crap get taken away. I don't trust this Merry person. She might try to stop them."

"You wanted this, Rags," Flint said. "Give it a chance."

"You know me," she said. "Guns blazing. Then we'll see."

"My temp's normal, by the way," Flint said. He'd stopped reminding her to take hers months ago, when it became clear she wouldn't comply any longer.

"I figured."

"Just one less thing for you to worry about," he said.

"I wasn't worried."

The two of them sat side by side for another moment before Rags rose and went upstairs to get ready. She'd been to war, and it was very hard to stand down even now, even after the last battle was long over. By the time she was heading out the door half an hour later, Flint was absorbed in setting up his workstation, the early morning spring light filtering in at a strategic angle to avoid any direct glare on his screens. The sweeping, abstract nature of his work required only bare-bones infrastructure: two big monitors, a robust CPU, and a heavy, old-fashioned black keyboard that clicked loudly as he worked. Rags could not understand why he didn't invest in state-of-the-art holo-projectors and digital paper. She chalked it up to skinflintedness, no matter how many times he'd tried to explain that software developers had settled on an efficacious way of working decades earlier, and nothing that had been invented since had improved upon it. Flint had his ear discs in, so that her movements through the house barely registered.

"Good luck," Flint said, not looking up. Rags knew they were heading into their own separate worlds for the day. She would begin to orient herself to the town's rhythms, figure out its factions, find her way to its secret-keepers. While he, she knew, would shut out the physical world almost entirely and plunge into the arcane virtual world of something he called "predictive analytics," hunting for "edge conditions" in complex models compiled with machine learning. Every time he tried to explain it—and he'd stop trying a long time ago—Rags found she just couldn't keep it straight. But then, he didn't fully understand her world either. Journalism, he declared, is an unreliable aggregation of "belief spaces." Rags felt confident in her ability to navigate these so-called belief spaces, which at least were grounded in the real world and not the rarified planes of abstract "information ecologies" that seemed to absorb most of Flint's waking hours.

Leaving Flint to stare at his blinking screens, Rags set out on foot to the newspaper office on Main Street, grateful for what she anticipated would be an easy ten-minute walk. *We should get bicycles.* The happy thought took her by surprise. She couldn't remember the last time she'd felt like this, practically innocent. She pictured the two of them stuffing groceries into bike baskets and saddlebags. Normal stuff. *A normal life—can we?* No need for a car in a town like this. As part of her research into Canary, Rags had discovered that years ago, Canary had been featured in an article about the most walkable communities in America. It ranked in the top five among towns with populations under 50,000. It was one of the few times Canary had been singled out for anything and everyone was proud. The *Canary Courant* apparently ran a front page story on it and shops pasted the article in their front windows, as if anyone who didn't already know about it was going to stop by and marvel.

During her brief walk, Rags forced herself to notice the clean spring air, the budding forsythia, the quaint houses with their neat little front lawns. Surely, many of these houses stood empty—vacant, rather than abandoned—but since they nearly all looked equally old and tired, their foundations sinking slowly and unevenly into the moist earth, it was impossible to tell. Perhaps, in a matter of weeks, many of these front lawns would be overgrown with new grass, giving away their status.

For now, the apparent normalcy was reassuring. Or at least, the semblance of normalcy. Every front door she passed held the same blinking green beacon of assured sanitation. Rags was reminded of the red crosses that marked hundreds of dwellings infected with plague across Europe in 1665. But she was determined to focus on the present: a shield against the past. Surely moving to this little town, where evidence of catastrophe was half-hidden by the slow, gentle pace of all-around decay, really was a good idea. *Go slow*, she told herself. *Take it in. Notice the moment.* These sorts of habits had fallen by the wayside a long time ago. In a crisis, everything happens quickly and there's rarely time to absorb what's right in front of you. You react first, think later.

But Rags's rare feeling of calm and safety was short-lived. Memories of her work in the city arose like a waking nightmare. She could not halt the flood of images forcing their way back to life. She is back in the city on assignment, tasked with filing a live spot for a national radio news program. Rags was among a handful of still-working journalists going at it nonstop, reporting in any media seeking an update—radio, print, or broadcast. She arrives at the apartment building on Hanover Street she was assigned to visit and rushes to get there ahead of any over-taxed ambulance. The boxy building is flanked by a CVS on one side and an abandoned gas station on the other. But she never even reaches apartment 602—the number indelibly etched on her memory—where she'd been sent to interview a family whose home-recorded songs had racked up millions of views.

The walls of the vestibule splattered with blood.

The bank of metal mailboxes, coated with viscous human matter.

Bodies piled between the outside door and the entryway to the main lobby. Men, women, and children together, a rictus of agony etched on each face.

Rags gags at the stench, despite the heavy-duty face mask and plastic shield she wears all the time. But she cannot turn away; she is obligated to report what she sees in real time. She steps back a few feet, keeping her eyes on the bodies so that she can accurately describe the scene. She phones in her report, barely aware that her words are heard by hundreds of thousands of people as she speaks them. She doesn't remember what she says, only the racing, spinning feeling that has taken over her nervous system and how she fights against that to speak into the microphone in a calm, matter-of-fact tone. Perhaps the mess on the floor belongs to the family of musicians she was sent to meet. Perhaps it doesn't. It doesn't matter.

And then the cruelest image of all: Maya is there, standing just outside the scrum of reporters and a medical SWAT team. Maya, jostled by everyone around her. Exposed. Maya, waiting for Rags to finish up so they can get out of there. Maya, in cutoff jean shorts and a yellow sweatshirt.

Maya. Maya. No.

Rags stood on the sidewalk, momentarily disoriented. She waited for her vision to clear, helpless, frustrated, and ashamed. She looked down and noticed a red tulip just pushing its way up through the soil, not yet opened. She knelt down to smell it and touch the velvety newborn petals. *I need this flower. This is real, this is right.* She yanked the tulip from the soil, knowing full well it would die within hours. But until then, the young tulip would be her talisman, a form of protection that she could not admit to anyone, even Flint, that she needed just to get through the next hour. She slapped her left cheek, hard, to quell the violent twitching that had resumed at the corner of her eye, but no slap could expel the sense of humiliation that had followed her here, after all, to Canary.

After a short walk that felt a century long, Rags arrived at the newspaper office. A thin man, cue-ball bald, dressed in ragged jeans and a T-shirt full of holes, sat on the steps leading up to the *Courant*'s office. Next to him sat a boy, maybe nine, Rags guessed, wide-eyed with a mop full of brown hair, and the spitting image of his father. The man stood up as Rags approached.

"You Goldner?" he asked, his thin lips barely moving as he spoke, as if he felt compelled to ration every word.

"Yeah," Rags said. "You're here to—"

"Porter. Got my truck here." Porter pointed to an ancient, beat-up flat-bed pick-up, a first-gen electric that looked ready to fall apart. Porter didn't bother to introduce his perhaps-son, who sat silently, like a well-trained dog awaiting orders. Rags didn't know much about kids, but the boy's stillness was unnerving. He was thin, like his father, and very pale.

"Come in," Rags said, forcing herself back to the present. "I need you to take almost all of it. You might need to make more than one trip." Rags had found Porter on a list of people who worked for the paper. He was the delivery man. On a hunch, she pinged his number shortly after leaving Merry the day before. She guessed—correctly, it seemed—that a grown man delivering newspapers could stand to make some extra currency. She didn't know why he'd brought the boy, but she wasn't going to ask. That was his business and she didn't want to know more than absolutely necessary. Another journalist might lust after the feature story suggested by the sad-looking boy and his dad. But not Rags. Poking around in people's personal lives, pulling out their sad and sordid tales of woe, was decidedly not her bag. Especially not now.

Rags was relieved to see that she'd beat Merry to the office, as she'd hoped. She already dreaded Merry's caterwauling about the changes she intended to make. Rags told Porter to remove all but three desks and most of the chairs, and to clear out all the junk lining the windowsills and the crappy melamine bookcases lining the walls, their shelves sagging with the weight of obsolete computers, desktop printers, even old telephone books. The dust-encrusted awards would have to go too, of course. The only old-fashioned printed material Rags decided to keep were bound volumes of the newspaper going back a century. Her journalist's heart still had a beat, and the newspaper archives were worth preserving, even if they were fundamentally useless. She planned to thumb through some of them, anyway, as a guilty pleasure—a pointless trip down memory lane, which would take her back to a time when the stories we told about our time and place exuded a momentous gravitas out of all proportion to the trivial reality they conveyed.

The year it rained so hard, all the basements in Canary flooded.

The year a sewer cover on Main Street blew off due to a leaky steam pipe underground, scaring the shit out of everyone and fortunately causing no injuries.

The year the Memorial Day parade had to be cancelled because the Canary police went on strike for better wages and benefits, and you can't hold a parade without police to maintain order.

As if any of that really mattered; as if any of that would change anybody's life one iota. As if these topics were matters of life-and-death—which, hah-hah, of course they were not.

Porter's boy didn't wait to be told what to do. He lifted a stack of yellowed papers off a shelf and carted it out to the truck. Porter, far stronger than he appeared, swung a table up in the air as if he were wafting balloons and followed his son out to the truck. They worked quickly and silently, barely a grunt passing between them. Rags appreciated their efficiency and wondered what else Porter might be good for. She sat at the desk she was claiming for herself—sturdy metal rather than the fussy, over-embellished oak furniture she was having removed. Her chair was the old-fashioned ergonomic kind, fake black leather; good enough. She'd claimed the newer tech, too, including digital paper (handy for taking notes) and a wireless screen. She opened the one drawer in her sleek metal desk and gently lay the tulip in it. The young flower already looked sad and desiccated, but Rags liked knowing it was there. She left the drawer open a bit, as if to allow the flower a bit of air and a glimpse of light.

She forced her thoughts back to business. Considering the resources the paper still (mysteriously) had, Rags couldn't imagine why Merry, or somebody, hadn't kept the tech up to date. Maybe small towns were stubborn that way—slow to leave the old ways behind, slow to adapt to anything that smacked of "the new." The illogic of it all irritated Rags, but news-gathering was still news-gathering, and that's what she was here to do.

Rags called up the Wednesday edition of the paper that had gone to the printer last night so that Porter could deliver them tomorrow. Merry had, in fact, changed the banner so the lead story was about the septic tank leak. As requested, the story on Effie the missing girl, which consisted of little more than a series of quoted lamentations and speculations from concerned residents, had been buried. At least Merry knew how to follow orders. The paper's actual printing press, shared by a handful of small publishers far too broke to print their own limited-circulation papers, was over two hours away, outside of Pittsburgh. Porter made the trip himself to load up his truck. Rags made a note to get eyes on the delivery schedule so she could be sure that Porter was getting the job done. She wondered, in passing, if Flint would bother to read the paper she was now charged with putting out. He had a habit, Rags knew, of building little micro-worlds for himself and living in them quite comfortably and obliviously. Perhaps that's how he'd gotten through everything that had happened without falling apart. *Stop*, Rags told herself. *Focus.*

Merry walked in just as Porter and the boy were finishing up. She dropped her large, shapeless bag on the floor and looked around. She appeared to wear the same clothes as the day before. Rags had a habit of doing the same thing; she'd thrown on old jeans, a flannel shirt, and her Free People brown suede jacket—a prized possession from the days when that sort of thing mattered. But bonding over the little things wasn't going to be *their* thing. Rags already recognized the icy stare. Tough shit, she thought. Merry can suck it up. Where else would she go?

"What the fuck?" Merry shot her already trademark glare toward Rags.

"Looks so much better already, doesn't it?" Rags said, goading her. "We've got some room to think, thank God, with all that crap out of the way. How did you stand it? We should dive into next Sunday's edition. Is there any evergreen copy that we can run?" Merry continued to stand in the middle of the floor, as if she was no longer certain where she belonged. "I left you two desks to choose from. So pick one and let's get moving."

Merry began dragging a desk to the far end of the newsroom—as far from Rags as she could get. "Where's all my stuff?" she asked, kicking a rolling chair toward her chosen desk. Rags pointed to a box filled with Merry's junk from her other desk. Rags wouldn't touch it, didn't want to look at it, so she'd asked Porter, who'd asked the boy to dump it all in there. This way, Rags had plausible deniability if anything went missing. Merry hauled the box to her new location and began rifling through it. Porter came in and stood by Rags's desk.

"Is that everything?" he asked, a film of sweat on his face despite the chilly spring air.

"For now. Thanks," Rags said. "Hold on." She logged onto her screen and transferred a payment into Porter's account. "There. All paid up." Porter nodded and turned to go, presumably to rejoin his son and hopefully get him a bite to eat, Rags thought. The kid looked under-nourished—but, she reminded herself, it wasn't her concern. "You up for more work, if I need you?" she asked. Porter nodded. "Anything you won't do—anything you'd object to?" Porter paused a moment, then shook his head. He walked out.

"Thanks for nothing!" Merry shouted after him. She returned to looking through her box. "I'm missing a pen."

"Good thing you won't need it," Rags said from her desk, several feet away.

"It's special. From before," Merry said.

"We've all lost 'special things' from before," Rags said. "But we're still here. Now, tell me about all these freelance contributors we're paying. Who's good? Who can we count on? Who misses deadlines?"

"Okay, but at ten I have to take a call," Merry said.

"What call?"

"For the ads," Merry said. "They give me the copy over the phone."

"You need to tell me more about how this works, Merry—the classifieds," Rags said. "Who is 'they,' for starters."

"But you want to talk about the freelancers."

"Both, Merry. We need to talk about both." Rags knew full well that Merry was being obtuse on purpose. She obviously ran on passive-aggressive fuel. Rags knew how to play this game. She would not let Merry get under her skin—not this way, at least. Merry's phone lit up. She looked at Rags, who understood instantly that Merry desperately wanted her to leave and let Merry take the call alone, as, evidently, she usually did. But there wasn't a chance of that, and Rags could see that Merry knew it. Merry stuck a disc in her ear. Rags watched her closely. She wouldn't interfere the first time so she could get a sense of how this weekly transaction went down. But soon, she'd need to figure out what this was really all about. The ads were the secret sauce that kept the paper alive and if Rags hoped to achieve a new status quo in her life, she'd need to understand if this really was a sure thing—which meant learning how and why this happened.

"Uh-huh," Merry said. "Uh-huh." She typed quickly, taking

dictation. There were easier ways to do this—direct voice-to-text, for instance. But Rags guessed there were reasons for the low-tech approach, which further raised her suspicions. "Reading back now," Merry continued. "'Looking for the vacation of a lifetime at bargain prices? Join the Syracuse Travel Club now for just ninety-eight credits a month. Over sixty fabulous deals that will take you anywhere from the vast beauty of Canada to the green mosses of Savannah. Download the free STC VR app or call us at 888-436-0962.' Okay? Yes, I see the logo coming through now." Merry looked at her screen. "Next?"

Rags watched Merry repeat the dictation exercise four more times. Each ad was more bizarre than the one before. There was something strangely, falsely cheery about each of them. They were breezy, wordy, and seemed to belong to a world that had nothing in common with the one they actually inhabited—an "alt" world where people had money to burn, lots of leisure time, and a sweetly innocent longing to find companionship with strangers. Rags tried to estimate how many column inches, at so many dollars per inch, these ads alone would generate. She recalled that the paper's budget clearly showed they covered a whopping ninety-three percent of the operating budget, with a mere seven percent coming from subscriptions. And these were just the new ads placed this week; the paper ran several ads on a bulk-buy basis. They ran for weeks on end, as if there were an unlimited appetite in Canary for splurgy vacations, expensive holo systems, gourmet cheese and wine clubs, hot-air balloon parties, and an assortment of other goods and services. Perhaps there was a side of Canary that Rags had not yet seen in her brief time here so far, but she seriously doubted it. Something just didn't feel right.

When Merry was finally off the phone, she turned her attention to her screen. Whether she was finalizing the ads for placement in the paper or working on something editorial, Rags did not yet know.

"So that's how it's done? Every week, just like that?" Rags asked across the room.

"Yup," Merry said, keeping her eyes on the screen. "Like clockwork."

"Huh," Rags said. She continued staring at Merry.

"What?" Merry said sharply.

"Who buys the ads, Merry? Where do they come from?"

Merry rose and began pacing around her desk. "Look, in case you haven't noticed, I've had to get this paper out all by myself—well, nearly—and I don't have time to worry about how our bread is buttered, okay? I don't know how you lucked into this job, but if I were you, I'd stop looking for trouble where there isn't any and start acting like a journalist who actually cares about what goes on around here."

Flushed, Merry sat back down at her desk. Round one to Merry, Rags thought. She would bide her time. She actually knew very little about the paper's owners—and presumably they were aware of, if not responsible for, the ad buys. The paper didn't have an advertising rep. The paper didn't have anyone besides Merry—and did she actually write any copy? Rags acknowledged she'd stepped into this thing knowing far less than she might in other circumstances. She'd clutched at it, without much forethought, and now here she was.

"What about the township meetings?" Merry said.

"What about them?" Rags asked. She guessed that Merry was referring to the local town council that governed Canary.

"I suppose now that you're here, you'll want to cover that yourself."

"As opposed to…"

"Brent will be disappointed," Merry said, crossing her arms. "And he needs the money. Probably more than you, Polly. I mean, *Rags*." Rags realized she'd have to meet with Brent and the other freelancers as soon as possible.

"Well, I should be there, don't you think?" It wasn't really a question. "Need to get my feet wet, don't I? It's tonight, right?" Just a guess, but why else would Merry put her on the spot? In a tiny town like this, population circa 4,700 in a post-pandemic world (a huge comedown from the 50,000 in better times), the township meeting would be ground zero for taking the political, cultural, and social temperature of the town itself. Rags couldn't miss it. But she didn't know exactly where or when the township meeting took place. She refused to ask Merry directly, as that would come off as some sort of weakness or concession to Merry's greater knowledge of the place. Rags hoped that if she simply walked around the two-block radius of downtown Main Street between six and eight in the evening, watching for people trickling inside somewhere, she'd find it. She'd walk out to the local high school, if necessary, on the assumption they had a modest auditorium that might double as a town meeting place. She thought again about how useful it would be to have a bike.

In any case, Merry could damn well hang back and slug whatever stories were ready to run—the last batch before Rags laid her editorial hands on all copy coming in, from business to sports to actual news of the day. Merry could handle the calendar listings; presumably that was her speed and she couldn't do much damage. And maybe, for now, Merry could pull some national stories off the newswire to fill in the bare spots. One way or another, they'd get next Sunday's paper out—with Rags's name and title on the masthead. Rags left Merry with explicit instructions. She figured a show of strength would go a long way with someone like Merry. Rags was determined never to show her a whiff of weakness.

3

Rags debated whether to go home and change before hunting for the township meeting but decided against it. What was the point? Who the hell cared? She called Flint and told him she'd grab a plantburger from the little café she'd spotted in town and see him later that evening. She didn't bother to ask if he wanted to come and he didn't offer. All he told her was that he'd had a good first day. He'd settled into his office nook, and the cherry tree buds had doubled in size since their morning coffee. She was glad he noticed; he wasn't entirely oblivious to his surroundings. She took that as a positive sign, a step forward for both of them.

Rags left the office before Merry, taking care to bring the wilted tulip with her and to leave no personal traces behind. She was sure that Merry would snoop around her desk the moment she was out of sight. She couldn't guess what Merry would be looking for, but probably anything and everything that she could use against Rags for leverage, blackmail, or some other way to puts Rags on the defensive. Rags wouldn't give Merry the satisfaction. As to why Merry had it in for her, and why they'd taken such a strong and instant dislike to one another, did it really matter? It was what it was, as Flint might have said. All that Merry would find, if she really looked, were some unlocked digital files holding evergreen feature stories that Merry already knew about and a shortcut to their shared cloud library of back issues. Rags hadn't had time to come up with any new story ideas yet.

Rags walked up and down Canary's small downtown grid of streets as the evening turned dark and chilly, looking for an open doorway, a lit window. She felt like a detective trying to solve a case without any clues. But she couldn't think of another way to jump-start her new job, which came without any meaningful guidance of the sort that a more ordered world had taken for granted years earlier. Maybe the township meetings were all posted on a municipal calendar, and she should have thought to look there first, but between settling in, arranging the office, puzzling over the ad situation, and sparring with Merry, she hadn't had time to think so logically. And then there were those moments when Rags's past overwhelmed her present, but she refused to factor those in. Instead, she cursed Merry for making this more difficult than it had to be. Then again, these days you could not count on the kindness of strangers; many people would just as soon threaten you with a baseball bat as say a friendly "hello." You never knew what you were getting into.

Downtown Canary, Rags decided, was just like a person who'd survived The Big One and bore the marks of a difficult battle: thin, wan, weak, pocked with scars, and looking older than their years. She again saw the woman with the dead eyes standing on the corner of Main Street and Chestnut, looking as though she was ready to take root there. A loose pack of dogs, collarless, their tongues lolling, trotted up the sidewalk as if preparing to take over. Rags approached the dogs, gingerly, and held out her palm. She was given a quick sniff and then the pack trotted on, searching, Rags supposed, for open garbage or street scraps. Nobody gave away food these days, not even to dogs with their ribcages showing.

The only place full of ordinary human life was the Canary Bar & Grill. It was packed, loud, and a throng stood on the sidewalk, smoking furtively, drinks in hand. They may as well have shouted in unison: *We're immortal now and we don't give a fuck anymore.* These were some of the so-called Luckies. They'd lived to tell the tale. They were, Rags thought, the post-pandemic counterpart to all the merry-makers who, at the height of The Big One, as people were dying by the thousands, committed themselves to hard-core self-indulgence. They worked at playing and said *fuck you* to everything and everyone else. The microbes may have been new but the behavior was the same as it had been in the plague-ridden Middle Ages. *Eat, drink, and be merry, for tomorrow we may die.* Rags wanted no part of it.

Around seven-thirty, she widened her search. She saw a couple of people, and then a few more, crossing an intersection just east of downtown. She followed them. If there was another big draw in Canary that night other than the township meeting (or the bar), she'd find out soon enough. She arrived with a small crowd at the low-slung, factory-like Canary Comprehensive High School, which did not appear very comprehensive even though the building served kids from half a dozen little townships in the northwest corner of the state. The school cafeteria, as she soon discovered, clearly served as the all-purpose meeting space for the school as well as the town itself. The school had been locked down for more than three years during the pandemic, and in the years since, there'd been little time or will and no public money to modernize it. Besides, the school was already behind the times when the building shut down and all students switched to remote forms of learning. *Just another example of the forlorn ye-oldy nature of Canary,* Rags thought. *The town that time forgot, more than once.*

A few dozen folding chairs were scattered across the hard, worn linoleum floor. Outdated plastic-coated posters of some absurd version of the USDA food nutrition pyramid were pinned to the walls, along with gold-blue banners celebrating the Canary Cougars high school football team and an illustrated guide to good manners. All the *ye olde* you could want; all seeming so beside the point now. A beat-up cafeteria table at the far end of the room was reserved, Rags assumed, for the town council leadership, or what passed for leadership in the context of Canary's anemic political infrastructure. Rags stood at the back of the room and watched people shuffle in quietly and take seats as far apart from one another as possible. Temporary social habits were now internalized everywhere except at the bars. Who knew if they'd ever revert back to the old ways? Never sit close enough to another human being to receive even a mist of breath or wayward spit. And no touching. Rags privately thought a lot of the ritualized behavior had morphed into reflexive bullshit. But she could not say that out loud without making everything complicated.

Rags watched as people greeted one another wordlessly with a nod or a curt wave. Even the elbow bump had fallen by the wayside as too risky. The reserved body language gave Rags the sense that nobody really gave a shit and they were just going through the motions. But perhaps they'd all simply buried their feelings in order to endure. If Rags felt like a walking volcano on the verge of erupting and dissolving into a steaming mess of hot magma, maybe everybody else did too.

The room was thick with unspoken knowledge. No one needed to say out loud that distance created a feeling of safety, and safety had become the deepest craving of all, the overriding need that drove most of the decisions, large and small, that people made, alone and together. Over half the people in the room wore respies—the latest generation of facemask respirators, which looked like translucent teardrops covering the nose and mouth; they simply could not believe that the era of contagion was actually over. Rags did not count herself among them, putting herself automatically at odds with many of those around her. At least no one was *required* to wear a respie now—a small sign of progress.

Still, a room full of Luckies.

They were alone, together, united by a common bond each of them distrusted.

They wondered, all the time, why they had lived when millions had died.

They worried about their purpose, their future—whether they should be doing more, doing something different, or perhaps throwing all caution to the wind and living only for the moment, whether in the local bar or elsewhere in their imaginations.

Rags noted how their clothing hung conspicuously loose; no one seemed to make much of an effort with personal grooming, save for the occasional slash of red lipstick some of the women made a point of wearing. There were no old people at the meeting; most were in their thirties and forties. No one had brought young children, presumably out of an abundance of caution—not only for health-and-safety reasons but perhaps because of the Effie situation. A thief of children in their midst?

Something else Rags noticed: people pointed their data-phones at one another, exchanging information. There were nods, murmurs, head shakes. She hadn't witnessed this kind of behavior in the city, where people still walked with their heads down and crossed the street if you so much as looked at them sideways. She edged into the room as unobtrusively as possible, trying to overhear the conversations between data exchangers. *Make it an even dozen… Four quarts… Ten pounds… Every Thursday at four… The last batch wasn't so good…* Then it dawned on her. They were bartering. Perhaps this was the basis of Canary's economy. That explained the pair on the street swapping a bicycle pump for a loaf of bread. And the woman standing on the corner? Waiting, perhaps, to make a sale—of something that had value to someone. Rags realized she'd paid Porter in old-fashioned digital currency. She wondered if he'd have preferred to barter, but she didn't have anything of tangible value to give him in return for his services.

"Hey, who are you?" Someone called to Rags from several feet away and it took her a moment to realize a muffled voice was calling to her. "I said, who are you?"

The uniform gave him away: thickly woven dark green canvas coveralls, a long-billed cap to match, and a badge that told Rags he was PHP—a member of the Public Health Police force that had emerged everywhere, even in tiny towns like Canary, midway through the pandemic. In Rags's experience, the PHP were uniformly petty bureaucrats who took the tiny inch of power allotted to them and ran with it. Many had been police officers, ex-military, even nightclub bouncers. As the economy tanked, thousands of people from these fields latched onto the chance of a steady paycheck that came with enforcement responsibilities. Rags had had many screaming matches with PHPs in the city, as they tried to block her from getting close enough to report grim disease scenes. This PHP accessorized his coveralls with gold hoop earrings and heavy black kohl eyeliner, so maybe he was more flexible. Short, straight, golden-brown hair swept back from a high forehead and arched eyebrows gave the PHP a look of dramatic surprise, even with half his face covered by a respie. Rags hoped this one was different.

"Rags Goldner. The *Courant*'s new editor."

"Goddammit!" the PHP said from behind an elaborate mask. "Terry didn't tell me. You should already have been scheduled for a dual inspection." Rags knew this meant the PHP would do a walk-through of the *Courant*'s office and her new home. Not so flexible, then.

"Nice to meet you too," Rags said. "I can't read your nametag from here."

"Piper Madrigal," he said from behind a respie. Piper wore thick latex gloves and clearly did not even consider shaking hands. He was perspiring heavily, his eyes glittering above the mask. Piper seemed like a coiled spring, just waiting to be sprung. "Contact trace." Piper spoke the words as a command rather than a data request. Rags held out her dataphone so that it beamed data directly to Piper's dataphone. She deeply resented the transaction over which she had no control. The big tech giants had collaborated years earlier to make it easy to suck personal information with pinpoint accuracy: specifically, where you'd been and who'd you been with over the last thirty days, and whether all parties had virus antibodies. This still went on, two years after the last case had been found. Infuriating, intrusive bureaucratic bullshit.

"Expect me at your front door early tomorrow morning, followed with a visit to your office tomorrow at eight," Piper said. Naturally, he would know where Rags and Flint were living; it was all part of the obnoxious oversight. Rags also knew the PHP collected a treasure trove of information about sanitary conditions, health risk factors, and more, for every residence and commercial establishment in Canary. She could already tell that Piper thrived on the power of it all. The day could not come soon enough when these mini-Nazis would be disbanded. When ordinary citizens would begin trusting their own instincts again, instead of blindly following anyone in a uniform telling them what to do.

A woman called the township meeting to order—Rags guessed this was Terry—and people took their spaced-out seats, keeping their elbows tucked by their sides. Terry was joined by two other people at the table. Canary had shrunk so much, only three people were apparently needed to govern the town, assess disputes, and oversee the collection of property taxes, which were meager. Rags wondered if the council had been called on to broker bartering disputes. As the meeting got underway, Rags watched Piper Madrigal pace the floor, too hopped-up to sit down. She wondered if the freelancer Merry had mentioned, Brent, was there to cover the meeting. She didn't see anyone who looked like a journalist, poised to record or take notes. Maybe he was simply unreliable, and if so, she'd have to do something about that.

Terry called out the top item on the agenda. It was about the Effie Rutter case. A woman in a threadbare woolen coat and long, stringy hair rose and began speaking without preamble.

"What are you people doing?" the woman asked, in a halting voice. "Why aren't you looking for my daughter?" Ah, Effie's mother, Rags assumed. "Haven't we all lost enough? Or is everybody too damn sick and tired to care? My baby was stolen and you all act like nothing's happening! Where's your humanity?"

"Thank you, Evelyn," Terry said. Rags immediately got the sense that Terry hoped Effie's mother, Evelyn Rutter, would shut up now. The room fell even more silent than it had been. No one looked Evelyn Rutter in the eye. Maybe they were ashamed, Rags thought. Maybe Evelyn was right: everyone suffered from compassion fatigue. There was nothing left in the collective tank. Someone's teenaged child had disappeared: what was anyone expected to do about it? Rags watched and waited for a sign of some sort, though she didn't really know what she was looking for. But there was no sign. Terry cleared her throat.

"You *know* this girl," Evelyn continued, desperately trying to get them to care. "She's a *good* girl. A cheerleader, for God's sake. What did she ever do to deserve this—to disappear into thin air?"

Evelyn looked wild-eyed. She spun around the room, her pocketbook swinging on her arm, trying to force people to pay attention.

"Look!" Evelyn said. "Look!" She pointed her dataphone at a wall in the cafeteria and projected a video of Effie practicing her cheerleading routine at home. The girl was dancing around an empty-looking room, kicking up her legs and laughing, her blonde hair swinging. Rags looked away. She noticed that many others did too. Rags felt the silence in the room as if it were a scream filled with misery and defeat.

"Thank you, Evelyn," Terry said when the silence became almost too thick to bear. "We do share your pain. We do. And you know this case is still a top priority." Terry scanned the crowd. "Isn't that right, Piers?" Rags followed her gaze and decided that Piers, dressed in a blue button-down shirt and dark blue slacks, a stun gun bulging on his belt, was the local peacekeeper—the current euphemism for local law enforcement.

Piers Olsson stood. He looked in Terry's direction but Rags thought his gaze seemed unfocused, like he wasn't looking anywhere in particular. He was tall and on the pudgy side, in contrast to most of the reed-thin men in the room. He ran his hair through thinning black hair. "Evelyn, we're doing our best. We've sent bulletins out all over the country. These cases take time." Piers sat back down in a heap. He's got nothing, Rags thought.

Evelyn was still standing. She began to cry.

"She could be dead," Evelyn sobbed. "She could be dead

and I'll never see her again. And nobody cares!" Evelyn shot an accusing look around the room and ran out into the night. No one went after her.

"Next item of business," Terry said evenly, closing over the gaping black hole of sorrow and loss that no one could heal.

4

The township meeting ended around nine-thirty p.m. There hadn't been any fireworks after Evelyn left, which Rags interpreted as a license to keep this story off the front page, for the foreseeable future. Rags had been a journalist long enough to see the strange irony in this situation; a story about a missing kid could be depended on to drive a news cycle for weeks on end. Early in her career, Rags would have jumped at the chance to cover a story like this and stick with it 24/7. But battle-scarred veterans don't necessarily run toward gunfire; they just don't have the heart or the stomach for it, and Rags was no exception.

As the meeting disbanded, the few dozen people who'd attended maintained their distance, though Rags had a hunch many of them would make their way to the bar in town, to tamp down all that volcanic activity. The bar was a place of magical thinking, she knew well, as all bars now were; a place where you pretended everything had returned to normal and it was your duty to have fun. Maybe she should begin to hang out there, with or without (probably without) Flint. She watched the downtrodden citizens of Canary file out of the cafeteria, many of them wearing the hollow-eyed, haunted look of people still counting up their losses and trying to figure out who they were now.

Rags went up to the three council members still clustered (but not too closely) by the front table. They exchanged introductions. Terry, the council president, had short white hair and a pointed nose that lent her an aristocratic air. Perhaps unearned, Rags thought. She was one of the few women present wearing lipstick. Terry struck Rags as the kind of person who didn't second-guess herself, which was probably why Canary elected her to lead the council.

"I hope you didn't come here to make trouble," Terry said to her. Rags instantly wondered why this woman was on the defensive when she apparently already had the town well in hand—at least, that's how it looked. She and Merry would sure make a pair.

"What kind of trouble?" Rags said.

"There's no reason to stir things up," said Missy, another of the three council members. She was as small as a child, yet her voice was deep and loud.

"Like what?" Rags asked, still probing.

"What we mean," said Keller, the third council member, "is that this is a go-along, get-along kind of place. We don't want any of your big-city muckraking." Keller had a long thin face covered with white stubble and tired, red-rimmed eyes. Wisps of white hair danced above his scalp. When he spoke, he sounded as if he were pleading—a sharp contrast to the two strong-willed women. Rags saw him glance toward Terry and Missy, as if seeking confirmation.

"So," Rags said, "you'd prefer it if the paper didn't make news. Real news. Just recipes, gardening tips, and crosswords. Is that right?"

"Of course not," Terry said sharply. "That's not what I said."

"But we expect the paper to respect the laws around here, which is what's keeping everybody safe," Missy said.

"Oh, you mean, don't question the PHP," Rags said.

"Well, yes," Missy said.

"Do your job, Rags," Terry said, "but don't go looking for trouble where there isn't any."

"But keep the Effie Rutter stories coming," Keller said. "Merry knows." He stopped himself abruptly.

"Merry knows what?" Rags asked.

"I just mean, Merry's good with the ads, so you have the resources you need to look into things like that, right?" Keller was red-faced and breathing hard.

"How *will* you cover the Effie Rutter case?" Terry asked.

"I'm keeping an open mind," Rags said. "But I won't keep

it on the front page if there's no new information coming in."

"Really?" Keller said, his voice rising.

"Is she a relative of yours, Mr. Keller?" Rags asked him.

"No, but—"

"I'll tell you what I *will* cover," Rags said. "That broken septic system on the south side of town. You said it yourself tonight: too much rain, saturated soil, sewage back-ups. It's a mess. *That's* a story."

Rags could see that none of them appeared mollified; she hadn't inspired much confidence. And that suited her just fine. Still, Rags clenched her jaw to hide her deep irritation; small-town busy-bodies already trying to tell her how to do her job. Exactly what she'd said to Flint on their way into town. Anyway, this case of the missing girl was far from the only thing weighing Canary down. How about a century of increasing isolation, economic dislocation and disinvestment, and then pile on a world-shaking pandemic. That's what ailed Canary. Whether or not a missing teen's disappearance would ultimately be solved would not, in Rags's estimation, much affected the trajectory of Canary's future. The town was already an afterthought in the grand scheme; she'd chosen it, she'd lobbied hard for it, exactly for that reason. Yet, this wasn't what she'd expected.

The cafeteria had almost completely emptied out except for the PHP, who rushed over to Rags and the council members like a truck barreling down a hill.

"Why wasn't I told?" Piper said, practically hissing through the respie. "You know better, Terry. Nobody comes into Canary without my knowledge. How else can I protect you and everybody else?"

Jesus Christ, Rags thought. Talk about delusions of grandeur. When the federal government had set up the PHP, they didn't grant them the right to bear arms or make citizen arrests; their chief function was to monitor, report, and enforce stringent local health laws and policies like Canary's, which required a health inspection of everyone who came through town and stayed more than four hours. But Piper made it sound like he was ready to roll out some kind of martial law with minimal provocation.

"Piper, you are absolutely right," Terry said. "This was an oversight on our part. But you and I both know that the publisher who hired her is like a ghost. We didn't get word." Terry looked at Rags like it was actually all her fault.

"We won't let it happen again," Missy added. "Public safety is our number one priority—we all know that."

Keller nodded.

So, this is how it is, Rags thought. An unofficial alliance between the council and the PHP. She wouldn't be surprised if Piper was allowed to weigh in privately on any proposed ordinance that even remotely touched on the council's area of responsibility—and maybe even beyond that, just to stay on their good side. *I bet you can't put up a new stop sign in this town without running it by the PHP.* And what about Piers, the peacekeeper? The *actual* law-and-order guy? Where was he in all this? He wasn't even in the room anymore. Rags had seen and heard enough to get the lay of the land. She knew she'd see the PHP soon enough—tomorrow morning, first at home, then at the office. There was no avoiding it.

As the lights flicked off in the high school, Rags found herself outside alone, in the dark. Canary didn't have many streetlights and none at all on side streets like this one. She looked up into the sky and took in the abundant starscape, including a creamy swath of the Milky Way. She knew she should go home to Flint. He'd probably kept something warm for her to eat, even though she'd told him she'd grab a bite in town. Feeding her was one of the ways he showed that he cared, without needing to put anything into words. Flint was stingy with words. Rags, a journalist, swam in words. It was one of the many 'opposites attract' things about their relationship that had brought them together—a long time ago, it seemed. But being new in this unfamiliar town made her restless and she wasn't ready to be cooped up. She decided to stop in at the unimaginatively named Canary Bar & Grill and figure out who the night owls were. Night owls were usually great talkers.

The bar was packed and a throng of smokers still congregated just outside the doorway in the chilly night air. There had been plenty of talk about outlawing all tobacco products at the tail end of the pandemic, but it still hadn't happened and many people now saw tobacco as a lesser among evils. Rags recognized Keller among the outsiders, hunched against the chill in a leather jacket, a drink in hand. He must have hustled over here in a hurry. He saw her and nodded but didn't seem interested in renewing a conversation. Perhaps he took his cues from Terry. Or perhaps, Rags thought, she was going to be held at arm's length in general because people assumed journalists were always trying to pry open their secrets. Rags prized truth over secrets (she told herself), although sometimes one led to the other.

Rags found a narrow opening at the bar rail, ordered a scotch neat, and looked around. *One drink. Just one.* This was the kind of place that probably hadn't changed much in fifty years, if not more. An old-fashioned flat-screen TV, turned off, hung over the bar. A blend of techno-rock music was loud enough to discourage easy conversation. The crowd, most on the verge of premature middle age, were mainly drinking in intimate pairs, whispering in one another's ears, laughing, touching. Public intimacy was the new sexy and still carried a whiff of taboo. She recognized a number of them from the township meeting, though now they'd shed all that stiff and distant formality. They appeared in no hurry to get home, either. In here, they put off their quiet, dour exterior personalities and behaved normally—in the old-fashioned sense of the word. Perhaps many of them were childless by choice—an understandable choice, given recent history—and so there was nothing to rush home for except another night of slow, cling-to-life, make-every-moment-count protected sex. Finding talkative night owls here was probably a long shot, at least judging by this night's crowd.

Rags finished her drink and thought about going home. She

thought about ordering another drink, too, and resisted. *The craving for a bicycle, the appreciation of the tulip, and now, limited drinking: all good signs.* Perhaps in time, the twitch would vanish as well. She unconsciously cradled her cheek. *What the hell.* She ordered a second scotch. Then she spotted a figure sitting alone at a table near the back of the bar. He had a broad back and wore a blue short-sleeve shirt. Piers the peacekeeper. He'd slipped out of the meeting quickly, before she could introduce herself. She walked over to him and got straight to business. She didn't want to give him the impression she was flirting simply because everyone around them was doing just that.

"Rags Goldner. The new editor of the *Courant.*" Rags sat opposite Piers. He looked up at her slowly with bloodshot eyes. He smiled a lazy smile and ran his hands through his hair.

"Piers Olsson. Peacekeeper."

"I saw you at the township meeting."

"Right," Piers said. "So you're the new face of the paper. Having fun yet?"

"Yup," Rags said. "Loads."

"Terry rip you a new one yet?"

This wasn't what Rags expected to hear. Was Piers on a different page? Is that why he'd left the meeting without sticking around to gossip?

"Why would she?" Rags said. "Don't I look friendly?" She sipped her scotch, watching Piers' rather rubbery face closely. He laughed—a bit too heartily.

"She likes calling the shots, y'know? She and Missy. What a pair."

"And what about you, Piers? You call the shots too, don't you?"

Piers gulped his beer, wiped his mouth on the sleeve of his blue shirt, and took out a small vial of eye drops. He laughed again for no apparent reason, as if he'd just told himself a private joke.

Holy shit, he's stoned.

"When that twerp doesn't get in my way," he said.

"Who?" Rags just wanted to hear him say it.

"Piper the peanut," Piers said. "That's what I call him. You won't print that, right?"

Rags shook her head. She couldn't help smiling.

"Hey, Tim," Piers call out to the guy behind the bar. "Can I get some curly fries, man?"

Rags asked Piers what his days were like, typically. She wanted a sense of who actually did what around Canary. He didn't sound too excited as he described the life of a small-town peacekeeper: breaking up domestic disputes, arresting the occasional "drunk and disorderly," issuing tickets to self-drivers who ran red lights, and once in a blue moon, responding to complaints about property theft, though there wasn't much around to steal, these days. He said people usually bartered for what they wanted or needed.

"You wanna know what really keeps this town going, Rags?" Piers said. She nodded. "It's not the peanut, though he thinks he's hot shit, that hopped-up little—no. It's all the black market shit. But hey, if nobody gets hurt, who cares, right?"

"You mean, like…the woman I keep seeing standing on the corner, waiting?" Rags pictured the woman with the dead eyes. Somebody ought to give a shit.

"You mean Camilla? Sex workers, sure." Piers waved that away, like it was obvious and also not worth commenting on. "But really, it's just people getting what they want and need." His fries arrived and he ate like a starving man. "I mean," he said, his mouth full, grease on his chin, "if somebody needs a satellite link-up and they can't pay the monthlies—and I mean, who can?—and somebody else needs, say, some help shoveling a pile of shit onto a vegetable patch. It's like that."

"And Terry?" Rags thought maybe this peacekeeper didn't know when to shut up, and that was a good thing.

"Oh, with Terry, it's all about the taxes. Property, sales, whatever, getting it filed on time—that's the shit she cares about. So anyway…where was I?" He ate another big wad of fries.

"What people need and want," Rags prompted.

"Yeah, so, you know, it's all about the trades. And as long as people feel they're getting as good as they give, why pry into it? Right? You see that, right?" Piers looked at her, his eyes clearer than before, but maybe that was just the drops. She had no idea what he was on, or how much of it.

"Don't go looking for trouble. Is that what you mean?"

"Yeah, pretty much," he said.

Rags sensed this was the bottom line in Canary. The unwritten rule. If she'd been forced to explain it, she'd guess it just boiled down to everybody feeling damn tired. They'd had enough. Been through enough. Live and let live—now that living was an option again. But the danger, as she saw it, was that this attitude ceded power to the ones who loved power. People like Piper and Terry and Missy. They'd probably fill any power vacuum available. It was in their nature. So maybe this little out-of-the-way town wasn't so different from the city, after all. *Why did I think I could get away from this crap?*

"What about Effie Rutter?" Rags asked, pushing her luck even further.

Piers shook his head.

"I don't know if that's some dirty black-market shit or... something else," he said. "She just fucking vanished. Nobody saw anything—or at least, nobody's come forward. We can't ping her because she left her dataphone behind, probably not on purpose. She was a cheerful kid, seemed pretty happy with her mother. At least, that's what I'm told. And, well, you saw. They only had each other after...after The Big One. If you can think of any way to use the press—you know what I mean—you'd be doing us all a favor." Piers balled up a paper napkin and threw it on his empty plate.

Shit, this is going to get tricky, she thought. A wave of exhaustion came over Rags. She left her second drink unfinished and cupped her left cheek. "We'll see, Piers," she said. "But don't expect any miracles. I don't do miracles."

Rags rose, and so did Piers, and they both walked through the crowded bar out into the night and headed off in separate directions. Rags tried to clear her head in the fresh spring air, to get her priorities straight.

She turned down her street in the dark and had to search the house numbers. Life here was still so new she barely recognized her own modest wood-frame house. The cherry trees helped her claim home, the scent from their blossoms wafting down the walkway. The house was dark save for a bluish glow in the parlor window, which meant, Rags knew, that Flint was still enmeshed. He hadn't bothered to turn on any lights. An old habit.

"Hey," Flint said, stretching. "You hungry?"

Rags gave him a brief, careless hug. "Nah, I'm beat. Long first day. Talk in the morning?"

"I'll be up in a little while," he said, his eyes already back on the screen. He'd flicked off his ear discs for all of thirty seconds, and now he flicked them back on.

Rags got into bed and willed her recurring nightmare to stay away. She also tried not to think about Effie Rutter and how she was going to get dragged into this whether she wanted to or not. Not thinking about Effie was like not thinking about Maya. Even putting all that aside, Rags knew that while newspaper editors had some say in shaping the news, they couldn't avoid actually reporting it.

5

I thought I was dreaming in my own bed.

Then I woke up. What happened is, they chained me flat on my back inside a van. I don't know how I got there. I remember the icy cold metal stinging my bare legs. The road rumbled through my body. My head hurt real, real bad. Oh God, I had to pee. I held it and held it until I couldn't. Warm piss trickled under my uniform, soaking the pleats of my skirt. I cried. It didn't matter.

When they pulled me out of the truck, two of them, sunlight drilled into my headache. My dried piss stung. They lifted me into a boat with a noisy motor. Pushed me onto my back, again, on the floor of the boat.

I call the older ones, the ones who took me and pushed me around, the sadists. The ones who boss the sadists around, I call them the overlords. They all dress the same, like they're going clubbing or something.

I learned what a sadist is in Mrs. Brennan's English class. Nobody thought I was paying attention, but I was. Didn't expect to meet any.

I can't picture Mrs. Brennan, but I can still picture Mom. Her hair is her worst feature. It's stringy and she never takes care of it.

I thought by going blonde I could inspire her. Or at least, not look like her. Maybe both. Doesn't matter now.

They took me to an island. Hauled me out of the boat. I almost tripped on the dock because my hands and feet were still tied together. My skin was rubbing off under the plastic ties. I felt raw all over.

Two sadists and an overlord talked near me, but not to me. They smoked. They made each other laugh. Then the overlord looked at me and handed currency discs to the sadists, got back into the boat, revving the motor.

And then I knew: The overlord had bought me.

Did that mean he owned me? Was I his slave?

I was shaking. My head hurt so bad. The sun hurt my eyes. Thought I would puke, but I didn't want to, in front of them. The overlord cut the zip tie from my ankles so that I could walk. I barely could. So he pushed me, pushed my back, until we reached a long shack, silver metal, like roof gutters stuck together. The sun bounced off the metal, making my eyes hurt even more.

A sadist came out from the shack. The overlord left. The sadist pulled my clothes off. Told me I could keep my underwear. My undies were stiff with pee. He squeezed my breasts through my bra. Then he threw my red-and-white cheerleader outfit into a barrel and set it on fire. I hugged myself tight and closed my eyes.

This wasn't happening. But it was happening.

I wanted to run so bad. But another sadist was there holding a mean dog on a short leash. The dog barked non-stop. I could feel its hot breath and see the fangs and the drool. Reminded me of the wild dogs in Canary, but a lot meaner.

The sadist who stripped me tossed me some raggedy old clothes. He cut my hands loose and told me not to run. There was no point, anyway, he said. Nowhere to run to except straight into the Hooper River or the Chesapeake Bay. The currents are swift, he said. So you're fucked.

He pushed me along a sandy path until we came to another building. This one was long, low, and all white brick. It had no windows and only one door.

He pushed open the door and another sadist appeared, a woman, her head shaved down to the skull. She threw a long white apron over my neck, tied it roughly around my waist, and shoved me over to the end of a very long metal table.

The room was filled with people my age—Black, brown, Native, white, the whole goddamn rainbow.

The tables were piled high with pink and orange crabs. The kids were holding sharp knives, picking the meat out of the crabs. Their hands were flying, bits of crabmeat flicked fast into buckets. Hardly anyone looked up when I came in. The stench was awful. Salty and rancid and bitter. Like the ocean itself had drowned. Nobody else seemed to notice.

I didn't even know they were crabs until Flora told me. They put me next to her, the first day. She didn't look at me even once.

Flora said, If I look at you, I'll cut my finger off. They won't care.

Flora was real skinny and the gums around her teeth were bleeding.

Flora was blonde, like me. I wondered if her color was natural.

Flora grew up in Missouri. She'd already been there half a year. Maybe. She wasn't sure. She overheard a sadist and an overlord talking one day, and that's how she learned that all of us were brought in to replace all the workers who'd died in The Big One. The government wouldn't let any migrant workers into the country to take their place. So we were it.

Flora said they'd figured out a way to farm the crabs year-round. So we weren't seasonal slave labor. We were permanent. That word—permanent—kept rolling around in my head.

We were the answer to the overlords' prayers. And we were making them rich. That's what Flora said, and I believed her.

I found a black Sharpie on the ground one day soon after I arrived. Don't know when exactly. That's when I had the idea. The bedsheet diary, I call it. I sleep inside the airless metal shack on a hard narrow bunk on top of my own words. The sheet's just a big scrap of cloth, anyway. When the Sharpie runs dry, I suppose I'll go crazy.

Did they throw away my pom-poms?

6

The doorbell rang at seven sharp the morning after the township meeting.

"What the hell," said Flint, still groggy. "We need a visi-cam. No more surprises."

"It's the PHP," Rags said, already dressed and putting on her high-top sneakers. She wore the same flannel shirt as the day before. "I forgot to warn you last night. Sorry."

"Now?" Flint said. "I haven't even taken my temp yet this morning. These people are relentless, aren't they?" Flint swung his hairy legs over the side of the bed and got moving. "Where are you going? You can't skip the inspection."

Rags handed Flint her personal thermometer. They both knew the drill: Piper would collect ninety days of temp data and re-calibrate their thermometers to ensure they were accurate. He would also collect Flint's contact trace data. Part of the routine procedure everywhere. Rags had hoped—futilely, it turned out—that this kind of shit wouldn't follow them out to the boondocks.

"I'll let Piper in. The PHP. He's a real treat."

Flint pulled on pants and followed Rags downstairs. She opened the door and Piper, in the trademark green coveralls, hat, gloves, and respie, walked right in without an invitation. Rags handed Piper her thermometer and slipped out the front door.

"Damn it, Rags!" Flint said. "What am I supposed to say?"

Rags was well aware she was leaving Flint alone to field questions about why her thermometer was data-less. And he'd have to let Piper get near his little village of electronics. Everything in the house would be laser-sprayed, releasing a high-powered disinfectant that was invisible to the naked eye. You could say this was overkill, as the house had already been cleared, but

Rags was certain that PHP Madrigal would never leave anything to chance. Rags also knew whatever Piper did would feel uncomfortably intrusive to Flint. And she'd willingly abandoned him. She filed that away for later.

An hour later, Piper walked into the *Courant* office, exactly as promised.

"You're out of compliance!" Piper yelled the moment he crossed the threshold. Runaway truck barreling into the building, careless of what or who got in the way. Beads of sweat shone on Piper's forehead. Rags expected this and didn't budge. Merry instantly guessed at the situation and got pumped up.

"If your temp isn't normal, I swear I will kill you myself, Rags," Merry said, keeping her distance. "After everything… You have no fucking right to put any of us in danger. You have no right to be here. We'll have to burn this place down. You realize that, don't you?"

"Calm the fuck down, Merry," Rags said. "It's over, don't you people get it? You're not gonna keel over tomorrow. Or the next day. No one is. Isn't that right, Piper?"

"That's not the point," Piper said.

"But isn't it true, Piper, that there isn't a single person in Canary who is currently spiking a fever or showing any signs of a virus, whether known or otherwise?"

"Because I'm vigilant," Piper said.

"There, Merry, you see? Everything's fine. Try and find a *real* reason to get all worked up, why don't you."

"You really have no fucking clue," Merry said. Rags ignored her.

"You've got thirty days," Piper said. "I'm coming back for your temp data, and if you're still out of compliance—"

"What?" Rags said. "You can't arrest me."

"You have no idea what I can do," Piper said. "Watch me."

"You should listen to him, Rags," Merry said. "This isn't just about you."

"Keep an eye on her," Piper said to Merry.

"Are you asking her to spy on me?" Rags laughed. "Well,

I'm an open book. So good luck with that. But you're right, Merry, this isn't about me. Piper, I'm asking you on the record to explain what's being done about the leaking septic tank on the south side of town."

"It's being handled," Piper said.

"That's not good enough," Rags said. "Tell me exactly what's gone wrong, who's fixing it, and when." Piper looked at Merry as if to say, *must I?* "Don't ask her. She's got nothing to do with this. She can't string two sentences together." Merry glared and sat down. Piper hesitated. "Where I come from, PHPs don't just practice health-care theater, Piper. They actually do the work. But I guess it's different here, in a backwater like Canary."

That bit of reverse psychology did the trick. Piper explained in a rush that the drain field needed to be replaced, which meant a lot of messy digging and the installation of new pipes. Rags asked several follow-up questions: Who was paying for the repairs? How long would it take? Would the affected homeowners have to boil all their water? The *Courant* had yet to dig into this properly and Rags was committed to telling the whole story. This was the stuff that local papers should live for. Did anyone else understand that?

Piper was bouncing on his toes. Eager to be off, bullying someone else, Rags supposed.

"That's it," Piper said. "That's all there is."

The PHP whipped out of the office, slamming the *Courant*'s heavy front door.

"You should show them some respect," Merry said.

"Piper gets what he deserves. *Sic semper tyrannis.*"

"That PHP might save your life one day. I hope I'm there to watch you beg for it."

"That PHP, Merry, is nothing but a jack-booted thug who will throw you in jail if you so much as sneeze."

Merry rolled her eyes and turned away.

Rags began organizing her notes from the interview with Piper. She kept half an eye on Merry, trying to figure out what she was actually doing. Asking Merry to explain her job, Rags knew, would not yield the exact truth. Rags suspected that Merry did just enough to literally get the paper published. Her role, her presence, did not make sense. She didn't seem to have any normal newsroom function, such as reporter, line or copy editor, proofreader, or graphic designer. She seemed to know Fred, the dead copy editor. But maybe she was just parroting what she'd heard others say. The only thing Rags had seen her really lean in to so far was gathering the ad info. Rags decided she'd quietly build her own journalistic case about Merry, and to do that, she had to let her go her own way, for now.

Rags realized she'd have to speak with the contractor digging up the septic field and she, or someone, would have to go out there and take pictures. She needed writers, real writers. The Sunday news hole had to be filled, somehow. As if on cue, the door opened and three people walked in, clearly familiar with the place. A man who appeared to be in his fifties, with the pallid look of a survivor, headed straight for Rags.

"Why didn't you talk to me first?" the man said, his skin turning a mottled purple. "That was a shitty thing to do. You could've at least asked." The other two, both women, also crowded Rags's desk.

"We know what we're doing," one of the women protested.

"We've been doing this a long time," said the third. "Ask Merry."

Rags turned to the man first. "What shitty thing?"

"The township meeting," he said. "I cover those. Always have. Merry told me not to show up. Said you wanted to handle it alone. Said you didn't need any freelancers messing it up."

Ah, the freelancers, Rags thought. And how clever of Merry to poison the well right away, so that she'd have to begin with them on her back foot. She could see she'd have to work quickly now to earn their trust and cooperation—which she should have by rights, as their editor. She wouldn't bother to refute Merry's lie, as she didn't want to start off on the defensive.

"I told them to come in this morning," Merry said from the fortress of her own desk. "Forgot to let you know."

Rags stood up. "Our first editorial meeting. Great! Everyone take a seat. Merry, you can stay where you are." The three writers pulled folding chairs into a widely spaced semicircle. They were not wearing respies, which Rags took as a sign that they were reasonably level-headed when they weren't upset. Rags pulled her own chair around to join them. Staying behind her desk, and lording her authority over them, would have been a boneheaded move.

"Tell me who you are, tell me your beats, and please, tell me you've got something worked up for the Sunday edition." Marginally mollified by the invitation, the writers introduced themselves. Brent, with a ring of light brown hair framing a shiny bald scalp, dressed in a soiled button-down shirt and equally soiled khakis, explained that he covered local politics and town business generally. He made a point of telling Rags that he hadn't missed a township meeting since the meetings had resumed after The Big One, and he didn't intend to miss another one and if she wanted to argue with him about it, he couldn't stop her, but dammit, he'd show up at the next meeting, regardless. He also, he said proudly, was the paper's self-appointed arts critic, covering the occasional choir concert, dance performance, or downtown art exhibit. These were becoming a bit more frequent, he said. "An encouraging sign, I think. And about time."

"You need to understand," Dineen said. "We're paid by the article. If we don't publish, we don't get paid. You have no right to take that away from us." Dineen was thin and seemed nervous, her face was etched with lines, although Rags would bet she wasn't even forty. A once-chipper blue-eyed blonde who wrote about education and also covered the obituaries. A weird combination, but she seemed fine with it. Rags had a hard time picturing Dineen as a mother herself, given the education beat. But one didn't ask about things like that; too much loss was still too present.

"As it is, I sew clothes, just to make ends meet," Ramona added. "Writing for the *Courant* doesn't pay the bills. You must know that." Ramona wrote about health care and local sports.

Another oddball pairing. She was small and muscled, probably pretty fast on the field with a hockey stick, Rags imagined. And surely she spoke with Piper on a regular basis. Rags immediately asked her to take some photos of the septic field site and knock on doors in the neighborhood. Ramona agreed. One down, anyway, Rags thought.

As they sat together for about an hour, Rags was finally able to piece together how the editorial side of the paper worked. The freelanced features, combined with national wire stories and other syndicated features pulled down to plug in any news holes, made up most of the paper. The filler helped: a puzzles page, a seasonal recipe or two, a syndicated self-help column (lame, Rags thought), and the occasional oversized photo accompanied by a caption and no story. Sometimes it was no more than a kid holding a garden hose while a puppy leaped in mid-air to drink from it. The Wednesday and Sunday editions weren't really all that different, though the twice-monthly Sunday paper devoted a full spread to local letters to the editor and opinion pieces. Rags knew she'd be sifting through those herself and writing Sunday's editorial column. She only had a few days to pull all that together. But there was one topic they hadn't covered.

"What about the investigative work? Who does that?" Rags asked. The freelancers exchanged a look.

"There isn't really anything to investigate in Canary," Brent said.

"Oh, come on," Rags said. "You're not serious."

"We're only expected to write features," Ramona said.

"Piers said something about a thriving black market, here in Canary," Rags said. The freelancers just shrugged. They didn't appear to be hiding anything; Rags guessed they just didn't care. Their own bartering needs were being met, she assumed, one way or another. And so there it was again: the tacit agreement that everyone was better off if they didn't tip the proverbial apple cart.

"Who's writing about Effie Rutter, then?" Rags asked,

looking at Merry. She realized she hadn't noticed the byline on the recent coverage, maybe because she was so intent on finding ways *not* to cover the story for the time being.

"That's handled separately," Merry said.

"What do you mean?" Rags asked, looking at all of them as if they were crazy.

"Well, nobody asked us to write about Effie," Brent said.

"We're not supposed to, anyway," Dineen said. "Like Ramona said, we're strictly feature writers."

"Merry, can you explain this?" Rags asked across the room.

Merry sighed dramatically. "That copy—everything about Effie—just gets sent to me," Merry said.

"It *what*?" Rags asked. What kind of newspaper was this?

"We run it as is," Merry said. "It's fine. It's good." Rags confirmed with Merry that the byline on those articles simply said 'By a *Courant* Editor.' Normally, an anonymous print byline was reserved for writers on strike; they deliberately withheld their names from appearing in print as a form of protest. Rags couldn't imagine running an investigative news story without holding a reporter publicly accountable. But apparently, Merry didn't worry about journalistic niceties like that. Rags was truly beginning to hate Merry for her seemingly deliberate passive incompetence. Redeemable? Hardly. Rags was tempted to call it sabotage. She couldn't begin to guess why this woman seemed hell-bent on screwing things up—for her and for the paper, generally—but there was no time to ponder that.

"We're not running any more stories about Effie Rutter until I say it's okay," Rags said to the room. "And if and when we do write about this, I will handle it. I will be the one on the record. Is that clear?"

"But—" Merry started.

"There is no 'but,' Merry!" Rags shouted across the room. "The *Canary Courant* will never ever run an anonymous news story again. Everybody got that?"

"We like our bylines," Brent said. "You get no argument from us."

"You can't just write whatever you want," Merry said. "Actions have consequences, you know."

"Oh yeah?" Rags said. "Thanks for cluing me in."

"But you have no idea—"

"You know what, Merry? Stop second-guessing me." Rags wanted the freelancers to hear this. "I'm in charge, like it or not, and you can stay or you can go. But if you stay, you'll have to trust that I know what I'm doing."

Merry put her face in her hands as if the world were coming to an end. Rags was already tired of her melodramatics. She told the freelancers to file their stories by five p.m. sharp on Friday. She said late copy would be rejected, which meant no paycheck. The writers left. Merry wouldn't meet Rags's angry stare. Rags pushed her chair back around to her own screen and stared blankly at all the words on the digital page, trying to figure out why things were so screwed up around here. She envied Flint, whose work seemed so straightforward, not subject to the illogical, duplicitous whims of human nature. He had it so much easier than she did. She chased away an unfair twinge of resentment.

7

Over the next several weeks, Rags thought of little besides getting out a paper that she could stand behind, despite all the nonsense that was printed. It felt good to finally have something that required all her attention. The trio of freelancers quickly forgave her for her perceived misstep (Merry's doing) and proved reliable. Merry had shown her hand with that little stunt and now Rags was on the lookout for other forms of sabotage. Dineen had called a few days after their initial meeting, asking if she could add religion to her list of beats. She told Rags she thought that not enough attention had been paid to the town's spiritual life, especially since the town was surrounded by three churches—Baptist, Catholic, and African Methodist Episcopal, or AME for short. Religion bored Rags to tears; she had absolutely no use for it. But editorially, it was a good idea, so she said yes to Dineen. She could ask the priests and pastors to write alternating columns on whatever pablum suited them; that would help fill column inches.

Rags wanted to put out a quality newspaper, one that upheld the best tenets of journalism. But putting her principles into practice was proving harder than she expected. As a crusader, she was clearly on her own. And in the absence of any feedback from the mysterious publisher, to whom she hadn't spoken since she'd been offered the job, it was tricky to figure out how hard, how far, and how fast to push. She wasn't afraid of any backlash from Terry or anyone else, but she didn't want to risk getting booted out, either. She felt like she was standing on quicksand, and that was not a good place for a newspaper editor to be.

The only bright spot seemed to be that Porter proved reliable; the papers landed on subscribers' doorsteps without fail. To show her appreciation for Porter, she told him she'd pay for any maintenance or repairs on his truck, if needed. Porter said he had that covered, but thanks, anyway. She guessed that Porter was engaged in an elaborate system of bartered trades, and perhaps truck maintenance was part of that web. She wondered, briefly, about his son.

Rags figured she'd better start getting to know the town she was supposed to write about in her Sunday editorials. So every afternoon, she left the office and set out on foot (the hunt for bicycles still hadn't happened) to call on the local businesses still operating. She had to start somewhere. In time, she planned to take a ShareCar out to the working farms in the area. Most of the light industry and technology start-ups that had once dotted the region outside of Canary—taking advantage of the open ex-urban land that came pretty cheap—had not returned since The Big One, which meant those jobs were gone too. As a result, the town of Canary was more self-sufficient than it had been in well over a century. Rags observed that most backyards were filled with vegetable gardens and many residents, she learned, had taken up canning and pickling. No doubt they traded food for other things. Ramona and Brent had each pressed on her jars of homemade preserves and pickles. Startled, she told them she had nothing to trade in return. Ramona told her that small-town hospitality wasn't entirely dead. The town as a whole felt, to Rags, somewhat provisional, as if it were still deciding whether it had a reason to exist, to keep going, to claw its way back up a shaky economic ladder—if that were even possible.

At the bar and grill, she met the owners, Ted and Roger Fallon. She recognized Ted as the guy who'd given Piers his curly fries. They were tall, lean, and bald (like so many of the male Luckies). While they didn't seem to mind Rags's unexpected visit, they remained behind the bar the whole time, evidently not eager to settle in for a long chat. Both wore denim work shirts rolled up at the sleeves, a bar rag slung over each of their shoulders. There was only one day-drinker in the bar that day: Keller, the township board member. Rags was surprised to see him there, looking flushed, hunched over his glass. He took his drink and removed himself to a far table as soon as she began talking with Ted and Roger. Clearly, Keller did not wish to speak with her and she wouldn't embarrass him by trying to make small talk. The man was evidently troubled about something, and that wasn't a matter for public record. Not yet anyway.

"We met at a big tech firm in Silicon Valley," Ted volunteered. "Coders, both of us."

"I grew up around here," Roger said. "When the shit hit the fan, I dragged Ted back. We sunk everything we had into this place."

"It was a disgusting mess," Ted said. "We think a bunch of people were actually living in here, in the bar, drinking up everything left behind by the previous owners when they died."

"I barely recognized Canary," Roger said, shaking his head. "It was...lawless. Reckless."

"Every man, woman, and child for themselves," Ted said. "That was the feeling. People did all sorts of crazy shit, like living in a bar, drinking themselves blind."

"Trying to wait it out," Roger said. "Maybe they thought alcohol would keep the virus at bay."

"It didn't," Ted said.

"We found two dead bodies in here, didn't we, honey?" Roger said. "Right there." He pointed to the middle of the room. Ted nodded. "Oh God, you're not going to write about this, are you?"

"Please don't," Ted said, frowning at Rags. "Don't. Nobody wants to dredge up old history. Besides, it isn't news. Far from it."

"I have zero interest in strolling down Memory Lane," Rags said, losing interest and patience with both of them. "I don't want to write about the past and nobody wants to read it, either. Do you read the paper?" Neither of them nodded. "It's about now, today, next week, not all that old shit." Of course, it wasn't about much at all, Rags thought.

"Well, so, what do you want from us?" Roger said. "We're

just small business owners, trying to make a living. End of story. I mean, there *is* no story."

"Without naming names," Rags said, "what do people talk about in here? What's on people's minds?"

Ted made a *tsk* sound. "We're bartenders, Rags. We can't tell you what anybody says. They'd stop coming."

"Haven't you ever spent time in a bar?" Roger asked.

"Oh, come on. I'm not asking you to give away state secrets. Just trying to get to know the place. What are people worrying about? What's on *your* minds?"

Ted and Roger exchanged a look.

"How's the black market affecting your business?" Rags knew this was a shot in the dark, but she took it anyway.

"Black market?" Ted said. "Our customers pay for their drinks."

"And we pay wholesalers in currency for our liquor," Roger added.

"If you're looking for trouble—" Ted said.

"Or trying to get *us* in trouble—" Roger jumped in.

"You won't find any here," Ted said. "We run a clean business. I'll show you our books."

"No," Rags said. "That's not necessary. Believe it or not, I came here for small-town gossip, not an exposé. I thought the bar was the best place to start. Guess I was wrong."

"Right," Ted said. He pulled the rag off his shoulder and began wiping spots off glasses.

"Effie Rutter." Rags turned. It was Keller who said it. She'd almost forgotten he was there. "That's what people talk about. And if you really gave a shit about this town, that's the only story you'd be working on."

Rags looked at Ted and Roger. They were wiping down the taps and preparing for the afternoon rush. She knew she'd hit a wall with all three of them, and pushing against that wall now could harm her chances of sounding them out later.

"Thanks, anyway," Rags said with an edge. "And don't worry. You didn't give me anything worth printing." Fucking

Effie Rutter. For someone who wasn't actually around, she sure seemed to be everywhere. What was the deal with Keller? Maybe he knew more than he was saying, but Rags knew this wasn't the time or place to figure that out. Not with Ted and Roger glaring at her, and not while Keller was so drunk.

Rags squinted in the sunlight after emerging from the dimly lit bar, a former chamber of horrors that was now just a regular old place to get drunk or have a laugh. The Fallons' story dredged up memories from her own past that she very much did not want to revisit. She'd stood there listening to them, awash in private images of blood and sickness and death. *Stupid to think I could really outrun it.* She was furious with herself for going at them so directly. That was clearly a mistake—journalistic malpractice. Her hand flew to her cheek, her index finger laid gently in the corner of her eye. A preemptive strike, of sorts.

She wondered if she would help her cause by introducing Flint to the Fallons. Maybe they'd bond over some nerdy tech stuff. As far as Rags could tell, Flint had barely left the house since they'd arrived except to forage for groceries, which, he'd reported, often required multiple stops. They weren't in on the whole bartering side of things—not yet, at least. He spoke even less than usual since they'd arrived in Canary and she'd been so busy trying to get a handle on the paper, she hadn't had the time or the energy to try to pry him open. Flint, it seemed, had bonded with his digital screens and little else. As a partner, he was steady and reliable, but their relationship took work. Too much work, maybe. The thought put her in a foul mood.

As she walked down Main Street, she saw the woman with dead eyes was there on one of the corners she frequented. Piers had said her name. Camilla? The woman beckoned to Rags. Up close, Camilla appeared older than Rags had imagined, her face lined and creased under a thick layer of makeup. Rags thought she was wearing a brunette wig, giving her big hair. Her eyes were deep brown pools of nothing.

"Are you okay?" Rags asked. She didn't want to say the

woman's name, since that would suggest she'd already talked about her behind her back.

"What do you like?" the woman said.

"Has anyone mistreated you?"

"I take food, currency, jewelry."

"Do you need help?" Rags asked. "Is there something I can do for you? Can I summon a ShareCar for you?"

The woman shook her head. "Fuck off," she said.

Rags would let her be. This would not find its way into the paper. She was beginning to understand there was no point in writing about, or printing, the reality that everyone in Canary was already living. That's why people preferred to see the crossword puzzle: a new distraction every week, all upside and no downside.

Rags left Camilla, if that's who she was, on the corner. She did not want to witness her picking up a customer. It was around three in the afternoon and Main Street was mostly dead. Rags avoided looking at the bright digital posters of Effie Rutter, though she could not shake the image of her blonde-haired, bright-eyed innocence still beaming uselessly from the small round projectors attached to the old-fashioned lampposts. The blocks were lined with old brick storefronts, many of them nearly identical to the *Courant*'s. Many were dark. Some were laser-gated—a cross-hatch of red clearly indicating that the premises should not be breached. Rags had seen this in the city, as well; it was a cordon intended to prevent contamination with sites that had been intense viral hotspots, like the vestibule of the apartment complex where all those people had died. No doubt Piper Madrigal had set up these cordoned sites and inspected them frequently. Rags wondered why he didn't just tear these places down, but she wouldn't put it past Piper to insist they remain as a warning—a way to keep people scared. *Never forget.*

She came to a block she hadn't walked down yet. A cluster of people, the only one she'd seen that afternoon, was going in and out of a storefront that stood apart from the rest. It was white, clean, and looked like new or at least freshly painted. Of course: the cannabis shop. The white neon sign over the door said Mellonia. Rags knew, without entering, that this must be where Piers shopped to keep himself well-supplied. And most of Canary, judging by the traffic. Customers came out of Mellonia ripping wrappers off edibles and other feel-good supplies. So when you came right down to it, this is what post-pandemic Canary had to offer: you could booze it up at the bar and grill or bliss out at Mellonia. You could have sex with a stranger in exchange for a crate of oranges. Many ways to take the edge off.

No wonder nobody reads the newspaper.

Rags felt an urge to get away from Main Street, away from Effie's gaze, away from the sad air of failed commerce, a town beaten into submission by death and its companion, defeat. Walking past an alleyway that ran perpendicular to Main Street, a flash of color caught her eye: a wall and a door, flush to the alley, splashed in bright pink paint. Apart from the tulips, cherry blossoms, and other brief profusion of spring flowers, Rags realized the town of Canary was mainly coated in drab brick-browns, grays, and dark blues; Mellonia's bright whiteness was a rare exception. She turned down the alley and paused in front of the pink explosion coating the wall. The painter hadn't bothered to square off the color lines where the door met the building's peeling stucco. Instead, the pink simply flared out in uneven brush strokes, with the doorway and several feet surrounding it thoroughly saturated.

The pink almost seemed to speak for itself: a challenge, a dare, a scream into the wind that not all was lost, that the business of living continued. The color took a bit of the edge off her bad mood. Alley doors were almost always locked, but not this one and thank God for that because Rags felt she had to find out what was inside. She entered a room flooded with light. Wide skylights that were not visible from the street allowed daylight to stream in. The walls were bright white, with the same pink traveling around the room's baseboard and crown molding. Huge abstract paintings, many colors blasted together, hung on the walls. And in the center of the room stood four white pedestals topped with white-and-gray marbled sculptures. Rags hadn't had time to figure out what they all were, but they almost appeared to be in motion, radiating energy.

"Hello?" Rags called.

"Be right there!" called a woman's voice. It came from behind a freestanding partition that ran the width of the gallery. Rags hadn't noticed it because it was white just like the walls. A moment later, Rags heard a clack of heels and a woman around Rags's age, thirty-two-ish, emerged, wiping her hands on a rough rag.

"Gesso," she said. "It gets everywhere, if you're not careful." Rags didn't know what she was talking about, which must have shown plainly on her face. "You know, the stuff you spread to prepare canvas? Kind of gunky? Well, never mind." The woman dressed unlike anyone else Rags had seen in Canary. She wore tall leather boots with a chunky heel, a full, multi-colored skirt, and a loose silky-looking blouse that hung off one shoulder. Her hair was long and thick and so black it almost looked deep blue. Her eyes were coal-black as well. The woman reminded Rags of the creative types she used to know in the city, a long time ago. She thought the breed had vanished, but no, for here was a perfect specimen. Rags realized she hadn't said a word; she was just standing there. "I don't recognize you," the woman continued, "which is probably why you're here. Nobody in Canary visits the gallery. If I put on a show and offer free wine and cheese, then they come—sort of. Otherwise, it's crickets around here."

"I haven't been inside an art gallery since…well, years ago… in the city," Rags said. "I'd forgotten…the colors, I mean… and the light. It reminds me…well, you know, how things used to be." *There's something about this place. Maybe the light. Maybe the art—which exists for its own sake.* "Why are you even here?"

The woman laughed. "You mean, here in Canary? I wasn't. I didn't plan to be. I came back after both my mother and father..." The woman waved off the rest of the sentence. "I had to figure out what to do with the house and all their stuff. My brother and sister were also gone by then. You know. The usual. And then, I don't know." The woman cast her eyes around the large, framed abstracts on the wall. "I kind of lost steam and just stayed."

"Brent must have done a story on you at some point," Rags said.

"Who?"

"You must know him. Brent. He writes about art, among other things, for the *Courant*."

"The what?"

"The newspaper," Rags said. "The *Canary Courant*."

"I guess I don't read it," she said lightly.

"I'm the editor," Rags said. "But it's okay," she added quickly. "Nobody actually reads it." Rags explained she was new in town.

"I'm Louisa Copperface. On days when I'm feeling grand, I call this the Copperface Gallery. Otherwise, it's just my studio with room to hang stuff."

"I wouldn't call it 'stuff,'" Rags said.

"What, then?" Louisa asked, and Rags felt the artist's dark eyes probing her, as if she were searching for a kindred soul. Rags felt an urgent need not to disappoint her—the first time she'd felt something like that since arriving in Canary. The first time, she realized, since Maya had come to live with her, years earlier.

"Each one is like a dance," Rags said. "I can almost see the paint darting around the canvas. But it's not an organized dance. More like a free-for-all." Rags stopped to see how Louisa was receiving her off-the-cuff comments. At least she wasn't frowning. "It's chaotic, but in an arranged sort of way. I'm sorry, I sound like an idiot."

"No, no," Louisa said. "I'm dying of thirst in the desert here. It's great to hear something, anything, to break the spell."

"You should go where you'll be appreciated," Rags said. "This town—"

"Yeah, I know. This town. But, you know, roots and all. Deep roots, actually."

Rags didn't know, but she didn't think she should probe further.

"Tell me about the sculptures," Rags said. She lightly touched one of the veined sculptures, her finger tracing its smooth curves.

Louisa explained that they were made from soapstone and each one represented a legendary encounter between a human and a beast—an ox, a bull, a tiger, a bear. The sculptures were meant to represent a moment when human and beast were one, with neither emerging as a clear victor. She drew on ancient lore from many indigenous cultures around the world, she said.

As Louisa spoke about the sculptures, Rags wished all of Canary could feel like this gallery and all of the residents could be like Louisa. Fresh, open, clean, no hidden agendas. The spoils of disease had been banished here—or so it felt to her. Wasn't that what she and Flint had come looking for in the first place? Rags wanted to lie down on the polished wooden floor, stare up at the bright skylight, and wait for peace to arrive.

"Rags?" Louisa said. "Rags?"

"I'm sorry, what?"

"I asked if you'd like to see my studio. Since you're from the city, not just another Canary hick, let me show you some new stuff I'm working on. It's a departure from the abstracts. I'd appreciate a stranger's eye—somebody who isn't an artist but knows how to look at art. Just give me a first impression, that's all I ask. It isn't often…" She again waved dismissively. "Well, you know."

Louisa led Rags behind the partition that ran wall-to-wall across the gallery. The working studio was a sharp contrast with the stark, spare gallery space. The studio, directly beneath a skylight, was cluttered with old saw-horse tables, rolled up canvases, frames on stretchers, and lots of paint cans and brushes scattered around. The floor was piled with art books.

"What do you think? Honestly?" Louise pointed to an

incomplete oil painting. It was a portrait, the planes of the figure's head delineated by sharp-edge colors, contrasting shades that cohered into a recognizable whole. Rags had seen enough art to know whose work she was reminded of—Lucian Freud—but she didn't want to say so.

"It's bold. Very expressive," Rags ventured. "Who is it?"

"Oh," Louisa said, deflated. "You don't recognize her?"

Rags stared at the painting some more. There was something familiar about the sitter's eyes, but she didn't know why. "I'm sorry," she said. "But I like it. I'm drawn to it, I mean."

"It's Effie Rutter," Louisa said. "I used the digital billboard as my source. I've never met her, of course. So I have to extrapolate, you know, to guess at how her features are arranged." Rags stepped back from the painting, as if Effie herself were about to leap off the canvas and scold her.

"I'm sorry," Rags said. "Maybe because the tattoo isn't there." The sunburst design on Effie's cheek, a monument to her innocence, to being alive.

"Not yet," Louisa said. She explained that she wanted to create a series of portraits reflecting people in crisis. She decided that Effie was a dramatic first subject for the series. Rags heard a ringing in her ears and wasn't able to take in everything Louisa was saying.

Maya, staring up at me, a look in her eyes that asked, 'How could you let this happen?'

She thanked Louisa, told her Brent would be in touch, and then she strode across the bright gallery floor and out into the alley. Her left eye began twitching rapidly.

Quit following me.

Rags could feel Effie's eyes—those digitally enhanced, larger-than-life eyes following her down Main Street. The same eyes that Louisa had painted. What was she thinking? A maudlin tribute? A mawkish fundraiser—the painting to be auctioned off to help poor Evelyn Rutter? Rags had left before Louisa could explain. Maybe there was no explanation. Artists did whatever they wanted.

What would I do, if I did anything I wanted?

Rags had no ready answer. She wrote news stories for a living. This was her path and not even a death-rattling pandemic could push her off it. She sat down hard in her office chair. Merry was out. Good. She forced herself to edit the stories submitted by the freelancers. She had to read the same lines over and over, bidding her wandering concentration to return. Ramona had filed an update on the repairs to the septic field, now well underway. She'd interviewed three families (in reality, they were Luckies, some related by blood, some not, who'd blended together to form new families) to learn how they were coping without running water. They all seemed downright cheerful—an outlook informed by having survived hell. Sometimes, survivor guilt morphed into a giddy sense of freedom. Ramona's photos were pretty good; Rags chose the ones to run with the story.

Once she'd finished the line edits to all the new copy, Rags sent a message to Brent, asking him to schedule a feature about the Copperface Gallery, with plenty of photos. She emphasized that he should only highlight the work for sale to the public in the gallery itself—not anything that Louisa still considered work-in-progress. Hopefully, that would keep the Effie portrait out of the story. She hoped he didn't make a mess of it. The moment came when she could no longer put off drafting her editorial for Sunday's paper. The obvious subject was Effie Rutter. But Rags couldn't bring herself to write it. And what was there to say that hadn't already been said? Instead, she wrote a fluffy feel-good piece about springtime in Canary, the enduring hope promised by the blossoming cherry trees and other crap in a similar vein. She knew the piece would be forgotten before the readers' eyes even left the page, but she didn't care. Nobody was going to read it anyway. She had just one job to do in Canary, and she found herself struggling to get it done. *This damn town.*

At home that night, Rags told Flint they should get bicycles. Even used ones would be fine.

"Why?" Flint asked.

"What do you mean, why?"

"Where would we go?" he asked, spooning rice and beans onto their plates.

"Well, we could ride out into the country. Out to the little farm stands. Just…out."

"You're already sick of Canary," he said. "I knew this would happen. I knew small-town life—"

"Canary is fine," she said. "Don't assume you know what I'm thinking when we barely have conversations lasting more than thirty seconds."

"You're never here," he said.

"That never bothered you before. And anyway, *you* never leave," she replied, "which is why biking would be good for us."

"You mean, good for *me*," he said. "You don't want me to assume I know what's going on with you? Fine. Then don't assume you know about me, either."

"Well, if you'd tell me, if you'd actually use words, then maybe I *would* know," Rags said. "I'm not a fucking mind reader."

"No, that's for sure."

"What the fuck is that supposed to mean?" Rags said, her fork clattering on the plate. Flint just shrugged. Rags knew he wouldn't say more than the little he'd already said. He was infuriating. Small-town life, sharing this quiet house, was turning out not to be a balm to their relationship. Rags was on the verge of regretting they'd hooked up four years ago, when neither of them was thinking straight; when the idea that normal civilian life might resume—gluing them together like any ordinary couple—seemed like a long shot. They brought their plates to the sink and retreated from one another. Later that night, when Rags woke suddenly from another nightmare, she discovered she was alone in bed.

The next morning Rags rose early, leaving Flint in a deep sleep at the far edge of the bed. She wondered if he was beginning to reverse his diurnal cycle—staying up all night doing God knows what, then sleeping most of the day. If that were true, that would obviously make it even harder to connect—or reconnect—on the same footing as before. Rags left the house angry and frustrated. The last thing she wanted to drag around with her in Canary was "personal problems." She didn't need the bullshit or the baggage. Why couldn't Flint become more normal, instead of less normal?

At the office, Rags banged out some quick, easy stories about a new hair salon opening up in town—the first in a long time—and an interview with a Maryland author who'd just published a book on small towns in Maryland, including a pitifully brief profile of Canary. Rags was well aware this was about as far from "investigative" journalism as you could get, but the pages had to be filled and investigations took time. She edited stories by Ramona about a new middle-school lacrosse coach and by Dineen, who'd interviewed the high school principal on her tenth anniversary as head of school—no small accomplishment in these times. Brent hadn't yet filed a story on Louisa's gallery but he did turn in a decent piece about the township's effort to attract a regional rural ShareCar hub. Rags doubted that would happen, given the zealous competition for new business and Canary's insignificance at large. The small-potatoes feel and general futility of it all only worsened Rags's mood.

A few minutes before ten, Merry trudged in. She went straight to her desk and a moment later, the phone rang. Ah, Tuesday, Rags realized: ad day. Rags stopped what she was doing to eavesdrop. Merry was as diligent as ever, taking down the copy verbatim, taking care to get every word right. And the ads were as weird as ever: an online course for growing bonsai trees, with precise information about tree heights; a verbose description about a chimney sweep service; another in a series of elaborate international vacation packages; and a handful of quirky personal ads, such as: *Military historian seeks like-minded time traveler to tour all 52,000 acres of Civil War battlefields in twenty-four states, looking for love and comfort along the way.*

"Merry," Rags said the moment she was off the phone. "Explain this to me right now. No more excuses."

"They'll only talk to me, you know," Merry said.

"That's not what I'm asking you, and you know it," Rags said.

"Without me, you couldn't publish." Merry sat in her chair and crossed her arms, looking like an immoveable object.

"That's bullshit."

"Oh yeah? Where's the money gonna come from without the ads? You know damn well *I'm* the one keeping this place going."

"This isn't about *you*, Merry," Rags said. "You're just the typist. Anybody could do what you're doing. *I* could do it—without you."

"No, you couldn't," Merry said.

"Why not? Give me one good reason."

"Because," Merry said, "I told you. They'll only speak to me. They won't trust anybody else."

"This is the weirdest bullshit I've ever heard, Merry. Do you even hear what you're saying?"

"Well, it's true."

"Oh yeah?" Rags said. "I'll call them myself. The publisher who hired me. I've got the number right here." Merry sat back and smiled, but it was a grim smile. Rags called the number on her dataphone. No one answered. "Give me the number they use to call you."

Merry kept on smiling. "I can't," she said, with a shrug.

"What do you mean, you can't?"

"I've got my own contract with them, Rags. This is the deal. This is how it works."

"You know what, Merry? You're fired. Take your stuff and go. I'll manage without you. I'm looking forward to it."

Merry laughed. "Good one," she said.

"What?"

"You can't fire me, Rags. I don't work for you. I work for *them*."

"Who, Merry? Why are you fucking lying to me? Why, Merry? Why do you do that?" Rags rose to her feet so abruptly that she sent her office chair rolling backwards, crashing into the wall. Merry laughed long and loud, a crazy sort of laugh that reminded Rags of the sound a wounded animal makes when it's cornered.

"Go fuck yourself, Rags," Merry said. So this was how it would be: all-out war between them. Rags vowed to find a way to evict her and figure out where these mysterious ads were coming from and who was paying for them—and why.

Piper Madrigal rushed into the *Courier* office, forcing Rags and Merry to call a temporary halt to their fight.

"Day thirty, Rags," Piper said, his dark-rimmed eyes flaring dramatically above the face mask.

"So?" Rags said.

"You owe me a month of temp data. It's the law."

"You and your fucking law," Rags said, feeling herself edging toward unreasonable anger. She didn't expect he'd hold her to it, and anyway, she'd forgotten all about it. "You're fighting ghosts, Piper. Why are you wasting my time with this bullshit? I'm trying to put out a newspaper—for the living, not the dead."

"Town ordinance," Piper said flatly. "Suck it up."

"Well, I don't have your fucking temp data, Piper. I stopped taking my temperature a long time ago. And maybe Canary should think about updating its laws. Stop wasting everybody's time."

"It's not up to you," Piper said. "You can say whatever you want in the stupid newspaper, but in the *real* world, you do as you're told."

"You think you're above the fuckin' law?" Merry shouted at Rags.

"Oh, shut up, Merry," Rags said. "Fine me, Piper. I'll dip into my meager savings, just for you, and that'll be an end to it, okay?"

Piper snorted. "Are you trying to bribe an officer? Merry, are you my witness here?"

"Oh yeah," Merry said. "That sounded like a bribe to me."

"Oh, for fucks' sake!" Rags said. "A fine isn't a bribe. I'm not offering to pay Piper personally, and you know it. Get the hell off my back, both of you!"

Piper and Merry exchanged a look, as though together they'd cornered a wild beast. Rags could feel herself turning into that beast, and she knew she had to get a grip on herself. But then Piers Olsson came in, his shoulders sagging.

"Jaxson Turner is reported missing," Piers announced to the room. Merry's hand flew to her mouth and she tried to stifle a gasp.

"Who's that?" Rags asked.

"He's sixteen, like Effie, a varsity running back for the Canary Cougars," Piers said with no emotion in his voice. "Big kid. Good kid, like Effie. Never came home from school yesterday. Absolutely vanished without a trace. Like...what the fuck, y'know?"

The newsroom fell silent, but Rags only needed a moment to begin acting like a journalist. This was an actual breaking story and she had no choice but to cover it, all of it, wherever it led.

"Piers, I need to know everything there is to know. Merry, call Dineen, explain to her what's going on and ask her to speak to all of Jaxson's teachers. His best friends too. She can send me her notes this afternoon." Rags was giving Merry one last chance, against her better judgment, to do something useful and good. She still intended to fire her, once she figured out the actual contractual arrangement. Merry gave her a thousand-yard stare.

Finally, the newsroom felt like a newsroom. The energy in the room wasn't fueled by hostility but the adrenaline rush that comes from working on a breaking story. Rags began to feel more centered. The story would cost her emotionally—she knew that. But this is what she had signed up for, and she couldn't look away now.

"She can't go anywhere," Piper said to Piers.

"Why not?" Piers asked.

"She's in violation of municipal law."

"I don't have time for this bullshit, Piers," Rags said, pointedly ignoring Piper.

"She failed to turn in her temp data—*any* data—since she arrived," Piper said.

"Shit, Rags," Piers said. "Why'd you do that?"

"Arrest her, Piers."

"Give me a fucking break!" Rags said.

"Nah," Piers said. "I don't think that's really—"

Piper was practically foaming at the mouth, the respie filled with ugly condensation. "The local ordinance clearly states that 'failure to comply after thirty days may result in a revocation of employment, up to thirty days of incarceration, and/or other punishment as deemed appropriate,'" Piper said.

Piers ran his hands through his hair, looking helpless and also conflicted. Then he laughed, which seemed entirely out of place and only reinforced Rags's view of his general haplessness. She quickly tried to think her way out of this. She didn't want to repeat her offer to pay a fine in front of Piers in case it was misconstrued, again. She didn't regret her actions— flaunting the temperature requirement—only the PHP's small-mindedness, which felt wildly intrusive and just plain stupid.

"House arrest. One week," Piers said.

"No!" Rags and Piper said together. Merry snorted.

"And she'll comply with the ordinance, beginning today," Piers said. "Right, Rags? Can you live with that, Piper?"

"That's only a slap on the wrist," Piper said. "Piers, you need to set an example."

"This is 'other punishment as deemed appropriate,'" Piers said. "You said it yourself."

Rags had no leverage. There was no immediate way to appeal the verdict.

"You're not really gonna make me do this, are you?" Rags asked Piers as he walked her home.

"I have to. You don't know Piper. Or Terry. They'll make my life a living hell."

"I'll work the story from home."

"I can't stop you."

"Piper's an idiot," Rags said.

"Yeah, but we need him, right? We can't afford to forget."

"Nobody ever forgets," Rags said. "That's the problem. A town like Canary can't move forward if everyone keeps living in the past." Piers just shrugged. Rags concluded she wouldn't be able to trust him—any of them.

When they crossed the threshold of Rags's house, Piers attached a device about the size of a quarter to the inside of her wrist. He activated it and her wrist blinked orange. It was a geo-lock. She couldn't leave the house without setting off an alarm on Piers's end.

"This really sucks," Rags said.

"It's only a week," Piers said. "You're lucky that's all it is. It'll switch off when your time's up."

"It fucking better." A week sounded like forever; she already felt cooped up and her confinement hadn't even begun. "And tell that fucking PHP to keep away from me."

Rags's brain was spinning: Effie, Jaxson, possibly others, mysteriously vanishing from this small, undistinguished town. Why? Where did they go? Who was behind it? She'd completely forgotten, for the moment, that her partner was home as well, just on the other side of the shallow vestibule. Flint, deeply entrenched in his virtual universe, was slow to respond to the pair's presence. But once he realized there were people in his midst—including his partner—he did not look happy.

"What the fuck are you doing here?" Flint said.

8

Flint Sten came of age just as Moore's Law was coming to an end. The famous prediction stating that the number of transistors that fit onto one integrated circuit would double every year, and later, every two years, had fulfilled its prophecy. The high priests of technology began delving into "deep learning," big data, and the new world of AI chips and other logic devices to power the cyber world everyone depended on for practically everything. Flint knew by the time he was fifteen that he wanted to live inside that world, one way or another. He attended Carnegie-Mellon, then MIT, and along the way, the skinny little nerd grew into a big, hairy bear of a man. He didn't say much, didn't pursue much of a social life, preferring his own thoughts most of the time.

Then came The Big One, steamrolling over everyone, reshaping the social order by force even as it killed off millions. Flint lived a coder's mindset: stay calm, break each problem into the smallest steps possible, and be patient and methodical as you root out the bugs in your code. This approach to life in general worked just fine when the world was at peace. But from 2023 to 2028, the world—the known universe, it seemed—went to war with an invisible enemy that made new and unexpected demands, terrible demands, on everybody, including Flint.

His older brother Harry died first. Then his mother.

After that, Flint stopped speaking to all remaining members of his family—cousins, aunts, uncles. He'd never known his father, so a part of him had always felt incomplete, and that wouldn't change.

As the world dissolved into crazy panic around him, Flint never worried about getting sick himself. He simply let that go. He let a lot of things go, beginning with family. Where others would cling to their families as if they were actual life rafts, Flint found the only way to get out of bed every day was to switch all that off. He felt he had to, to avoid drowning in a roiling ocean. He told himself every action he took, every decision, was in service to survival. Life reduced to a pinpoint. He kept his head down, lived like a monk, and took each day as it came—a cliché with life-saving qualities. He avoided the news and all the noise of the collateral damage around him. He went out each evening and came home with a plastic bag filled with crappy food—whatever he could get easily. Noodles. Cheese spread. Hot dogs. Fried chicken. Chocolate pudding. He willed himself into a state of numbness that was akin to hibernation—body and soul in hiding. He made ends meet by working remotely for a big tech firm. As millions of small businesses imploded, the overwhelming size and market advantages that the tech giants had amassed enabled them to power through. Flint would never be out of a job. The work didn't particularly move him or challenge him but it provided financial security, which in turn afforded him the isolation he felt he needed just to get by.

One evening, after foraging for food, Flint had been walking with his head down, as usual, his face curtained by long, shaggy dark hair and an unkempt beard. He nearly tripped. He looked down at the obstacle in his path. It was a dead body, covered in the filth and excrement that were hallmarks of the disease raging around him. He stepped around it, knowing that someone would come along shortly to scoop it up. He felt…nothing… and continued walking. He decided to throw away his shoes in the bin outside his apartment building, just to be safe. His socks too. He took a scalding shower as soon as he got home and washed his clothes in the sink, hanging them up in the shower to drip-dry. He wondered if something was really, irretrievably wrong with him. He was broken, perhaps. Had he done this to himself or did circumstances do it to him?

Flint was twenty-eight years old, and this was his life.

Is this it? All there is?

At night, he dreamed, and when he woke, he knew he'd never share what his dreams taught him, as he did not want to put any of it into words. He dreamed he was in Poland, running from the Nazis as they invaded Warsaw. He knew, somehow, it was Warsaw. He himself was a Pole and a helmeted Nazi carrying a rifle was chasing him, getting closer by the second. Dead bodies lay all around on the cobblestoned streets. The cobbles were slick with blood. He was running for his life but at the same time his dream self was telling him another story, a parallel story. He told himself that just as people around the world would tell stories endlessly, for decades, about the war—the Nazis, the Allies, the way death entered little villages, taking everyone by surprise before they'd finished their morning coffee—so too would people tell stories about The Big One and death's fresh forays into unsuspecting villages. That story would go on and on.

The big tech firm he worked for directed Flint and every other programmer to drop whatever enterprising new projects they'd been working on to focus exclusively on developing new tools to analyze big data sets tracking the virus. He thought about quitting. He didn't want the virus to dictate to him. He began thinking about going out on his own as a consulting developer, where he'd be free to seek out clients still willing, he hoped, to pay for him to do the kind of work he was really interested in. As a graduate student at MIT, he was deeply influenced by the ground-breaking work of Pauline Benjamin. She'd played a key role in figuring out the importance of introducing diversity into densely connected networks.

The famous example, which had obsessed Flint for months, was about the behavior of self-driving cars. Imagine what happens when hundreds of driverless cars merge onto a California highway, while a few miles ahead a raging wildfire blocks the roadway. The self-driving cars were never taught to detect a wall of fire as a threat so they steer straight into it—putting their passengers in immediate danger. Now imagine a handful of faulty self-driving cars stalling out unexpectedly on this same highway, forcing vehicles otherwise headed straight for the fire to detour around the stalled vehicles onto other, safer roads.

The defective cars—introduced into this otherwise rigid network of programmed behaviors—function as agents of diversity that unwittingly short-circuit the stampeding herd mentality of the doomed vehicles.

Flint was shut down on the outside, but on the inside, intellectually, he continued to ferment. He began thinking he wanted to become a code-breaker—to be the one who probes and tests for weaknesses in the machine learning systems that were supposed to keep us safe. He imagined becoming one of a handful of people in the world who could identify the next "driving straight into the fire" problem and find ways around it. This was about building safe information ecologies. This felt to him like a way to be useful while staying in his lane. Some day.

Nearly four years into the pandemic, Flint realized that even crises like the one he was living through undergo a lifecycle with discernible stages. The wild entropy of the first two years—terrifying death rates, economic collapse, social disregulation on a mass scale—gradually gave way to a cautious new-normal. Danger was weighed in relative, rather than absolute, terms. People gradually resumed a kind of half-life, a life of compromises.

Around that time, as Flint was still pondering his professional transition, he met Polly Goldner, who called herself Rags, which he found unaccountably funny. He actually laughed, for the first time in a long time, when she introduced herself to him as "Polly, but everyone calls me Rags." They'd been living for years in the same city, but of course he didn't know that. If you'd told him the day they met that in a few months' time he'd thank her for saving his life, he would have assigned a very low degree of probability to the idea.

Flint's boss had asked him to meet with a reporter doing a story on the marriage of AI and epidemiology in the fight against the virus—the very thing Flint hated but knew a lot about. He couldn't imagine why his boss wanted him to do the interview, unless it was because Flint's taciturnity practically guaranteed he'd say as little as possible and wouldn't embarrass his employer in some way. He resented that he had to leave home and come out for this, but limited personal contact among people who had been medically cleared was permitted and both his boss and the reporter seemed to demand it.

Something about Rags: he couldn't put his finger on it. She was like an elegant string of code—not physically elegant, but structurally sound. Neat. All of a piece. What was it about her that made him suddenly sit up straighter and wake up to the world around him when she walked into the sanitized conference room to interview him? He never really found an answer. All he knew was that a responsive chord shuttled between them; he learned later that she felt it, too, and was as surprised as he. Flint didn't think he judged her on looks alone; she was of medium build and height with straight, shoulder-length brown hair. She was dressed all in black the day they met, which made her skin appear sallow. But all that aside, when she looked at him with bright green eyes, he felt he was looking back at someone true and real, someone who would not bend or sway. And suddenly, that felt just like what he needed—and wanted.

Rags sat down and activated with a wave the recorder built into her dataphone, asking for his permission to record even as she began doing so. She explained, succinctly, that recording guaranteed accuracy, and she was a stickler for accuracy. Flint was entranced by her air of certainty. She cut right to the chase, which she did a lot, he learned.

"How are you using technology to bend the curve of this crisis?" she asked, looking straight at him.

"That's a broad question," Flint said. "I really don't know how to answer that." He didn't mean to be difficult, but he had no idea what kind of response she wanted or expected.

"Okay," she said, "let me ask it this way. Are you like a detective who uses data instead of, say, ballistics or, oh, lipstick on a collar, to track down the killer?" Rags smiled—a sardonic smile, Flint thought. He liked her slyness, as if they'd already tacitly agreed that the world was an absurd place.

"That's a good way to put it," he said. He then tried to explain to her, in earnest, about proven patterns and pilot-mapping exponential derivatives and how predictive analytics provided the clues for him and his colleagues to follow.

"Whoa, whoa, whoa," Rags said, her lips twisting into half a smile. "I knew this would happen. You're giving me geek-speak. I need you to use plain English. It's not that I'm stupid, Flint, it's that your vocabulary isn't, uh, widely shared. You do know that, right?"

Flint pushed back, explaining to her that precise language was important in his line of work and he didn't want to give her any misleading impressions. "For example," he said, leaning across the table unselfconsciously, "if you throw data at a really sophisticated machine learning system for six hundred hours, you get a beast with one-point-five-billion parameters. That's not easy to explain."

"Sure, if you say so, but what's that got to do with using big data to run simulations about ways to kill the virus, or slow it down, or just figure out who gets sick next? Can you just explain *that*?"

Flint recognized that she was just doing her job, trying to get him to create a sound bite—he was pretty sure that's what you called it—that she could put into her article. He knew he couldn't wiggle out of it. So he spent the next hour talking through the kind of work he and his colleagues were doing, striving to speak in plain English and backtracking whenever she flagged him for retreating to geek-speak—as she called it. When she finally stopped asking questions, she stopped the recorder and rose to leave.

"That's it?" Flint asked. "Did you get what you need?"

"Well, I got what you were able to give me," Rags said. "I'll make it work. I always do." He watched her walk out of the room. *Isn't there more?* he wanted to ask. *More that you need—from me?* Ordinarily, someone like her would disappear from view and that would be an end to it. He'd go back to his tiny apartment and re-immerse himself in his screens of data. And it would be as if the interview had never happened.

But Flint felt an unaccustomed need welling up, an urgent clamor in his gut that he found impossible to ignore. "Hey," he called to Rags. She stopped and turned around. "Will you have dinner with me?" She smiled and looked at her dataphone. She said okay. They worked out the details. Flint went back home and for the first time since his mother died, he had trouble concentrating.

They met up at a Middle Eastern place that both of them liked. Restaurants were open but they had all erected partitions so that people could only dine in pairs. No groups, no parties, no large public celebrations or gatherings. You'd walk into almost any restaurant larger than a food truck and you'd see a maze of temporary walls. A server escorted you around one corner after another until you were at your own cozy little nook. This improvised solution—which turned into a city ordinance—had the effect of making eating out almost unbearably intimate and sometimes, unexpectedly romantic. It was one of the rare secret pleasures of the pandemic.

Flint and Rags discovered that neither of them ate out often. Hardly ever, in fact. They also discovered, as they talked, that they had both kept a cool head amid all the madness. Rags explained that as a journalist she had to gather facts, focus on details, and bring some kind of objective reality into her reporting, even if the story itself was horrendous. She told him that the story she was working on about artificial intelligence and epidemiology—the story she'd interviewed him for—was the most cerebral piece she'd been assigned in months.

"I've been on blood and guts duty for a long time," she explained, dipping pita bread into a dish of hummus. "I think my editor is almost feeling sorry for me." She paused and put the pita back on her plate.

"Because why?" Flint asked, feeling obtuse and wondering if he seemed just too dense for anyone to bother with.

"Because my body count is so high. I'm like a reporter working nonstop in a war zone, in a conflict that never seems to end. And because, well, shit happens along the way, you know?"

Flint watched her pick up the bread and hummus and chew and swallow quickly, as if tasting the food, and enjoying it, were beside the point. He didn't tell her about nearly tripping over the dead body, many months earlier. He just said he'd been muddling through and doing okay. As they sat across from one another in their intimate little dining space, Flint noticed that Rags had a twitchy eye. The twitch seemed to go off at random, like a faulty alarm, and when it happened, it wasn't just her eye that blinked rapidly, her cheek muscle was involved too. He wondered about this: whether it was something she was born with, or whether it had developed on its own. He thought of it as the chink in her armor—a secret story that he wanted to learn more about.

After that first dinner, things happened quickly—much more quickly than Flint could have imagined. But then, he never quite knew what to expect of the so-called real world.

9

They found a new place to move into together. It wasn't easy. Hundreds of apartments throughout the city had fallen vacant. But that simply meant they weren't occupied. Often, the detritus of lives that had ended abruptly still filled these places. Furniture. Unmade beds. Refrigerators and freezers filled with rotten food because the electricity had been cut off. So-called smart appliances were useless without power. Flint and Rags would walk into one of these "corpse homes," as they were called, and gag. More than once, they nearly stumbled over the decaying skeletons of cats and dogs left behind unintentionally, their fur all mangy, their eyes milky white. Flint thought again of the human corpse he'd stepped over. He wondered if he'd do that now, just pass it by, if Rags were with him. He hoped he had changed, that she had changed him. But he wasn't entirely sure.

The hunt for a new apartment was further complicated by the scarcity of real estate agents. So many had gone out of business, fled the city, or simply died off. But Flint didn't find the process all that frustrating. It gave him a chance to get to know Rags. Every time they'd walk into another corpse home, she'd put her elbow up across her face and say, "Oh, fuck this." And then they'd walk through anyway, driven by a shared morbid curiosity. *There's no one on the planet like her*, he thought.

The hunt for a new living situation also gave his days new definition, something to look forward to. For the first time in his adult life, he had a reason to leave his own tiny apartment at the end of the day. She'd call him at odd hours to say, "I've got a live one." That meant she'd found a place they needed to look at as soon as possible. She took the lead on this, she seemed to want to, and he was happy to let her. In exchange, he took the lead on finding new restaurants for them to try. They began to hope they could find a place to live that wasn't too far from their favorites, including the Middle Eastern place they'd gone to on their first date.

As the months wore on, they took turns spending nights in each other's narrow beds. They had quickly figured out that neither of them was a Lucky: they simply hadn't ever gotten sick. And furthermore, neither of them worried obsessively over it with respect to their individual well-being, even while taking sensible precautions. They weren't reckless, just comfortable with their own rationalizations. It's just how they were each made.

Their biggest discovery together, however, in the third week of their relationship: both of them were virgins. They weren't ashamed. It wasn't uncommon, under the circumstances. In the movies, people fuck like bunnies in a disaster. But in The Big One, intimacy could spell death—or so people thought at the beginning. Many people forced themselves to shut down, to ignore biological urges (or take care of themselves as best they could) and pour their energies into the awful slog of staying alive. Flint was aware he'd done this and was relieved to find he wasn't the only one.

The first time they had sex, they'd gorged on peanut sesame noodles beforehand. Flint never forgot the nutty umami scent on Rags's breath as he hungrily connected his hulking body with hers, the two of them sitting upright, gripping one another's backs, their legs entwined, smashing the thin mattress of Rags's unmade bed. For a long time afterwards, that sense memory alone was enough to arouse Flint.

Afterwards, he lay half on top of her as the narrow bed couldn't hold them side by side. "Finally," he said, laughing sheepishly.

"Me too," Rags said.

He looked at her naked body, observing the way her rounded breasts flopped towards her chest wall. He traced the U-shaped parabolic curve of each breast, noting how they were both alike and different. She told him that felt nice and he should keep doing it. They made love again and then slept, pushed against one another.

In the morning, Flint admitted, first to himself, then to Rags, that he was enormously relieved to remove himself from the virgin column. She just laughed. It took Flint a long time to figure out that Rags actually laughed very little. The early stages of their relationship, as they began the slow and wary process of falling in love, had unlocked something in her, and she laughed often and easily—in daylight. After their first several weeks together, however, in the safe glow of their relationship, Rags woke up at least once a week from a nightmare that left her sweating and panting. At first, her intense dream life—seemingly more vivid than his own—disturbed him. If he'd had to plot her on a graph, he'd put only a handful of data points above zero on the axis; the rest would dip below. Not an easy trendline.

Flint gleaned only incoherent little bits of the story from her nightmare: she was soaked in blood, she couldn't breathe, she was being devoured by some kind of evil creature. *Maya!* she cried out. But she never said more and Flint was afraid of what she might say or do if he pushed her. It took him a long time to figure out that the laughing Rags reflected a temporary and artificial state—a standard deviation from her core personality. Sometimes, he resented what felt like a bait-and-switch. Other times, he looked at her with a quick flash of empathy. No wonder she hardly laughed, after everything she'd been through—at least based on the little he knew.

One day in June, toward the end of the fourth year of the pandemic, when they'd been a couple for several months, two things happened. Rags had spent the previous night at Flint's. He was on his computer, sitting naked in his crappy plastic chair, his sweaty body sticking to the chair so that it made a slight sucking sound every time he shifted. He called out to Rags, who was just coming out of the shower.

"Look!" he called. "You gotta see this!"

Rags wrapped a thin towel around her body and came and

stood behind him. She knew not to let her wet hair drip onto his keyboard. This was one of the mornings after her recurring nightmare, which they tacitly agreed to ignore in the daytime. Flint pointed to his two big monitors, the exact same monitors he would eventually bring to Canary.

"What am I looking at?" Rags asked.

"There!" Flint said, pointing. "It's right there! Do you need glasses?"

"I see wavy lines going up and down. It's the same curve as always, isn't it?"

The progressive curves tracking rates and levels of the virus were so ubiquitous, they were easy to tune out, like an annoying commercial that played its obnoxious, insistent jingle everywhere you went. Rags's own newspaper put the data on the front page every day. She'd grown tired of looking at it, but Flint couldn't imagine *anyone* turning away from new data.

"But the curve is almost flat, Rags, see? The end is in sight."

She peered at the screens, pointing. "Oh, here, where the lines go way down."

"Yes! I ran all the CDC and WHO data against my own algorithms, and it checks out." Rags stepped away to get dressed. "You know what this means? Maybe, finally, I can quit my job. I can leave this prison—I can leave epidemiology and death rates and infection spikes behind, for good." Rags remained silent, her back to him. Her body, her posture, seemed off in some way, but he didn't know why. "You don't seem excited." She slipped on an old pair of sandals. The straps were literally held together with duct tape. When she turned back to him, tears were running down her cheeks.

"What?" he said. "Did I say something wrong?" He put his big hands on her shoulders. He felt he was in uncharted waters, caring for this woman. *Should I have anticipated this? It's only data. What is this really about?*

"Too little, too late," Rags said, wiping snot from her nose. "Never mind. Ignore me." She pulled away. "I have to get to work. I'm profiling a woman who's a hundred and four. Can you believe that? A hundred and fucking four! She gets to keep on living while other…other people don't." Flint knew there was still a lot he did not know about Rags, but he didn't feel equipped to pry it out of her, and anyway, prying probably wasn't the right approach—if there even was a right approach.

Later that same June afternoon, Rags got a call from one of the handful of realtors she'd reached out to. A deal had just fallen through on a great place—two bedrooms, polished hardwood floors, great light. Was she interested? Flint rushed over to meet Rags there at five-thirty. He worried about the state he'd find her in. He didn't know whether her tears in the morning would spill out again in the afternoon. *I really suck at reading people.* He was relieved and surprised—and maybe also a bit confused—when he got to the apartment and found her dancing, or what looked to him like dancing, on the polished hardwood floor.

"It doesn't smell!" she said.

"Good light," Flint said, looking around. "Do we like it?"

"Don't be mad," Rags said. "I signed the lease." Flint raised bushy eyebrows. "I had to, or we'd lose it. But it's ours—our place. The signature was just a formality. So?"

Flint strode through the apartment, the late-afternoon sun streaming through the tenth-floor windows. This was so much more luxurious than where he'd been living—and that place had always been just fine, for him. But now he was part of an *us,* so it made sense that something better was required. If he was being honest with himself, he didn't really care about his surroundings; they didn't affect his mood or his ability to work. *It's just four walls and some stuff.* But if Rags liked it, then he liked it.

"I'm going to put my desk right here," he said, pointing to a blank wall opposite one of the windows. Technically, it was the living room, which was separated from a modest wall kitchen by a built-in breakfast bar. Once he could visualize where he'd be working, the place felt real to him.

"Perfect," Rags said.

That night, they brought in pizza and red wine and sat on the floor.

"Something's different," Flint said, licking tomato sauce off his fingers.

"Well, yeah," Rags said.

"This feels so…normal," he said. "Or, at least, I think so. I don't really know what 'normal' is to other people. Is that weird?"

"I knew you were weird five minutes after meeting you, Flint. Weird, in a good way."

"Explain to me what 'normal' means, to normal people, I mean."

"You think I'm normal?" Rags asked. "I think I just fake it better than you."

Flint had absolutely no idea if that was true. He liked Rags a lot, he thought he probably loved her, but he couldn't easily describe where she was on the weird-to-normal spectrum. Far closer to the normal end than he was, he suspected. Then again, she had those nightmares, while he slept like a baby most of the time.

"I'm just a bag of tricks, Flint," Rags continued. "A bunch of bits and pieces and loose ends cobbled together so I can get through this thing. Under all that—masses of scar tissue. That's about it. Maybe whatever we mean by 'normal' is beside the point, now. Maybe nobody will ever be normal again. I don't know."

"That should work in my favor," he said, only half-joking. "If everybody is weird now, then I'll seem closer to normal." Rags laughed—the laugh that would not last.

10

Finally, the unimaginable happened. The thing that nobody had the capacity anymore to believe in. The pandemic ended. The Big One was declared over. Flint didn't believe it simply because he read about it in the news (sorry, Rags). He believed it because the data told him it was true. There were still active cases here and there and little micro-bursts of contamination. But overall, the rate of new infections in his city, across the U.S., and around the world were at or near zero.

They moved their bits of furniture and clothing into the apartment on the tenth floor. Everything fit, with room to spare. Neither of them had accumulated much. Flint didn't care and Rags hadn't seen the point, knowing she might be dead in a day, a week, a month. The only new thing they bought together was a king-sized bed. Flint woke up the first several mornings in the new place feeling completely disoriented, which turned immediately into hopeless anger. Where was he? What was he doing there? What was the source of this disruption? He worried, in those waking moments, that something had been taken from him, something that he required to stay calm, stay focused. Then he blinked and felt Rags's warm body stir beside him. He made a conscious effort to let go of the anxiety and the anger. He made an effort to be, to act, like a normal person. A normal person makes his lover coffee and breakfast, so that's what he did on the mornings she did not rise before him.

One morning, Flint woke up and saw Rags gliding between yoga poses on a dark blue foam yoga mat she'd lain at the foot of the bed. She wore loose shorts and a tank top. He watched her in silence from bed, wondering how she got her body to bend that way—knees up by her ears, then a moment later, arms stretched behind her back over her head, her shoulder blades flexed like tiny wings.

"Come here," he said when she was finished. He loved the salty taste of the thin film of sweat that coated her collar bone. So this is what life is like, he thought.

Week by week, the locked-down city began to unfurl for the first time in nearly five years. Flint could no longer count on one hand the vehicles on the street below, as ShareCars began once again to crawl up Charles Street at a slow but steady pace. He wanted to chart the flow longitudinally, on a minute-by-minute scale. He thought about setting up his dataphone to record the vehicles and pedestrians on the street below, so he could later turn action into data—the data always more real to him than the action. But he didn't have time to mess around with that.

He continued working from home even as most of his colleagues had returned to the glass-walled headquarters that fronted the harbor downtown. He wanted to break free, to start over. Acquiring a personal life—which he never saw coming—made him more determined than ever to take control of his entire life, including his intellectual output. That was the way forward.

So he began writing simulations, probing for weaknesses in machine learning systems. He knew that the output of deep neural networks could be easily altered by adding relatively small perturbations to the input vector. That's how he put it to himself. To Rags, he explained that he was beginning with a project that he assigned to himself: identifying "fooling attacks" on facial recognition systems. It was too easy to do: someone wearing a pair of brightly patterned eyeglasses could confuse an AI-based facial recognition app so that it misidentified that person. All it took was changing one pixel. Flint hated the idea that a malicious human could sidetrack an otherwise beautifully written program. He disliked the mischief in the machine. He planned to write up his methodology and findings and use that as a calling card to land independent contracts.

Each evening when Rags came home acted like a shock

to his system. As if he had to continually retrain his brain to remember that he was no longer alone. *You want this. You need this.* He cooked for them both as a way to keep her alive in his mind when she wasn't there.

"Oh, you're here," he often said when she clicked the door behind her and slipped off her shoes. He could practically hear his own gears grinding. "I made paella. It might be a little dry."

Flint ventured out mainly to shop for groceries, which Rags never seemed to think about. He made food magically appear on the table, and she made noises of gratitude. He didn't bother with a ShareCar. He put a large backpack over his shoulders and walked three miles to Trader Joe's in Canton, the only decent grocery store in the city that had survived the long clamp-down. Outside the store, a kiosk-style holographic projector let approaching shoppers know "We're fully stocked!" As a precautionary holdover, a PHP stood outside the store, only letting a handful of shoppers in at a time.

Each time he set out, Flint reminded himself that he would not encounter any dead bodies on the street. He could afford to look up, look around, observe the other life forms: the September sun slanting through the trees, a few children playing tag in a park where the grass had grown wild, suited office workers speaking to the ether, walking briskly as though to make up for lost time, lost years, loss itself. Many people still wore masks—but many did not. He couldn't shake the feeling that life in the city remained provisional. They could all topple back into darkness—disease, pain, death—if a swath of microbes landed *here* and not *there*. He trusted the data—but not people. He felt he could literally only get through this one day at a time.

Later that month, Flint read a story online that Rags had written for the national wire service she was now stringing for, about how people of all ages and races burst into tears in public—moved by the beauty that still existed in the world and overwhelmed by the feeling they were still around to enjoy it. They stood there, tears streaming down their faces, neither ashamed nor embarrassed. He read this kind of stuff now out of loyalty to Rags. Otherwise, general news failed to hold his attention beyond the headlines. The news told stories, but not necessarily truth. He didn't share this view with Rags. A photo ran with the story, showing a Black woman Flint guessed to be in her mid-fifties. She had tears on her cheeks, and she was quoted as saying that she thanked God every day for sparing her, but at the same time, she could not forgive him for taking away so many people she loved. Flint knew, without Rags telling him, that writing this kind of story marked a 180-degree turn away from covering an endless series of tragedies. She would call this "fluff," and he assumed it came as a welcome relief. She'd been recalled from the battlefield.

"Why are we still here?" Rags asked Flint, the day that story ran. He knew she was asking the big question, not the little question. He wanted to tell her the story had forced him to think about his mother and his brother, Harry, both of whom had succumbed early on. *Moving but inconsequential.* He wanted to say, *We carry on because we must and because we can.* Instead, he recited a snippet of poetry from his meager store. "Miles to go before I sleep."

"But why?" Rags repeated. "Why us? What's a random universe for? Do you think about these things, Flint?"

He was afraid to disappoint her. He wracked his brain for something he could say that was true—for him—not merely something she expected.

"I don't feel guilty because I survived," he said slowly. "So much in the universe isn't random. And so much of it is still so beautiful." He watched her. She waited for more, he could tell. "We can still depend on things," he said, reaching for her hands.

"I don't know," she said, her eyes filling with tears. She looked away. The story must have affected her more than she admitted. He'd come to notice that she did not like him to see her when she felt this way. "I don't think so."

"The world is still symmetrical," he said, the words failing to convey what he meant to say, to reassure her. "Look." He tossed a spoon up into the air and caught it. "All the fundamentals, all the building blocks, are still here. Gravity, for instance. We can count on them. They won't fail us. And that means—"

"That means what?"

"That means, well, we aren't going to fly apart."

"Emotionally?"

"I won't leave you," he said. The only response he felt safe giving.

"That may not be enough," Rags said, putting a hand on his arm. "But we can only do what we can do, right?"

By October, the streets and parks were once again filled with people running, biking, admiring the leaves tinged with red and gold. The restaurant partitions came down, replacing hushed intimacy with noisy release and celebration. Nobody had much money, but that didn't seem to matter. Going out for a couple of beers with friends in a newly crowded bar was enough of a thrill for lots of people. Flint assumed that as a journalist always in the thick of things, Rags would be bursting to socialize. He hadn't known her in "peace time," and figured that despite her fierce independence, she'd want to mix and mingle just like everyone else as soon as the restrictions loosened. Turns out, she didn't. He was relieved at not having to give up his introverted ways, and also puzzled. *The pattern will grow clearer,* he told himself.

Rags brought back reports from the outside world, a world larger than his weekly hike to the market. "The PHP are out in force," she said. In the city, they wore dark green coveralls and matching watch caps, which made their white masks stand out. White-snouted pigs, was how Rags described them. Self-important bastards, she railed. Checking everybody's IDs and demanding contact trace data. Sticking thermometers against the foreheads of random people. One day she came home more worked up than usual. Flint tore his focus away from the silent, ordered world of neural networks and forced himself to train his eyes on her: on her restless, loose-limbed energy, her anger, her unending impatience with the universe, or so it seemed to him.

"You won't believe this," she started, pouring a tall scotch. "So I see this PHP stop this girl. Probably fifteen, if that. She's tiny. Carrying a pink polka dot umbrella, for God's sake. The PHP slaps a thermometer on her, reads it, shakes his head. And then guess what? He calls the police. The fucking police! And she's just a girl! A squad car pulls up. I stand there watching them trap this girl with her stupid umbrella between them. And then the cop hauls her off! I mean, what the fuck!"

"She must have had a fever," Flint said. "They were just protecting the public."

"They're not supposed to act like fucking Nazis, Flint," Rags said, gulping her drink. "It was a disproportionate response."

"Maybe," he said.

"Maybe? Do you *want* to live in a fucking police state? Doesn't it bother you that's what this city's becoming? All those happy people drinking and hanging out in bars again. It's a lie, you know."

"What do you mean? What's a lie?"

"Because there's a curfew. You know that, right?" He didn't know, but he had no reason to, as he wasn't interested in being out late, anyway. "Streets empty by ten p.m. or else."

"You mean, they're arresting people who break the curfew?"

"That, yes. And charging all these public places with hefty fines if they break curfew, just when they're barely surviving. Even the fucking laundromats. And where does that money go—all the fines they collect? Huh? Do you know? 'Cause I sure don't." But this wasn't even the worst part, she said, refilling her glass. Flint asked if she was hungry, if she wanted to wash that down with some food. She told him no. He put a square of lasagna on a plate for her anyway.

Later that night, Flint found Rags crashed out on the bed, still fully clothed. He gently undressed her and tucked her in. She half-woke.

"The worst part, I didn't tell you," she said, half into her pillow.

"What's that, Rags?" Flint asked, sitting on the edge of the bed, pulling off his socks and taking deep, even breaths, so that whatever came next, he'd be ready to take it in.

"My editor said no," Rags said. "I pitched the story. About the fascists taking over the city. And the arrests. And the fines. And she said no. Leave it alone, she said."

"Well, that's bullshit, Rags," Flint said.

"Thank you," she said, falling back to sleep.

November arrived. The apartment was pitch black by five-thirty in the afternoon. Flint didn't notice. "Jesus, Flint," Rags said when she walked in at six. "It's like a fucking cave in here. Why don't you turn on the lights?"

In mid-December, a rare ice storm coated the city, forcing everyone to retreat to an all-too-familiar state of hibernation. Rags insisted on bundling up and going outside, to see what she could see. Did he want to come with her, to check it out? Her editors expected something, anything, to be filed, storm or no storm. Working the phones was fine, but it wasn't enough, she explained. She was still mad as hell about the investigative piece her editor had killed. Flint looked down at the thick socks on his feet, and at the knobby knees below his boxers, and he knew that *she* knew he didn't really want to. He wanted to get back to the recursive algorithm he'd been working on for two days. He wondered about the boundaries of a relationship: Must he subsume his needs to hers? Or was he still entitled to put himself first? He wished this could all be reduced to some kind of equation—but he also told himself that healthy relationships could not be reduced in that way.

Rags went out alone. When she came home an hour later, she had a massive dark purple bruise spreading on her right hip, where she'd slipped and smacked the ice hard. She lay on her left side in bed, speaking notes into her dataphone, which she'd shape into a *vox pop* story later. Wouldn't take long, she told Flint, as he brought her hot tea loaded with honey. She would just toss something off and be done with it.

"Guess who I saw?" Rags asked, wincing as she shifted to drink the tea.

"The PHP?"

"Yup. Guess who else?"

"Hmm. An ice cream truck?"

"Good one," she said. Flint still tried to make her laugh from time to time, and always felt better when he succeeded. "Actually, nobody is out. The ice is an inch thick on the sidewalks, the trees, everywhere. So why is there still a PHP standing on the corner? Huh? What's he doing? What's the point?" Flint shrugged. "I'm telling you. This city isn't recovering. It's devolving."

The winter wore on. The days were short. The curfew emptied the darkened streets, making them feel even darker, Rags reported to Flint. The cost of living in the city skyrocketed. Their landlord raised their rent by twenty percent in mid-lease. He said the city was allowing anyone who owned property to make up for revenues lost during The Big One. Flint was shocked to see how much prices were jumping at Trader Joe's. He bought more rice and beans and skipped the avocados. He understood basic market forces and the laws of supply and demand. But living the lesson was uncomfortable. He wished he could simply review the data in a series of neat graphs on his screen. *It is what it is,* he told himself.

On the way home from the market late one January day, he got a bigger shock. A gang of teenagers—boys and girls—surrounded him on the sidewalk just off Boston Street. They were uniformly thin, pale, and scraggly. Their jackets were too thin for the cold. As if on cue, the kids formed a circle around him. Someone shoved him from behind. Not hard, just enough to seem angry. A pimply-faced boy who looked barely fifteen took a handgun from his pocket and pointed it at Flint, who remained completely still. Flint felt his heart racing. He was alert rather than frightened. He couldn't imagine these kids as killers or criminals. Still, he only had thirty dollars in his wallet and wondered what they'd do to get it.

"What's in the bag?" asked the boy pointing the gun. He meant Flint's backpack.

"Food."

A girl behind him yanked the straps off his shoulders and unzipped the bag. In a frenzy, the gang dove into it, pulling out apples, oranges, canned soup, a bag of rice. They seemed to forget he was there. Flint began to slowly walk away, leaving it all behind for them to pillage. The boy with the gun paused to look at him, then pushed his way back into the pile of food and canned goods spilling out onto the sidewalk. A few people walked quickly by, hunched in the cold, and didn't even glance over.

Flint kept his eyes to the ground the rest of the way home. He walked briskly, thinking about the dead body he'd tripped over, the oranges rolling toward the gutter, the kids who came out of this thing—alive, yes, but at what cost? And what next? *Fuck. This is the pattern. Clear now.*

He arrived home and waited for Rags. For once, he didn't look at his screens. Instead, he stood by the window and counted ShareCars and pedestrians on both sides of South Charles Street. He constructed a memory palace of the east- and westbound flows: which side bore more traffic; whether the cars were traveling any faster than the pedestrians on the rush-hour city street below him. *Why anybody did anything, went anywhere.*

The lights came on, startling him.

"In the dark again," Rags said, irritated. "What are you doing? Flint?" He realized he was still staring down at the street. He forced a smile.

"A weird thing happened." He told her about the gang and that he'd have to find a new backpack. A cheap one.

"I'm sorry," Rags said, wrapping her arms around his bear-like frame, thinner than before. "We've been running stories on these gangs all week. A lot of them are orphans, roaming around because everything and everyone is still too fucked up to sort them out. Hopefully, you weren't too surprised." Flint didn't contradict her. There was no point. "Don't cook tonight. We'll order Thai." Flint thought of Rags smelling like noodles, which reminded him of sex. But the memory just sat there, dull and distant.

That night in bed, they lay side by side on their backs, their arms barely touching. Flint wondered how Rags tasted, but he felt as though he couldn't move. And neither, it seemed, could she.

"If this is how it's gonna be…" She let the sentence drift off, leaving him to wonder if she meant the two of them. If she was about to leave him. And if she did, it hit him that he'd be alone in a way he'd never felt before. He already knew that. Growing up without a father had created one kind of hole. Losing his mother and Harry, a larger hole. But life without Rags, now that he had her…he couldn't picture it.

"If what?" Flint asked, terrified of what she might say.

"Everybody's losing their fucking minds," she said.

"You mean those kids?" Flint exhaled. She wasn't laying any blame on him, it seemed.

"Yesterday, somebody called our office to say they were going to plant bombs all over the city. They called it a 'cleanse.' Said the PHP weren't doing enough to purify the city. Make it safe."

"Shit," Flint said. "Are they for real?"

"Do we want to wait and see?" Rags asked, turning her face toward him in the dark.

"What, then?" he asked.

"I can't write another story about people crying into their beer. Or turning all their leftover face masks into a stupid quilt."

"But isn't that better than writing about stacks of corpses and rising death tolls?" he asked. Flint really wasn't sure *what* she wanted. It seemed she was never satisfied.

"Yeah, but…none of it feels…real," she said.

"We're real, Rags…aren't we?" He wasn't sure what she needed, where she was headed, or how he was supposed to follow. He wanted one thing, at least, to be clear, to be true for both of them.

"This city isn't real anymore. It's an ash heap of death with sprinkles on top."

"You think so?"

"Let's get out," she said, tapping the back of his hand.

The next four weeks went by so fast, Flint lost track of the days. Once Rags told him she was determined to leave the city, he spent two days quietly frantic. Would he follow her at any cost? And did she want him to—was that assumed? Could he ensure that he'd have an income, wherever they landed? *What do I want?* The question echoed within him, over and over. She continued going into her office, roaming the streets, filing stories. He committed to making himself portable so that he felt ready to leave, when the time came. He made lists. He focused on practical matters.

He began reaching out to the big private firms, the winners in the pandemic's economic war of attrition. He heard back from a federal military contractor, interested in his work on resiliency. He'd co-authored a paper that he'd posted to a non-classified, open-source forum for developers working on integrating AI in military weapons systems. In the paper, he discussed how intelligent systems cannot be brittle—military intelligence, above all. *They must handle overload conditions gracefully and recover quickly. They must be able to indicate when they are operating with low confidence, and they cannot simply freeze.* Flint readily cast aside any lingering ethical qualms he may have had about strengthening military resources. War had come to seem like a humanely organized way of exercising aggression compared with an invisible virus that killed stealthily, relentlessly, and randomly. The work would pay well and was about as secure as you could get, given the times. His buttoned-down way of living would help ensure he could get a top-secret clearance, which he'd need. And he could do it anywhere.

Rags came home one night and said that a second and then a third bomb threat had been phoned in to the wire service's editorial office. The caller went on and on about cleansing the city of its remaining scourge and filth. The FBI had descended to investigate, but nobody knew anything. Rumors were flying. All the editors had gotten into a fight over whether to publicize the rumors—thus legitimizing the caller—or to keep it secret. Until something happened. And then they'd all be inhabiting a fresh hell. Meanwhile, the PHP were going crazy, stopping more and more people, as if body temperature were an indication of guilt. She told Flint she saw no point in waiting for the shoe to drop.

"What will you miss?" he asked her over a supper of boxed macaroni and cheese. He hoped that asking the question out loud would make their departure seem real to him. She paused before answering.

"Anything I would miss…is already missing," she said. He waited for her to continue, to open the door to the secrets she still held on to, the nightmare she could not shake. Instead, she cleared their plates and changed the subject. "I think I've found a new job."

Riding in their ShareCar on the outskirts of Canary, Flint saw out of the corner of his eye the big, boxy crematorium. He was trying to figure out what it felt like to experience high death rates in a small town compared to the city, where it had been awful but the proportions were different. Would Canary feel as if Death itself had permanently taken up residence? He looked down, trying to parse his own line of thinking.

"Ah, crap," Rags said, as they turned on to Main Street. And then he saw Effie Rutter, first motionless, then smiling through the lens of his dataphone, her lanky blonde hair swinging from side to side. *Yes. Death lives here still.*

11

Rags stood by the front door, counting down the seconds until her weeklong house arrest expired. She stared at the blinking orange light on her wrist, willing it to turn off. She'd had a week to build her rage into a smoldering fire: gritty gray ash on top, hot as hell underneath. The claustrophobia that had begun to crush her in the city was nothing compared to how stifled she felt now. Every morning for the past week, Flint held out her thermometer before she'd even had a chance to brush her teeth.

"C'mon," he'd said. "Just do it. Stop making it into such a big deal."

"It's health-care theater. It's stupid."

"It's the law," Flint said. "Why get all worked up about something you can't change?"

"But it's a pointless invasion of privacy," she said, yanking the thermometer from him. "Everybody needs to move on."

"Yeah," Flint said. "'Cause that's what you're doing, right? Moving on?" She watched in the bathroom mirror as his bearded face curled into a sneer. The expression made him look deranged. She almost hated him this way—challenging her.

"The whole point in coming here…" she began, still facing him in the mirror.

"Is? What?" he asked.

She turned around to him. She could smell his minty breath. She wanted to grab him, hold on to him—and to push him away at the same time. So she did neither.

"Are you happy?" she asked. She was sorry the second she said it.

"Are you?"

"Do we deserve to be?" She let the question hang, knowing

he would not have a ready response. He wasn't glib, and she counted on that.

All through that week, they foraged for food on their own, abandoning communal mealtimes. They retreated to separate corners whenever possible. Rags knew Flint needed his space and lots of time to think, though she could not have explained what he thought *about*, exactly. He had mentioned something about AI and defense logistics, and the moment he said that she decided to put up an invisible wall that she would not breach. She would not "play" journalist with him about the military, the war-industrial complex, etc. Their situation was tense enough. They went on a sex fast. Flint usually came to bed a few hours before Rags awoke. She wanted him to want her as before, but she didn't want to make the first move. She stopped practicing yoga in front of him.

Each day during her forced confinement, Rags sat at the small, battered kitchen table and edited a newspaper that had begun to feel like a figment of her imagination, rather than a real ink-on-paper enterprise that was supposed to capture Canary as it was lived, to reflect the town back to itself in the form of living, breathing stories. Rags had wanted to become a journalist since she was twelve and, like Flint, her vision never wavered. She wanted to figure out what was true and then share that truth with others. The first time she said something along those lines out loud was in college, at Swarthmore, and her roommate, a whip-smart econ major, just laughed at her. So Rags never said anything like that again. She majored in journalism, interned at the *Boston Globe*, took a detour to NPR to cover labor issues, and then returned to print at the *Baltimore Sun*.

She racked up a number of regional press awards and thought about putting out feelers at a bigger paper, maybe the *Washington Post* or the *New York Times*. Then The Big One descended out of nowhere and there was only one story to tell, over and over again, the story leaping and lurching as reality reformed itself. Sometimes a fresh lede followed by grafs of recycled material was all she and her colleagues could manage, as they often filed two, three, and sometimes four stories a day, alternating between print and online deadlines.

Once the first wave of exhilaration had passed—*this* was the story of a lifetime, and she was there to cover it; she wasn't the only reporter who dreamed of a Pulitzer—a deep, despairing lassitude set in. For the first time, putting a story together, triangulating sources, checking facts, became a painful, wearying grind. For Rags, fear arrived only much later because she refused to let it in until it forced itself upon her like an earthquake splintering the ground beneath her feet. Fear coupled with loss. And guilt. And self-loathing for her inability to do things any differently. And then, telling the truth felt like being flayed alive. She left the *Sun* and became a general assignment reporter for Global Wire, thinking this would free her, somehow.

Now, in Canary, Rags forced herself to admit that the *Canary Courant* was not, after all, a better paper, or even a different paper, under her stewardship. Snappier headlines and openings, maybe. Better grammar, certainly. But better stories? Not really. Rags spoke with the freelance trio every other day from home. They were working on the usual assortment of stories: the resumption of the annual garden show after a seven-year hiatus; the end-of-year high school robotics league competition; a follow-up on Canary's bid for a ShareCar franchise. None of the writers said a word about her quarantine and Rags wasn't entirely sure they knew about it. Then again, in a town this small, it was hard to believe they didn't. Merry had probably told them. Rags had not spoken to Merry all week and didn't plan to. Brent told her that Terry was convening an emergency township meeting to discuss the situation about "the missing kids," as he put it.

Rags also called Piers every day to learn if there were any new leads in either case—Effie's or Jaxson's. She swore she could hear him toking over the phone. He told her no and she wasn't sure whether to believe him. Dineen had spoken to a few of Jaxson's friends and teachers, as she'd asked, and turned her notes over to Rags. There was little to go on—not enough for a story. Jaxson's best friend called him "a kick-ass quarterback." Not exactly world-shaking news. His teachers all said he was a solid B student, diligent but not extraordinary. A nice kid, everyone said. Where would a "nice kid" go all of a sudden?

For the upcoming Wednesday edition, Rags decided to run Jaxson's photo with a caption along the lines of: "Second Canary teen goes missing...police following all leads...anyone with information is asked to call..." To do any more than that would turn her newspaper into a screaming tabloid, and she was willing to draw a hard line to prevent that. Rags did pick up one new tidbit on one of her nagging calls to Piers for fresh intel.

"Say that again?" she said to Piers on a vid call. "Jaxson lives with whom?" She wasn't sure she'd heard correctly.

"Yeah, Tim and Roger took him in," Piers said. "After, you know, like, you know." No one, it seemed, ever completed a sentence about death in Canary.

"The Fallons?" Rags said. She couldn't picture it. And she was miffed that they hadn't said a word to her about being the guardians of a minor when she'd interviewed them at the bar. "They could've told me," she muttered. More missing teeth among the Luckies, she thought. Jaxson was yet another orphan forced to find a new home. But what, if anything, did the missing Jaxson's living arrangements have to do with his disappearance? Nothing in this town, she decided, was quite as it appeared.

On the last night of her house arrest, Maya came to Rags in her dreams. The old nightmare was replaced, at least for the time being, by something that seemed sharper, more immediate. Maya sat with Rags in the parlor downstairs. She wore her yellow sweatshirt. In the dream, Rags wondered what had become of that sweatshirt—Maya's favorite—and now her dreaming self knew that Maya still had it.

Maya leaned forward and spoke to Rags. "Imagine if I were simply missing," Maya said.

"Simply missing," Rags echoed in the dream. Her younger

sister sat motionless in the chair, only her mouth moving. Her light brown bangs fell into her eyes. There'd been no time for a haircut and all the salons were closed anyway. And then it was too late. Maya's nose ring, which she'd gotten over Rags's strenuous objections when she was fourteen, glinted in the dark parlor.

"If I were missing, you'd do everything to find me," Maya said. "I know you would."

"I would," Rags replied with great effort, barely able to form her lips around the words.

"So please try," Maya said. She rose and walked out of the house without another word. Rags wanted to call after her, to hold her back, but she couldn't move.

Rags woke with tears on her cheeks on the morning she was set free. She saw no point in waking Flint, who'd probably only come to bed recently. Rags realized that since no one seemed to know whether Effie and Jaxson were alive or dead, she couldn't possibly be held responsible if the worst came to past.

Not my fault. Not my fault.

At seven on the dot, the orange light blinked off and beeped. Rags tore the device off her wrist and darted out of the house. The bright morning sunlight nearly blinded her.

Evelyn Rutter lived in a narrow wood-framed house with peeling green paint on a block where all the houses appeared to lean like tired old people who find they can no longer straighten their spines. Rags's only exposure to her had been at the township meeting, when Evelyn accused Canary of turning a blind eye to the horror she was enduring as the parent of a missing child. Rags figured Evelyn had a point and Maya's dream directive, "please try," haunted her. Rags did not imagine that Evelyn was out working somewhere. She pictured her as someone who mainly stayed at home, wandering from room to room like a ghost, looking for all that she'd lost. Maybe she lived off meager savings. Maybe she depended on the local food pantry. Maybe she bartered for everything she could.

"Can I help you?" Evelyn said tonelessly in response to Rags's insistent knock. She had a long sad face, drooping eyelids, and stringy hair, and she may as well have said to Rags, "Go away." Rags was determined to avoid putting her off as she'd done with the Fallons at the bar.

"I've been meaning to stop by," Rags lied. "Rags Goldner. I edit the *Courant.* I heard what you said at the township meeting, and I can't stop thinking about it."

"So?" Evelyn Rutter said, still holding the door open just a few inches.

"I want to help."

"You with the police?" Evelyn squinted.

"No. Like I said, I'm the newspaper editor. I'm new in town."

"Piers says they're working on it. Doing all they can. You believe that?"

Rags knew she'd have to tread carefully now.

"I think Piers is probably doing everything he can. But that's not much comfort, is it? I can only imagine how awful this must be for you, and how worried you are."

"You got kids?" Evelyn asked, cracking the door open a few inches wider.

"No," Rags said.

"Then I don't see how—"

"I had a sister. She died. I watched her die." Rags knew she had about four seconds to let the image of Maya's final agony tear through her before she'd have to let it go and refocus. *You asked, Maya, and this is what it takes.*

"Well, that's…" Evelyn said. "What do you want?"

"I'd like to talk to you, if you'll let me. I want to learn your side of the story." Rags didn't say that the conversation would be on the record and find its way, in one form or another, into the newspaper, eventually. One step at a time. Evelyn remained standing in the threshold.

"I already spoke to someone on the phone," Evelyn said.

"Spoke to who?"

Evelyn waved vaguely. "I don't remember. He wasn't from around here."

"I'm sorry, Evelyn," Rags said. "May I call you Evelyn? Who are you talking about?"

"The day after Effie disappeared. Maybe two. I dunno. Somebody called me and asked a whole bunch of questions about what I remembered about her disappearance. What I knew."

Rags recalled Merry's cavalier explanation about the paper's early coverage of Effie's disappearance—that the copy had been "supplied," though Merry could not or would not say by whom. It was the oddest thing Rags had ever encountered in journalism. And it made absolutely no sense. Could the anonymous copy and the crime itself be related? How? And why? Rags didn't bother asking Evelyn if she read the paper.

"Well, look," Rags said. "I don't know anything about that. I wasn't here when all that happened. But I'm a really good listener. I pay close attention to what people tell me. So, if you're willing to go over it again—if you can stand to do that—maybe I can help discover the truth." *The truth: I said it.*

"Find Effie, you mean?"

"Yes. Maybe. I can't promise. But I want to try." Rags felt Maya peering over her shoulder.

Evelyn hesitated. She reached over her splintered porch railing to snap off a slim branch of blue hydrangea hanging over the railing. "The flowers bloom no matter what happens, don't they?"

Rags touched the flower. "I know exactly what you mean," she said. Evelyn opened the door and Rags entered.

Once inside, Rags felt oriented at once. The layout was nearly identical to the house she and Flint were living in. The interior was darker, however, and more sparsely furnished. As her eyes adjusted to the dim light, she saw that the parlor, the same size as her own, had almost no furniture in it. She had the sense that pieces had gone missing; surely it hadn't always been like this. Evelyn said nothing, made no apologies for the barren rooms. The parlor contained only two hard-backed chairs, a small round table, and an antique clock on the wall.

Rags wondered if Evelyn had grown up in this house, if it had been in her family a long time. It had a deeply settled feel to it, even amid the emptiness. She decided to start with questions about the past, rather than diving right into the hard stuff. At last, her journalist's instincts were kicking back in.

Evelyn spoke freely about happier days, though the tone of her voice, low and croaky, sounded sad. Evelyn's great-grandfather had moved into the house as a boy when it was brand new in the early 1900s. The street was just packed dirt dotted with clots of horse manure back then. "We're dry cleaners," she explained, meaning that successive generations of her family had run a dry cleaning store, with back-room tailoring, in downtown Canary for decades and decades. She spoke about the past as if she'd been there herself. When Evelyn reached into the drawer of an old side table for a dusty photo album, Rags knew it was time to bring the conversation back to the present, even if that meant causing Evelyn pain. This is the job, she reminded herself.

"Tell me about Effie," Rags said softly. Evelyn held the photo album in her lap. "What's she like?"

"She's not a natural blonde, you know," Evelyn began. Rags pictured the wide-eyed poster of the blonde Effie that hung over Main Street like a cruel reminder of—what, exactly? "Her hair's dark brown, like mine is—or was. But she begged and begged and finally I let her dye it. In the kitchen sink." She glanced back toward the kitchen. "That was just...days before...before she disappeared. Maybe that was a mistake. Maybe going blonde made her, uh, conspicuous." Rags wondered if the dye job was part of a plan, on Effie's part, to leave town? She didn't dare say that out loud.

Evelyn talked about Effie for an hour. It seemed to Rags that all she needed was an appreciative audience. Rags surreptitiously recorded their conversation on her dataphone. She didn't intend to trick Evelyn—that wouldn't be ethical. But she did intend to build as much rapport as possible before springing on her the fact that this was for the *Courant*. Rags learned that it was just the two of them in the old house. Effie's father had vanished when she was born, she said matter-of-factly. Evelyn had worked as a classroom aide while Effie was growing up. The dry cleaning business had closed years ago, a victim of high-tech household washers and dryers that did the job for you. The two of them didn't need much; the house was free and clear, she explained.

"When The Big One came, we weren't spared, not entirely," Evelyn continued, her voice empty of the anger and despair she had unleased at the town council meeting. "But my girl and I, we got through it. Took care of each other. We stayed in. I taught her gin rummy." Evelyn paused to look at Rags. "It's an old card game, you know. No tech, thank goodness."

"So you and Effie, you're Luckies," Rags ventured. Evelyn just shrugged. Very few people in Canary seemed to feel that surviving conferred luck.

Nothing Evelyn had said about Effie made the girl stand out in any particular way. She got decent grades. Hated math and history. Tolerated English. Joined the junior cheerleading squad. "That was her best day, I think," Evelyn said, pulling a crumpled tissue from her sweater. "I really thought we *were* lucky, then, so lucky." She pressed the tissue to her eyes.

"What happened that day? The day Effie disappeared?" Rags asked softly.

"She didn't come home after cheerleading practice," Evelyn said, sniffing. "She walked off that field at six o'clock every day after practice and she was always home before six-thirty."

"Except that day last October." Evelyn nodded. Her eyes were red.

Rags could see she was exhausted. She didn't think she could push much further. "What about her friends? Did they see anything?"

"I went over all this with Piers," Evelyn said, closing her eyes.

"Of course," Rags said. "And her behavior hadn't changed at all, in the days leading up to…to that day?" Evelyn shook her head. She got up to open a hall closet and came back with something in an old plastic bag. It was a shiny red Mylar pom-pom, the thin ribbons of material shaking and shimmering in the dim light of the parlor. Rags thought that Effie seemed like a girl who might have stepped right out of 1950 or 1960, based on Evelyn's description. She certainly didn't seem like the kind of girl desperate to leave home in 2029.

"Piers brought this back to me," Evelyn said, holding out the pom-pom as if it held magical properties. Didn't pom-poms come in pairs? Rags wondered. She took it and put the cloth strap across her hand, just to get the feel of it. Cheerleading hadn't been on her radar growing up. Maya might have liked it, though, she thought, if things had been different.

"Piers found her dataphone on the ground," Evelyn said. "He kept it. Will you tell him I want it back?"

Rags realized she'd need to ask Piers for the incident report. She doubted he'd let her handle any evidence, including the dataphone, while the investigation was ongoing. But at this moment, she knew she was on the verge of overstaying her welcome, so she got up and thanked Evelyn. Hugs were as rare as gold coins, but Rags opened her arms and the two of them embraced briefly.

"I don't know why I survived," Evelyn said, looking straight at Rags. "Do you?"

On her way out the door, Rag said softly that she planned to write another story about Effie when the time was right, hoping it would add pressure to the investigation. She had taken a 180-degree turn since arriving in Canary, and this is where she now found herself: committed to investigating the disappearance of a girl who was nothing like Maya yet felt exactly like Maya. *But this time, it won't be my fault.*

Back out on the street, Rags felt lightheaded. She hadn't eaten since the day before so she walked into town, to the little café where she liked the plantburgers. The café was just a room with a long counter, old-fashioned swivel stools, and a handful of tables and chairs. It was lit up—aglow, actually—with pale pink and blue neon and run by machines. You ordered at a kiosk and retrieved your food from a compartment in the wall. The place was called Eat Clean, and Rags could see why. The only other person in the café happened to be Piers. Rags nearly shuddered at the coincidence, but she realized there were only two places to eat in downtown Canary—here and the bar. Perhaps Piers rotated between the two, depending on how high he was. She sat on a stool next to him.

"Crime spree keeping you busy?" she asked. Piers seemed to live on french fries. He dove into a plateful of them.

"This town used to have six on the force plus a desk sergeant, if you can believe that," Piers said. "I was just a rookie then. Low man on the old totem pole."

"And now you're all they've got."

"Last one standing." Piers shrugged and took another mouthful.

Maybe he's just like everybody else, Rags thought. Seen too much. Worn out. Done sticking his neck out. What lay beneath that stoned, placid exterior of his?

"I guess it must've been pretty rough," Rags said, watching him. He paused and licked his fingers.

"Well," he said, "it's a lot easier to get through the day if I just don't think about it. A lot of shit under the bridge, y'know?"

Rags pulled her order from the slot: an omelet, whole wheat toast, and a large coffee. "Seems to me that Piper thinks about nothing else," she said.

"Always on me about somethin'. Let me give you some advice."

"Yeah?" she said.

"Steer clear."

Rags waited for him to continue. But he stopped and slid off his stool. "Of?" she asked.

"Piper. Terry. Missy too. You leave them be, they'll leave you be." Rags clearly remembered the first thing Terry said to her was not to make trouble. They must have felt like they had carte blanche, those three, especially since Piers, the only other official in town who could legally make things difficult for somebody, clearly followed his own advice.

"Well, Piers, I'm going to do what I need to do. I spoke with Evelyn Rutter this morning. At length."

Piers looked surprised. He finger-combed his hair. "And?"

"I want to read the incident report," Rags said. "And I want to talk to you on the record about the case."

"Can I just text you a statement?" Piers asked.

"If you do that, you're telling me you have nothing substantive to say about it. Is that what you're telling me?"

Piers hesitated. "We've got zero hits on the national missing persons database. Maybe this girl really doesn't want to be found."

"Why would you assume that?" Rags asked, raising her voice. "You seem awfully ready to blame the victim." Rags had thought along similar lines just an hour ago, but now she did not really believe Effie had brought this on herself.

"I didn't say that," Piers said, standing awkwardly in the middle of the empty café, sucking down the last of a chocolate milkshake.

"Let me see the incident report, so I can draw my own conclusions," Rags said.

"I can't do that. It's an ongoing investigation."

"Rapidly turning into a cold case," Rags said, glaring at him.

Piers grew quiet. "I tell you what," he said. "Let's make a deal."

It was only noon but the day already felt old. Rags knew she should head to the office, but she didn't want to face Merry's smarmy snarl. Besides, the news hole wasn't in bad shape, given all the work she'd done from home. She wanted to think about how to handle the interview with Evelyn Rutter before slugging it. And she wanted time to sort that out before tackling Ted and Roger Fallon about Jaxson. Trying to run both cases to ground at the same time wouldn't necessarily yield better or faster results—and could potentially spook an as-yet undiscovered source. And she needed to read Piers's file—assuming she could get it, based on their deal. It would be so easy to ask Flint to hack in to the peacekeeper's database and download it for her, except that he had scruples, and while she might be willing to bend them in pursuit of the truth, she knew he'd never go for it. She'd have to do this the old-fashioned way.

The June afternoon was growing hot and Rags felt a sudden yearning to stand in the middle of Louisa Copperface's crisp, clean gallery and drink in the artwork. Studying a canvas, she would be free to make up any story about the images that confronted her, any stòry at all. No need to obsess over "the truth" or which angle to play. She could let art wash over her without any right or wrong to it. What a relief. Brent had yet to file a story on Louisa's gallery and she wondered if he was lying about his interest in covering the arts in an effort to seem more versatile than he was. Was there anyone in Canary who wasn't lying about something? Louisa. She was a straight shooter. She had to be.

She walked the two blocks from the café to the alley and stood across from the gallery entrance, gazing at the pink explosion that had drawn her in before. The pink was still shocking—like jumping into an ice-cold river on a hot day. She crossed the boundary from the hot, defeated reality of Canary into the cooler, streamlined world of Louisa Copperface's self-made gallery. Louisa was standing precariously near the top of a tall ladder, trying to hook a large painting to the wall. Rags hurried over to steady the ladder.

"Oh, thanks," Louisa said, as if she'd been expecting Rags. "But I'm used to it. This probably looks more dangerous than it is." Rags gazed up at Louisa and the canvas, which was over six feet tall. Louisa held the hanging wire attached to the painting a few inches away from the wall. She peered down behind the painting to see the hook. Rags thought she looked entirely different from her first visit. She wore a sleeveless white tank top under paint-splattered overalls, her heavy black hair haphazardly pinned up off her neck. Still holding the ladder, Rags looked around the gallery and was surprised to see that all the paintings were new.

"You must paint nonstop," she said.

"I just follow my muse," Louisa said. "There!" she said as the wire caught the hook in the wall. "You can let go now." Rags realized she'd been gripping the ladder tightly, as if an accident were imminent.

"What happened to the others?" Rags asked.

"What others?"

"The paintings that were hung before. Did you sell them all?" Oh, that was rude, Rags thought. But Louisa didn't seem put off.

"Actually, I did. But don't be too impressed. I don't charge much. I mean, you can buy a Copperface for, like, five hundred dollars. I'm not exactly in the big leagues."

Surely not enough to live on, Rags thought. How does she do it? She could barter art for food—but would there be any takers? Rags knew that people kept body and soul together in Canary in all sorts of ways, and it was probably best not to look too closely at how they managed it. It would be like asking people to show you their underwear. Besides, she didn't want to treat Louisa as a journalism assignment. Brent was supposed to handle that.

"What do you think?" Louisa asked, gazing around the gallery. "I've been in a figurative mood lately, so these are a bit of a hybrid. I think it's the portraits, egging me on."

Rags steeled herself to ask to see the portraits. Louisa referred to more than one. She was ready now. But first, she took a moment to absorb the new work on the walls. She dredged up the vocabulary she'd learned from college art history. "I like the pentimento. That's what you call it, right? The layers of paint, with the bare hint of limbs, bodies, faces barely showing through underneath. Kind of like, when you look at the moon, sometimes you see a face, sometimes you don't."

"I'm giving you an A in my class, Rags. Brava. Do you know, you're the first person to walk in here and 'talk art'? I didn't realize how much I missed those conversations. Canary is so fucking boring. Don't you think so?"

Rags smiled. "Professionally, I'm not allowed to be bored."

"I've started reading your paper," Louisa said. "I mean, after your last visit, it seemed only fair. You've seen my art, so I wanted to see yours. To be honest, not a lot happens in Canary, does it?"

"If you don't count teenagers who vanish into thin air."

"Of course—that," Louisa said. "But can I be honest?" Rags nodded. "The classifieds are the best part. That's where all the action is! All those exotic vacations. And the personals? Where are those people hiding? I want to meet them. Oh, and the bonsai class—I might sign up for that." Rags rolled her eyes. "What? It's for real, right?"

"Will you show me the portraits? They weren't finished last time."

Louisa led Rags back into the messy work room. The soapstone statues she'd seen before were clustered together in a corner, perhaps awaiting buyers. Rags thought she was mentally prepared, but the two larger-than-life faces in thickly textured oil paint, propped on black easels, packed a wallop. There was Effie with her dyed blonde hair, looking like she'd just finished cheerleading practice. The sunburst tattoo had been added, delicately feathering Effie's cheek. Louisa had also painted Jaxson, a square-jawed redhead with a light spray of freckles across the bridge of his nose. Two all-American kids, two Luckies, two teenagers gone to who knows where or why. Louisa told her she hadn't decided what to do with them. She wouldn't sell them, of course. But she was afraid to offer them to the parents, for fear the wounds were too fresh.

"And anyway," Louisa said, "I don't want anybody thinking this is hagiography. You know, some kind of idealized portrait that feels like a memorial. Can you tell me anything, or is that confidential?"

"I don't know," Rags said. "That's the truth. And if I did, I couldn't tell you. I couldn't tell anyone."

"But are you...I mean, is anyone..." Louisa said, looking at the portraits.

"Yes. We're trying. I'm trying. I promised I would." Rags stopped herself.

"I'll never have kids," Louisa said matter-of-factly, "so I can only imagine. But loss is like common currency now, isn't it? It's something we all trade in."

The two women stood together for a moment in silence.

"Louisa," Rags said. "Would you like to come to my house for dinner one night next week? Flint is an excellent cook." This would be a first, Rags realized. Not once in the city, or so far in Canary, had the two of them entertained anybody. At first, it wasn't safe or practical, and then later, it didn't seem to occur to either of them to try. Until now. Rags had to believe that Flint would not object, that he'd fall in line with the plan. And it would save the two of them from another evening of half-begun conversations and awkward silences.

"I'd love that!" Louisa said. "Can you believe, in the three years since I came back, nobody has asked me. So, yes, absolutely. I'll bring wine."

Rags took another long, hard look at the portraits, especially Effie's, before leaving the gallery. Perhaps because she'd spent the morning with Effie's mother, or because Maya felt like an ever-present force hovering just beyond reach, Rags felt an uncomfortable prick of obligation to do something, anything, whatever it took, to find the girl. If only all the other stuff weren't piling up on her—Merry, the strange ads, the vaguely threatening Piper Madrigal, and wheedling the evidence file from Piers.

12

They feed us crap that looks like dog food. The water tastes like dirty metal.

Mom makes the best hash browns. I smell them. Don't think about it.

I smell like a fucking crab. I stopped wearing underwear. Better this way. The metal sleep shack reeks so bad that the sadist only pops his head in to count us and yell at us.

The scraping sound the lock makes when he shuts us in at night...makes my teeth ache.

He says we're fucking lazy. He says we're all replaceable. Disposable? He says we get out of line, they'll toss us into the bay and put somebody else on the line before we even hit bottom. He says there are thousands of us ripe for the plucking, everywhere.

Sometimes I imagine walking into the bay and swimming until I can't.

Often I imagine taking my knife and cutting the sadist's throat. Any sadist around. I would if I could. I swear. But there's always a guard dog nearby, ready to chomp on me. And the short-haired sadist takes the knives from us at the end of each day.

I'm worried about Flora. She looks like shit. I put my hand on her forehead, like Mom did when I was little. She's burning up. She holds up her thumb.

It's swollen way up, red and black. Something's wrong with it.

They must have taken Flora away when I was sleeping.

Now I stand next to Henry. He keeps muttering about how he's getting out of here. He's not.

I think my seventeenth birthday is next week. But I'm not sure.

I shouldn't miss Flora. It's not worth it.

13

The emergency township meeting drew a larger crowd than the snoozy one Rags had attended weeks before. Chairs were pushed out to the walls in a bid to maintain social distancing while accommodating as many people as possible. The high school cafeteria, which absurdly lacked air conditioning in 2030, was stiflingly hot. Still, many people wore respies or at least clutched them, ready to protect themselves if anyone so much as coughed in their direction.

Rags understood why things were ratcheting up. Effie's disappearance was alarming, but that was just one kid—somebody else's bad luck. But now that Jaxson was gone, everybody was bracing for a pattern to emerge. People were conditioned to look for patterns. The Big One had been a giant honeycomb of patterns that people obsessively watched over: infection rates, geographic hot spots, contact trace data revealing immunity gaps, death clusters, and so forth. So now, if two kids were missing, surely that was an early indicator of a multiplier effect. Whose kid would be next? And how could this be stopped? Rags had received several letters addressed to the editor expressing these concerns in one form or another. She would run a few of them, and then no more, as the redundancy served nobody's interests.

Once again, Rags watched the survivors—the Luckies—trickle in, only this time, there was a hum of anger and anxiety filling the room, replacing the usual sense of tired apathy. She could see it in the dour expressions all around her, the whispered conversations. Everyone looked at Evelyn Rutter and Roger Fallon when they came in, and then they all looked away, as if they feared that children going missing was a contagious condition that could be caught with merely a glance.

Paranoia and justice did not mix well. Rags pondered writing an editorial about that, and filed the idea away for later.

Rags noted that Louisa Copperface wasn't there, and she wasn't at the last meeting either. Not much of a joiner, Rags thought. What a luxury, to live above and apart from the fray, dwelling in a kind of timeless present. That's how Rags thought of Louisa. She didn't hold it against her.

Piper Madrigal stood in a corner bouncing on his heels, hands behind his back, in protective gear as always, watching everyone suspiciously. The familiar kohl-rimmed eyes glowed with menace above the rim of a respie—or so Rags imagined. Was this the town's real enemy hiding in plain sight? Was Piers right about Piper—or merely giving voice to his own stoned paranoid fantasies? Because she couldn't get back at all the PHPs who had made life so difficult in the city, Rags longed for a shot at just one—but her only weapon was the newspaper and she couldn't simply print whatever she wanted.

Somebody grabbed Rags's arm. She jerked away quickly. It was Keller. He was flushed and reeked of alcohol, his white wisps of hair sheened with sweat.

"I've got to talk to you," Keller said, his unmasked mouth exhaling damp alcoholic fumes. Rags took another step back. She instinctively wiped her face with the back of her hand, which she then wiped on her pants. He stood uncomfortably close. "The ads in the paper, they're—"

"Keller!" Rags needed to cut him off. Whatever he was about to say, she knew she didn't want anyone else to overhear. "Come to the office tomorrow morning."

"I can't," Keller said, weaving slightly. "Find me at Ted's joint. Tonight." He meant the Canary Bar & Grill. Ted had to mind the place, which was why Roger had come to the meeting alone. Rags nodded and Keller tottered off. She doubted he'd be in any kind of shape to make sense later on, but she had to try.

Brent found her just before the meeting began. "You're not tag-teaming me, Rags, are you? This is my turf." He held up his tablet. "I know all the players. And how to read between the lines." His implication was clear. Rags held out empty hands.

"No notes, see?" she said. "The story's all yours. But try to make the lede snappy, okay?" Brent frowned. She sensed he'd tolerate her as his editor, he just didn't want her poaching his journalistic territory. She already expected that he'd turn in a fairly superficial write-up of the meeting, without a lot of local color.

Terry flicked a bright red laser pointer on and off toward the ceiling.

"This emergency session of the Canary Town Council is now called to order," she said, her sharply cut white hair conveying a sense of professional authority, with a voice like cut glass to match. Missy stood a few feet apart from Terry, watching the assembly through narrowed eyes. Rags saw this for what it was: a public performance. Public officials, she knew, used every trick they could think of to intimidate their constituents and remind everyone who was in charge. As a journalist, she felt herself to be immune. Terry and Missy took their seats at the battered table, and then Keller did likewise. Rags wondered if Keller had an actual say in policy matters when the three of them met alone together. She guessed not.

Terry began the meeting by calling on Piers to report on any updates in the investigation. "Or rather, I should say, investigations, plural," she added.

Piers stood and ran his hand through his hair. His other hand rested on the hilt of his stun gun, as if he were poised to use it, though Rags did not think he had the gumption. Maybe it just makes him comfortable, knowing it's there. Piers explained he'd called in a pair of peacekeepers from nearby towns to comb the areas where both children were last seen. They'd spotted some tire tracks and were still in the process of analyzing detailed photos of the prints. They were also still analyzing the two dataphones recovered at the scenes. However, Piers said, both phones had been mysteriously wiped clean, so retrieving trace data on them was proving difficult. This was all news to

Rags and she was furious. He could at least have told her about these developments when they met at the café. But instead he'd played dumb—dumber than he actually was. Tire tracks? There weren't that many cars in Canary. How hard could it be? And Flint could crack those phones in an instant, she thought. *Piers is way out of his depth.*

Roger Fallon stood up and interrupted Piers.

"What about the FBI, Piers? Why haven't you called them to help?"

"I did, Roger, but they don't have any field officers available right now," Piers said, shrugging, as though all of this was completely out of his hands. "They're already stretched thin. You know how it is."

Evelyn Rutter had shot up from her seat. "You're not trying hard enough! When are you gonna take this seriously?" The room burst into applause. "When is *anybody* gonna start caring about our kids? Wait'll they take *your* kids," Evelyn said, looking around the room, while Roger nodded vigorously. "Then you'll wanna see results in a hurry!"

"Evelyn's right," Roger said. "This isn't just happening to *us.* It's happening to *all* of us. Most of you know my son—Ted and I call him our son now. You watched Jaxson Turner grow up. You watched him lose everybody he loved. How can you just stand by and do nothing?" More applause. Everybody wanted something to be done, but nobody knew what. Rags felt it was a pointless rerun of the earlier township meeting.

Piper stepped forward and caught Terry's eye, seeking her permission to speak. She gave him a curt nod.

"I'm asking everyone to consider another troubling factor in these cases," Piper said, pacing in front of the table where the council members were seated, in a voice pitched to reach the back of a large theater. "It is possible—entirely possible—that whoever is behind these crimes comes from well outside Canary's borders. In all likelihood this person, or persons, entered our town in the dead of night, skirting all our requirements for contact tracing and temp checks." He shot a glance in Rags's direction. "There could be another outbreak brewing in Canary right now, for all we know. It's entirely possible. So we really have got to take this seriously." Piper looked around the room as the words sank in. And then Piper lobbed a bigger bombshell. "And if that's the case…if there's a new strain coming in…with no vaccine…well, then…"

Suddenly, everyone began talking all at once:

"Erect an electric fence around our borders!"

"Nobody gets in or out!"

"Make respies mandatory!"

"Stop the super-spreaders!"

A woman Rags did not know pointed at Camilla, who had been seated quietly in a far corner. She was less recognizable without her big wig; she looked like any other woman in Canary, wan and dull-eyed, with thinning hair. "It's *her* fault," said the accuser. "Camilla's a super-spreader!" Rags observed several men in the room pointedly looking away from Camilla while she remained the center of attention.

"I'm no different from any of you," Camilla shouted at them. "No better. No worse, either. I give and I take—to survive—just like all of you. So quit spreading damn lies about me."

Terry did nothing to de-escalate the tension in the room. Rags wondered if this had been orchestrated—if Piper, Terry, and Missy had planned for the PHP's little speech. As if getting people worked up, putting them on edge, would somehow work to the trio's advantage. But how? Rags thought about what Piers had asked her to find out and she knew she'd have to call on Terry as soon as possible.

Piers issued a piercing two-fingered whistle. Then he flopped down hard in his seat, as if he'd discharged a taxing duty. As soon as the room quieted down, Roger was back on his feet. "Stop it! All of you! What are you getting so worked up about? You're all safe right this very minute. You'll sleep in your own beds tonight. And you'll wake up in the morning, still safe. But what about Jaxson? He's not safe. He didn't just disappear. He was stolen. I don't know how. I don't know why. But your kid could be next. So if you wanna worry yourselves sick, then worry about that!"

The room erupted in loud cross talk again. Evelyn burst into tears but Roger was the only one to go over and comfort her. He put his arm around her shoulder, the rarity of the gesture casting a kind of spotlight on the pair of them. Everyone else in the room seemed to clear an extra space around them, as though the two of them were contaminated.

Missy climbed up onto the table to be heard as well as seen, as she was so tiny. Her deep voice rang out. "Hey!" she yelled, waiting for the room to settle down. Piers whistled again. "Hey! I'm sorry your children disappeared," Missy began, dark curls framing her small face. She sounded angry, not sorry. "But if PHP Madrigal is right, then we have a much bigger problem than your kids, or even the next kids, and we need to put all our resources into prevention." Many in the room were nodding and muttering, *She's right.* "We can't afford… Canary can't live through…another holocaust. A missing kid is bad, but letting death back into our homes…that's unthinkable."

"She's right, people," Piper said loudly. "Population-protection protocols always need to take precedence."

"Health first!" somebody shouted. And then the room grew noisy again. Missy climbed down off the table. It seemed Missy had lobbed a second bombshell that exploded all around them, with Piper's help, and Canary's residents were taking it in, probably imagining the worst, Rags guessed. A few people were once again pointing and yelling at Camilla. Evelyn and Roger looked downhearted, defeated. Piper stood, arms crossed, looking smug and satisfied. Rags could swear she saw the PHP and Terry exchange an almost imperceptible nod. Had this been orchestrated, then?

Rags thought again about her idea for an editorial—how paranoia and justice do not mix. The former short-circuits the latter. When people are frightened, they take refuge in groupthink and grow susceptible to bending and breaking rules that come between them and a feeling of security. And justice be damned. Rags had seen it all go down in the city. She didn't want to see it again in Canary. Somebody had to find Effie and Jaxson—or at least figure out beyond a shadow of a doubt what had happened to them. Justice had to carry the day. She was thinking about a headline for the piece: "'A Town Bends Over." That would get their juices flowing, wouldn't it? She'd spell it out in her column, surely making her even less popular than she already was. Tough shit.

The meeting broke up quickly. Nothing much had been accomplished. Several people collected around Piper who stood now with arms clasped behind his back, radiating a satisfied authority, pleased to be at the center of attention, Rags thought. She saw Camilla make a quick exit, away from the pointing fingers.

Evelyn stopped Rags on the way out. "Big help *you* turned out to be," she said. "I spilled my guts—for what? You haven't done shit. You're as bad as the rest of them." Rags wanted to tell her to be patient, to give her a chance. She wanted to explain that she'd made a promise to someone that she intended to keep. But Evelyn didn't wait for a response. She walked out into the warm June night alone.

Rags did not want to be seen just yet with Keller, so she let him leave for the bar first. She knew by now that he had probably reached a stage of drunkenness where he would remain fairly coherent for a little while longer, even if he kept on drinking. And she wanted a word with Roger before he darted out of the cafeteria. She called out to him. He looked at her glumly. Clearly, she was not his favorite person to talk with, but she went over to him anyway.

"Quick question," she said, looking up at him. He might have been six-five, she guessed, a tall stick of a man. He looked her, his mouth set in a thin line. "Did you or Ted, by any chance, get a call from a stranger asking you a bunch of questions about Jaxson's disappearance?" Roger's expression changed. He colored and looked uncomfortable, as if she were trying to trap him.

"We really have *no* idea who that was on the phone. Absolutely no idea," Roger said.

"I believe you."

"You do?" Roger said.

"Why wouldn't I? What did this person ask?"

"I didn't talk to him. Ted did. But I think he—"

"So it was a man who called?"

"Yes," Roger said. "He—" Roger stopped. "I don't want to be quoted in the newspaper. You're not going to quote me, right?"

"I'm not taking any notes, Roger. I'm not going to quote you. This is strictly off-the-record. Do you know what that means?"

"I know what it's *supposed* to mean," he said.

"So tell me. Please. Every little bit helps."

"Well, Ted said he spoke quickly and asked if we knew exactly where Jaxson was when he disappeared, what time of day it was, what he was wearing, if anybody saw him right before that. Ted finally asked the guy who he was and what he wanted. And then he hung up."

"Who hung up?" Rags asked.

"Ted did," Roger said. "The guy was being weird and intrusive, and Ted didn't think he was a peacekeeper or from the FBI or anything like that. And then…" Roger said.

"And then what, Roger?"

"Well, you don't need to know this. But then we both cried. A lot. We love Jaxson. We're desperately worried."

"I know," Rags said. "I can only imagine." Roger nodded imperceptibly and seemed to soften a little.

"Goodnight," he said and walked quickly away. She didn't know if she'd see him at the bar moments later, but she knew he had nothing more to say to her, or she to him, for now.

Moments later, she spotted Keller at his usual table at the back of the bar. The place was packed, and she avoided looking around in case anyone else wanted to start up a conversation. She brought her scotch from the bar and joined him. His face had turned deep crimson and his gray nylon shirt was soaked with sweat.

"I used to be in manufacturing, did you know that?" Keller asked her the instant she sat down. Rags shook her head. Better to let him set the pace, initially. At least he couldn't whip out an old photo album. "Aluminum extrusion. Made parts for solar panels. Biggest in the state, we were. Complicated stuff. Couldn't just rely on so-called machine intelligence, y'know? People intelligence—that's what it took. Whole thing fell apart." Keller waved his hand, assuming Rags knew the story, or stories like it. "They call us the Luckies. Ah, that's bullshit. Nothing lucky about it."

Keller held up his empty glass high above his head and signaled for Ted to bring him another. Rags wondered if he was burning through whatever savings or pension he had, spending it all on alcohol. Maybe that was his plan. What did he have to barter?

"You wanted to talk about the classified ads, in the *Courant*," she said. No point in letting him continue to wallow in the past if he was willing to get to the point now—before he passed out. Ted brought Keller another bourbon and whisked away the empty glass. He didn't even look at Rags, who was still slowly sipping her scotch. "I've been wondering about that, since I got here." *And what on earth does it have to do with you?*

Keller leaned forward. Rags leaned toward him but kept her face down toward the table to avoid his wet, foul breath. "The ads contain coded messages," he said. Rags's first thought was that he was completely insane, and this was a waste of time. But she waited for more. "Addresses, times, locations."

"For what?" she asked.

"It's how they coordinate the kidnappings."

"Who?"

"I can't tell you that."

"How do you know they were kidnapped?"

"Well, taken," he said. "What else would you call it? They weren't abducted by aliens. Though maybe that's next."

"How do you know any of this?" Rags said, as matter-of-factly as possible, fighting against the pumping surge of adrenaline coursing through her. She decided to ignore the comment about aliens and assume, for the moment, that he was trying to tell the truth, or as much of it as he knew. "Did Merry tell you? Is she wrapped up in this, Keller?"

"Can't speak to that." Keller knocked back half his bourbon. "I'll tell you this: Merry is good people. You can't blame her."

Rags would unpack this later. She didn't want Keller to stonewall her about Merry, in case he shut down on her completely.

"Does Piers know?" she asked. Keller shook his head. That was almost better news than the news itself; finally, she had a jump on the investigation. "The PHP?"

"That asshole knows shit," Keller said. "It's none of his fuckin' business." So he too would toe the line in front of Piper and then quickly diss him behind his back. Exactly the kind of cowardly hypocrisy she expected not just from him, but most of them.

Rags waited. She didn't want to pummel Keller with too many questions. She sat back and tried to appear relaxed. Just having a drink with a "friend."

"Tell me about your family, Keller," Rags said.

"Lost," he replied. "All gone. I moved into one of the survivor studios on Main Street. Solo. So…low. Get it?" He laughed bitterly, revealing yellowed teeth.

Keep him talking.

"What do you think I should do with this—this information you gave me?"

"Find Effie Rutter," he said.

"And Jaxson Turner?"

Keller nodded. "Evelyn can't take much more of this. Everybody has their breaking point, y'know. Ted and Roger"—he jerked his head toward the bar—"they're not the boy's blood kin. Not the same thing."

"What about you, Keller? Do you have a breaking point?" She risked the question to glean what she could about his state of mind and whether he might be depended on to tell her more, another time. If he *knew* more.

Keller smiled at his glass. "Not anymore. Now, I gotta take a piss. When I come back, I don't wanna see you here."

Rags walked home quickly through the June night, questions piling up in her head. How much did Keller really know? Was he somehow directly involved in the kidnappings? He didn't seem to feel guilt, only bitterness. And his desire for the kids to be found seemed genuine; after all, he'd said it more than once. Maybe he was protecting someone else. But who? Merry? And why? Rags wondered if she had an obligation to report the little she knew to Piers—and quickly decided against it. She wanted time to figure out more of this on her own.

She arrived home to the usual scenario: Flint at his desk, the bluish glow of his screens emitting the only light in the house. The windows were open to let in the scant evening breeze. The house was so quiet, Rags heard the sound of crickets floating in from the yard. Flint was beginning to seem like a ghost who haunted the house, not the flesh-and-blood man she'd let herself fall for almost four years ago. But tonight, she wanted something specific from him.

"Can I interrupt you with a question?" Since their last fight, they'd both made an effort to tiptoe politely around one another.

"Sure," Flint said, stretching in his chair. "What time is it?"

"Nearly ten."

"Oh, wow. How was the meeting?"

"You should come to one. I think you'd find it interesting, you know, anthropologically speaking. Get to know something about the town you're living in. It's called Canary, by the way."

"Hah-hah. There's more than one way of knowing, Rags."

"I'm starving," she said, not interested in debating epistemology with him. He told her there was cold potato salad in the fridge and she filled a bowl.

"What's your question?" Flint said, joining her at the kitchen table. He squinted in the glare of the light. *He's practically nocturnal, like a lemur.*

"Suppose you had a bunch of printed material that contained

coded messages that helped somebody decipher dates, times, and locations for some kind of event."

"Okay," Flint said, "that's random."

"No, it isn't. In fact, it's probably a matter of life and death."

"Never a dull moment in the life of a journalist, eh?"

"I'm serious, Flint. Just because I'm not inventing a new algorithm or whatever."

"No, I know. Sorry. Go on."

"How would you go about cracking the code? Figuring out what the messages actually mean?"

"Are you asking for my help?"

"Yes."

Flint surprised her by asking for something in return. He liked watching her do her yoga routine on the mat. He wanted her to resume doing it in front of him. It struck her that he must have given this quite a bit of thought. She readily agreed. This felt like a détente and Rags truly did not want to be fighting on more than one front at a time. Before heading up to bed, she decided to take advantage of their mutual thaw to tell him she'd invited Louisa Copperface to dinner the following week. She told Flint that Louisa was the closest thing to a cosmopolitan citizen Canary had, and that she thought it would be a good idea to try and do something that normal couples do.

"Oh, are we back to playing that game?" Flint asked with a rueful smile. "How normal are we?"

"Well, we should try it at least once," Rags said. "And it gives you a chance to cook for someone new for a change." So that was settled. Rags had never had much need for close female friends, but something about Louisa reminded her that the world was a big place, bigger than Canary, bigger than the corrupted city she'd fled, bigger even than a killer disease And that felt like something that needed to be remembered too.

Early the next morning, while Flint slept, Rags hurried to the office, bringing with her the biggest backpack she could find from their meager store of supplies. She went through the paper's archives, scooping up as many back issues as she could fit into the pack. She gathered at least two years' worth—hopefully enough to provide Flint with enough raw data to decipher patterns from the printed ads and extract something that made sense. Maybe he'd find something that would eventually show that Keller was telling the truth—though she was still a long, long way from solving this troubling puzzle. Rags didn't know whether Merry would discover the missing papers or not, and even if she did, she was happy to put Merry on notice that the time for business as usual was over.

14

I didn't vomit today. Guess that's progress. The sadist doesn't care.

Still dizzy, though. Chanelle says I'll get used to it. She'd know. She's been here over a year. I don't see myself lasting that long. I can tell after only three days.

I fucking hate chickens. Hate hate hate them.

I miss crab island. Almost. It was super-shitty. But this is super-shittier.

Chanelle and I aren't friends. Nobody here is friends. Just stuck. No, caught. Like lightening bugs in a jar. I used to snatch them and fling them into an old mayonnaise jar, then screw the lid on so they couldn't get away.

Didn't know I'd turn into a lightning bug. Snatched, stuffed inside, with the lid closed so tight there's no escape.

At the super-shitty place, I didn't vomit, even though the smell was real bad. Crabs aren't as disgusting as chickens. Their parts are way smaller.

But the crab juice burned like hell in all the cuts that crisscrossed my fingers and palms. I can still see lots of little scars from the shells, which are sharper than they look. The knives too. The gloves they gave us were a joke.

One morning after Flora disappeared—if that's what you can call it—I woke up with shooting pains in my wrists. My hands got a mind of their own, curling up like claws. The sadist with the shaved head gave me two aspirin. Said I'd get used to it and I couldn't slow down.

Pick, pick, pick. They think our fingers are wings. Or machines.

Sadist approaching for bed check. Must tuck this away soon. My new bedsheet diary.

Good thing I keep the Sharpie tucked down my pants.

But I want to get this down. Out of me.

They put me on the evisceration line. I didn't know that word. Still not sure how to spell it. But I'm living it.

I remove the viscera. Heart, lungs, stomach. All the fatty slops.

Rip, rip, slide, plop. Rip, rip, slide, plop. I hear the rhythm of falling guts when I close my eyes at night.

I still gag. But at least I don't spew.

The naked yellow chickens dangle from a metal conveyor rod, all dead and defeated, like us. Hundreds and hundreds of them come at me, an army of pimply corpses. The line moves, moves, moves for hours and hours. My head buzzes. My hands burn and sweat inside thick rubber gloves.

Guess what they feed us? Chicken.

I can't eat that shit. Can't eat any of their shit.

Can't sleep. Writing in the dark.

Shooting pains across the back of my neck and shoulders. Like I'm an old lady now. Pains in my stomach, like I'm being stabbed.

Tried closing my eyes, walking through my favorite cheerleading routine.

Step, hop, hop, step, kick, kick, left arm up, right arm up.

Rip, rip, slide, plop.

Can't remember the rest. Everything hurts.

Another day. Maybe two. I want to chop off my hands. It's their fault. They stopped working on crab island. One morning, I couldn't hold the knife. It clattered to the floor. My hands contracted like an eagle's talons. The shaved-head sadist yanked me off the line.

What the fuck's wrong with you, she asked. You shirking? Are you?

She brought me outside. Called the bed-check sadist over. They grabbed my wrists roughly, turning them over. Shooting pains tore up through my wrists, elbows, shoulders.

The bed-check sadist calls out, Transfer!

He tied my hands behind me and wrapped them in a dirty cloth. Can't let them think you're damaged goods, he said with some type of smile. Bad for business, he said. A few hours later, a van pulled up.

I was almost excited when I saw the van. It meant I was leaving crab island.

But then I was terrified. Where would they send me? Would I be forced to strip again? Would the new sadists and overlords be even worse? Was that possible?

Still: sky and air.

And the thought, just before I was made to step into the van:

Run, run, run. Run to the sea.

Can't run. The dog is there, always waiting for us to mess up. And they have stun guns that take you down hard. Helen said she was blind for a week after that. What happened to Helen? When was that?

15

Flint was in the kitchen making sure he had not over-salted the pot roast when there was a knock on the door. They still had not installed a visi-cam. It was on his to-do list. He heard Rags open the door and speak in a voice that seemed to emanate from a complete stranger. It was what his mother would have called a company voice: a bit high-pitched, bright and friendly, many words stretched out for no particular reason.

"Thank you sooo much, Louisa!" Flint heard. "This looks amaaazing!"

Why was she acting this way? Her tone made him wary, as if he needed to be on the lookout for something, but he couldn't say what. Rags brought Louisa into the kitchen, and they got through introductions. Rags simply said, "And this is Flint." She opened Louisa's wine, a light ruby-colored Beaujolais, and poured for each of them. They didn't own wine glasses, so she used the same cheap, flat-bottomed glasses they used for everything.

"A toast!" Louisa said. Flint paused, his glass near his lips. "Let me think. Hmm. I know!" Louisa raised her glass:

"Nights were not made for the crowds, and they sever
You from your neighbor, so you shall never
Seek him, defiantly, at night.
But if you make your dark house light,
To look on strangers in your room, You must reflect—" she paused and looked at the two of them—"on whom."

"Wow," Rags said. Who was this enthusiastic person? Flint wondered—meaning Rags, not Louisa. Louisa did not look like anyone he'd seen on his trips to the markets in Canary. Her lustrous dark hair, dark eyes, and bright floral sundress reminded him of city girls. He could tell she was wearing make-up and her long, bright, dangly earrings caught the light. He didn't mind that Rags never dressed up, but he wondered what she'd look like if she did, just once. Rags had on the same thing she'd worn all day, some kind of loose cotton pants and a gray T-shirt. She wore the same sandals she'd had in the city, still held together with duct tape.

Flint was glad he had to get food on the table because it excused him from making small talk. He was terrible at it and didn't really want to do it better. He told Rags and Louisa to go sit in the parlor and he'd call them when everything was ready. To his surprise, they instantly obeyed him. He could hear the rise and fall of their easy conversation. He imagined Rags and Louisa exchanging more words in fifteen minutes than the two of them had exchanged in a month. He envisioned a dual line graph, comparing the different trajectories, wondering how he'd scale each axis. How many words did one person typically utter over thirty days? After several minutes, he called them into the kitchen. There was just enough room for the three of them to squeeze around the battered gate-leg table.

"Pot roast, crescent rolls, and salad," he announced, feeling stupid since the food was right in front of them. "And brownies for dessert. From a box, though. Not from scratch."

"Delish," Louisa said. Flint had never met anyone who said this word, but he thought this was probably a reflection of the extremely small social circle he traditionally inhabited. She refilled Flint's glass, then Rags's, then her own.

"You really should see Louisa's gallery," Rags said. "Art to soothe the savage breast."

Louisa laughed. "I think that's a reference to music, but I'll take it."

"Am I the savage breast?" Flint said. Both women laughed. Louisa asked for seconds. They finished the wine. Rags found and opened another bottle. Flint observed a bright flush on both women's faces. *She needs this. Maybe I'm in the way.* He grew more quiet as they grew more talkative. They spoke at length about Louisa's paintings, putting him at an obvious disadvantage, since he'd never seen her work. He listened to Rags fling around an art-world vocabulary, using words like *gouache* and *golden ratio.* He'd never seen her try to impress someone before. It revealed a new side of her—a side he didn't care for. She seemed to want it too much, whatever *it* was.

At some point, Louisa asked him about his work. She had no idea what he did. Flint looked briefly at Rags, remembering the first day they met, when she interviewed him and he kept falling back on what she called geek-speak. He took a stab at it.

"I use AI to help recognize patterns in data."

"Uh-huh," Louisa said, clearly expecting more. Rags began clearing plates, as though she couldn't sit still another minute to hear him explain how he filled his time.

"Patterns help you spot flaws, mistakes, so you can fix them. Or figure out if there's danger ahead. Like, say you've got a whole bunch of seismic data that records underground waves, shifts in the earth's movements." He decided it was wise to steer clear of the military as well as medicine. "I can train a model to analyze lots and lots of seismic data so that it's looking for unusual patterns, which might tell you where an earthquake is likely to happen."

"Oh, so like an early warning system," Louisa said, finishing her wine.

"Yeah, that's a good example," Flint said. At least she'd made an educated guess. He couldn't remember the last time Rags had done that. Rags brought the plate of brownies to the table. Flint had cut each brownie into a perfect square.

"The geometry is fantastic," Louisa said, turning the plate slowly. Flint had stacked the brownies in a pyramid, each square turned ninety degrees atop the brownie below. "You *do* have an eye for patterns, Flint. You weren't kidding. This is almost too beautiful to eat. *Still Life with Chocolate.* That's what I'd call it. Wait a minute." She dipped into her large colorful tote bag and pulled out her phone to take a picture. Rags snatched a brownie from the side, ruining the symmetry. Flint felt a twinge of irritation. Did she really have to do that?

Louisa reached back into the tote bag. "I almost forgot," she said, chewing. "A gift for the host and hostess." She pulled out a very small painting, about six inches square, mounted inside a simple gold frame.

"Let me see," Rags said, snatching the painting from Louisa's hands before Flint could even lean in for a view. "Oh, wow." Her second *wow* of the night, Flint observed. "So completely different from your other work." Flint sat back in his chair. He'd wait to be included. Louisa took the painting from Rags and handed it across to him. He studied it closely. It appeared to be a meticulous nature study: a wooded area, not dense. The tree trunks were narrow and grew at odd angles, some straight, some bent over. They were widely spaced, giving an ample view of a gray-white sky. Grasses, ferns, and a tangle of brambles grew wild, creating an unkempt forest carpet. He noticed how precisely she'd placed each brush stroke. He couldn't imagine the care and patience required to achieve the total effect. He felt, in some deep way, that his own work was like this: a careful accumulation of details adding up to something greater than the sum of its parts. But he didn't dare to share this thought. He didn't think he could find the words to express it without sounding ridiculous.

Flint smiled and told Louisa he thought the painting was excellent, every detail seemed so real. He asked her where she painted it.

"I can't tell you," Louisa said, looking serious. Flint saw that Rags was as surprised and puzzled as he was. So this wasn't some typical artist's ploy. "It's a site that is sacred to my people," she said. "I'm descended from a long line of Carolina Algonquians. Some of them settled not far from here, in the woodlands near the river, over seven hundred years ago." She touched the frame of the painting. "These woods are like a palimpsest—scraped, cleared, settled, burned, planted, abandoned, and so on, for centuries. My own blood is there, soaked deep into that ground. We have to protect it from looters, especially nighthawks. So only a few of us know the actual location."

"Looters?" Flint asked. "What's there to steal?" He didn't

know what a nighthawk was and decided he'd look it up later.

"Artifacts," Louisa said. "Like these." She showed Flint photos stored on her dataphone: arrowheads, spear tips, potsherds, other fragments. He gently laid the painting on the table.

"Are you sure you want us to keep this?" he asked softly, looking at Rags.

"What do you call it?" Rags asked Louise, her voice restored to its normal register. "I noticed in the gallery that all of your paintings have titles. So I'm wondering."

"It's called the *Potrero Complex*," Louisa said.

"What does that mean?" Flint asked.

"Well," Louisa said, "like everything that once belonged to Indigenous people, the name of the place was imposed by outsiders. It's a mish-mash. A 'complex' is what archaeologists call any site where a bunch of different cultures lived, and left artifacts behind, over a long period of time. My painting just shows a tiny fragment of the site, which covers a couple hundred acres. As for the *potrero* part..." Louisa paused. "Do you really want to hear this?"

"A *potrero* is Spanish for a field or something, isn't it?" Rags said.

"Close," Louisa said. "It's Spanish for paddock or pasture, or even a vacant lot." She shrugged. "Whatever my ancestors called this place is lost to the mists of time. Oral history is fragile. But they were here: that much is certain. And the record of their life, their culture, belongs to the place where it was created. Their spirits rest there, and always will—as long as the land remains undisturbed by outsiders."

Flint and Rags both pressed Louisa about whether she really wanted to part with the painting, which clearly was important to her. "We're friends now," she said. "I don't really have any friends in Canary. I want you to have a little piece of me. Besides, this is just one in a series." Flint couldn't think what he could possibly give to someone like Louisa in return, if they were ever invited to her place. He thought he might actually like to see how and where she lived.

Louisa kissed each of them once on both cheeks, European-style, which they received in stunned silence, as it had been so long since anyone attempted something like that. She shouldered her large tote bag and left.

"That went well," Rags said, as they washed all the dishes by hand. "The food was really good. And I know you really tried."

"I *tried*?" Flint said. "I'm not a seal you can train, Rags. You can't toss me a piece of raw fish and expect I'll jump six feet out of the water for you."

"That's not—"

"Then what?"

"Why are you so touchy?" Rags said.

"I'm sorry," he said.

"I'm sorry too." He was washing. She was drying. They kept their eyes on their tasks.

"I see why you like her so much," Flint said.

"She's better than this place. Better than all the shit that goes on around her. Around us. Do you know what I mean?"

"Sort of." He squeezed the sponge and set it by the sink. "I want to put her painting on my desk. So I can look at it some more. Do you mind?" She didn't seem to hear him.

"I don't want to look for Effie Rutter," Rags said. Suddenly, she had tears in her eyes. "I don't want to know."

He began to understand: this is what lay behind the company voice. The little dinner party was a form of distraction. As tears rolled down her cheeks, her left eye began to twitch. Slowly, tentatively, Flint took her in his arms and held her.

16

Rags felt a permanent scowl settling into the furrow between her eyes. A couple of days had passed since the dinner with Louisa. She'd slept badly, her nights filled with vivid dreams where Maya and Effie took turns reproaching her, calling for help, melting into puddles of molten lava, running away from hulking monsters. She woke feeling as if she were awash in danger. Running a newspaper was beginning to feel like an inadequate way to express what needed to be said—and done. Still, she knew she couldn't take her eyes off her actual job. She rose in the morning, gritty-eyed, and banged out her longest editorial yet for the Sunday paper on the theme of paranoia and justice, inspired by the tensions at the township meeting. *A town bends over.* It was intended as a warning, but she doubted many in Canary would heed the call.

She and Flint had warmed to one another again. She didn't know how long it would last. There was a need there; she couldn't quite nail down what it was about. For either of them. But she kissed the top of his sleeping head before heading to the office. The early July morning was already hot. She'd thrown on a wrinkled, sleeveless shirt, wrinkled capri pants, and her semi-broken sandals. Her thin brown hair fell in uneven waves to her shoulders. She had yet to get a haircut since moving to Canary. She just couldn't work up the energy. The brilliant spring flowers she'd passed on her first walk to the office, and that newborn tulip, had been replaced by clusters of greenery, already wilting under the dry summer sun. The vacant houses were still vacant, looking as if they'd never come back to life.

Welcome to the new normal.

Merry was already at her desk when Rags walked into the

Courant's office. She sat hunched over, her head in her hands. She snapped to attention the moment Rags stepped inside, but still, Rags had caught her out.

"Looking for something to do?" Rags asked. Merry's eyes looked puffy, which Rags attributed to careless living. Her long gray hair appeared more tangled than usual. Rags desperately wanted this useless excuse for a news employee to be gone. But now, based on what Keller had said about the classified ads, she needed Merry to stick around. "Call Porter and check on his next run to the presses." Rags was confident that Porter would do exactly what he was supposed to do, but she wanted to make Merry do *something*.

"I read your opinion piece, for Sunday," Merry said, not looking directly at Rags.

"Uh-huh."

"You don't understand a thing about this town. You never will," Merry said.

"And what do *you* know that *I* don't know?"

"People are in danger here. You act like nothing's going on."

I know something about danger. What it does to you. To people around you.

"The damn virus is over, Merry! You and Piper—you're clinging to all that like it's the only way to feel like you matter. Like you want starring roles in health-care theater. That's total bullshit." Rags sat in her chair and spun it around to keep her from walking over to Merry and trying to slap some sense into her. She felt like she could actually do that, in the moment. "Why don't you get a fucking life!"

"I *had* a fucking life!" Merry said, standing, but keeping her distance. "And everything got taken away from me. And they still keep taking! And there's no end to it!"

"Who, Merry? Who is taking anything from you at this very moment? Because as far as I can tell, you're getting paid by a mysterious stranger to do absolutely nothing. And if you had an ounce of self-respect, you wouldn't be sitting here right now. Far as I can tell, a lot of people in Canary are a lot worse off than you. At least you don't have to sell your body to make ends meet, like Camilla. Ever think about that?"

Merry swept up her bag and headed for the door. "Camilla is making the best of the options available to her. She might not feel like she has a choice. And neither do I."

"There's always a choice, Merry. Always something to choose between."

Merry made a sound halfway between a laugh and a strangled cry. She left the heavy door gaping open behind her.

Rags had already thought long and hard about how to approach Merry about the ads in a way that wouldn't send her running or force her to instruct Keller to stop speaking to Rags, or both. She had imagined asking Merry straight out about whether the ads were coded information somehow related to the kidnappings. But she was convinced, based on what she knew about Merry, that a direct question would get her nowhere and would probably jeopardize Rags's independent investigation. She still had no answers as to who paid Merry and why and no ready way to find out; there was no paper trail to follow. She needed Flint's help, that much was clear. She just had to hope that he'd make time for her, though she didn't really have anything special to offer him in return. Maybe that was part of their problem.

Rags breathed easier with Merry away from the newsroom. There was something about that woman that made her feel as if she were choking, as if Merry poisoned the air by her presence. Rags opened all the stories filed by the freelance brigade in advance of their bi-monthly editorial meeting. By the time Brent, Dineen, and Ramona arrived, Rags had done a light editing pass on their stories about summer football tryouts, gardening tips, and summer squash recipes. She couldn't help but feel that all this was merely a veneer of normalcy, slapped like a thin coat of paint on a rotting corpse. Was that fair? Rags wasn't sure.

Dineen brought a bag full of tomatoes from her garden. Ramona brought snap peas, and Brent brought homemade cookies. Rags knew by now that this was simple small-town hospitality, not an opening gambit to barter. Unless, perhaps, it was their tacit way of asking Rags for permission to continue following their editorial whims, within reason.

They formed a spaced-out semicircle, as usual, next to Rags's desk. Rags walked them through her edits, explaining why she moved paragraphs around, shortened quotes, or rewrote ledes. She excluded Brent's piece on the township meeting, focusing instead on a short piece about the local fire station—the only one within thirty miles—needing a new roof. There was no public money to pay for it. They wouldn't be able to barter their way out of that one, Rags thought privately.

The freelancers still had a tendency to ignore the classic news-story inverted pyramid: most important information up front, followed by key details, and then additional information in the tail of the story. They often wrote their pieces backwards, boring readers with background before getting to the heart of the story. Working on editorial quality under "peace time" conditions still felt like a luxury. The writers took it all in stride, nodding in response to her comments. Rags hoped the constructive criticism helped them become better writers. She liked this part of her job. That was something, at least.

"Now, who's got something new for next week?"

Ramona and Dineen exchanged a look. Ramona spoke up first. "Rags, maybe it's time to start up the obituaries again." The *Courant* had stopped accepting or running obituaries during The Big One, she explained. There were too many deaths. The three of them, who'd split the duty of writing them in better times, couldn't keep up. And even if they could, the sheer number of announcements, or even just a list of names, would have overwhelmed the paper. The *Canary Courant* would have turned into the *Death Courant.* And nobody wanted that—not the writers, not the readers. Even Frank, the dead copy editor, had asked that the paper *not* run an obit for him, Ramona said. Two years after the official end of the pandemic, the paper had not resumed printing obituaries. Nobody wanted to read about death anymore.

"But we think it's time to start writing them again," Dineen said. "Beginning with Effie and Jaxson. Out of respect."

"Why on earth would you suggest that?" Brent said. "You don't need an editor to tell you that's totally and completely inappropriate!" He backed his chair a foot or so out of the semi-circle, as if in protest.

"It could say, 'missing and presumed dead,'" Dineen said. "Not like a standard obituary."

"People need closure," Ramona said.

"I mean, it's not like they're going to find them," Dineen said.

"You don't know that!" Brent said.

"Sooner or later, the paper has to say something. Take some sort of stand. Isn't that true, Rags?" Ramona asked.

"These are open, ongoing law-enforcement investigations," Rags said evenly. "Brent is right. We don't know exactly what happened. When there is something new to report—"

"Then the *Courant* will report it," Brent said, crossing his arms defiantly. "Talk about good journalism!" He let the thought hang.

"I understand what you're saying, about people wanting closure," Rags said. "We all do. We'll all sleep better when we know what happened."

"And why," Ramona said.

"We may never know why," Rags said. "We might have to settle for finding them, or finding out what happened to them. That might have to be enough."

"But if we don't find out why it happened in the first place," Dineen said, "then how do we know it won't happen again? That kids won't keep on disappearing? I have an eight-year-old niece I adore. I can't stand the thought of something like this happening to her—and she ends up God knows where. After everything else. It's not fair."

Rags shrugged. What was fair, anymore? There was no easy answer. They all knew it. Sometimes, merely asking the question seemed like a form of progress. They all sat for a moment. Rags could feel the waves of helplessness and general resentment. But she hated wallowing. She told them it made sense to resume writing obituaries for confirmed deaths, but certainly not for unconfirmed ones. She ended the meeting and asked Brent to stay behind. They sat facing one another in their respective chairs, spaced several feet apart. Rags was grateful that Merry had not returned. She wanted to deal with Brent and his version of the township meeting without a glaring witness.

"Brent, why did you lead with that stunt Missy pulled at the end of the meeting? That was entirely beside the point."

"I disagree," Brent said, his pale skin turning a shade whiter. "What Missy said, about prioritizing protection for the community as a whole, that *was* the point. That was the most important thing that got said all evening. You just told us to lead with the main point. Well, I did."

"But you twisted the story," Rags said. "The meeting was about sharing information on the kids' cases and trying to learn if anybody had any new information."

"And nobody did. And Piers didn't have a lot to say."

"And that's what you report," Rags said.

"You're asking me to bury the lede," Brent said. "I won't do that."

"Missy's not in charge. She doesn't have the last word. She was floating an opinion. That's all." Rags felt herself growing impatient with Brent's stubborn bias. "And the PHP was also expressing an opinion, not a fact."

"Well, I think you're wrong about the whole thing."

"I'm sorry, Brent. I'm going to rewrite the piece."

"Suit yourself," Brent said, clearly angry and heading for the door. "You're the editor. I'm merely a contributor. Lived here my whole life, but, hey, that's not important, right?"

After Brent left, Rags realized she still hadn't asked him why he hadn't visited Louisa's gallery and filed a story about it. Now she wasn't sure she trusted his ability to treat Louisa's art with the respect it deserved. Nothing she'd seen of Brent so far convinced her he knew anything about art, anyway. Covering amateurs was one thing, but Louisa was a professional. Rags acknowledged her own bias in the matter, but she knew she'd never run a bungled story about Louisa or her gallery. Now she thought she'd have to watch him—and whatever he filed—more closely.

She began a rewrite on Brent's township piece. Merry returned. She threw her bag on the floor next to her desk and sat at her computer, staring at the screen and checking her dataphone as if her life depended on it. She and Rags did not exchange another word the rest of the day.

On the afternoon of the Fourth of July, Terry sat with her elegantly silk-shorts-clad legs crossed on her pristine patio. A cut-glass decanter of lemonade stood beaded with sweat on the latticed iron-work table. Rags hated lemonade and was deciding whether she ought to take a sip just to be polite. She didn't ordinarily "do" polite, but sometimes, you just had to bend. She ran her fingers along the cold glass while Terry reminisced about her adventures in corporate law in DC. Rags figured that explained the wealth on display, beginning with her modern, boxy wood-and-glass house, so incongruous among Canary's tired streets. Rags imagined that something old had been torn down to make way for this showy replacement.

"That's great," Rags said tonelessly, waiting for the end of Terry's pointless story about a big case she'd won back in 2018, the case that propelled her to a partnership in her law firm. Rags knew without asking that the firm no longer existed, a casualty of The Big One. But Terry had clearly already made her financial "nut." Terry, seemingly hungry for a new audience so she could relive her glory days, sipped from her glass as if it were a vintage wine.

"So," she said, recrossing her legs, her legal exploits finally over. "I'm glad you called. We got off on the wrong foot. Telling you not to make trouble—I shouldn't have said that."

"What are you worried about?"

"Not worried," Terry said. "Concerned. And I didn't want you jumping to conclusions. What do you think of Canary?"

"What do you mean?"

"Your honest impression, so far. About the town. How it seems."

"You mean, apart from Camilla, who solicits on the corner of Main and Chestnut?" Rags said.

"You just made my point."

"Which is?"

"Things of that sort may be legal, but that doesn't mean they're ethical. Canary is…drifting," Terry said. "Losing its way, in every sense. I should know. I grew up here. When The Big One hit DC, I left my firm and moved back. I didn't even have any family here anymore. But it felt like the right thing to do. Where I belonged. The best place to wait for, well, for things to return to normal."

"But you didn't exactly wait, did you?"

"No, you're right, Rags." Terry smiled. "I'm not really the waiting type. I saw a way to help and I jumped at it."

"The council, you mean."

"The council, of course. Toward the end of the pandemic, the council was more of an idea than a governmental body. I mean, let's face it: practically everybody who'd run this town for years had died."

"And you, being a lawyer, as well as a native daughter, were the logical choice, I suppose."

"I don't believe in false modesty," Terry said. "Yes, I was not just the logical choice but the best choice. But I'll be honest, Rags." She uncrossed her legs and leaned forward. "We can do better. We *must* do better. Coming from the city, you must see what I mean."

"Well," Rags said slowly, "with no disrespect to you and the council, I suppose there's room for improvement. The Effie Rutter investigation, for instance."

"Yes!" Terry said, more animated that Rags had seen her. "That's it, exactly!"

"You think the investigation is—"

"He's botched it," Terry said quickly. "Piers, I mean." Rags nodded. She didn't want to get out ahead of Terry. She needed Terry to show her hand. Lawyer or not, Terry wanted things to go her way and Rags could see she wouldn't be shy about pushing for the upper hand.

"What about Piers?" Rags said.

"It's not only the investigation," Terry said. "He's wrong about Piper Madrigal and always has been. Piper is the best thing to happen to this town in a long time. The PHP is all that's standing between us and another round of black death. We can't keep sitting around and hoping for the best."

You've got to be fucking kidding me.

"And I need you to see, Rags," Terry continued, "that you were wrong to claim that putting the public's health and safety ahead of other priorities makes us paranoid or somehow blind to justice. I'm a lawyer. You think I don't care about justice? Of course I do. It's not either-or. But if we lower our guard for even a split-second, then nothing else is going to matter, is it?"

Rags wondered when Terry would bring up the editorial, which she'd expected her to hate. And she suspected that what Terry knew about justice would fit on the head of a pin. Still, she needed to press her further.

"Does Piers get stoned every day, do you think?" Rags asked.

"Probably." Terry said. "I don't know. But I do know he's useless. He's not what we need around here. He's only got that job because he's a Lucky. That's all. Everybody else in that office was mowed down. We can't afford to keep incompetent people in important jobs. There's just too much at stake. You must see that."

"What do you propose?"

Terry refilled her own lemonade glass and topped off Rags's, even though she'd barely touched it.

"We—the council, I mean—are overhauling all the local law enforcement ordinances," Terry said. By *we*, Rags assumed Terry really meant herself, with Missy's enthusiastic backing and Keller's indifferent assent. "There are gonna be some big changes around here. And they're for the best, believe me."

"Such as?"

"I can't give you details yet, Rags. But I'll tell you this: there will be winners and losers."

"You're talking about a shift in authority, aren't you?" Rags said. "Can you really do that?"

"I've already been in touch with some friends at the state level and the feds too," Terry said, looking satisfied.

"And Piers?" Rags asked. Terry shook her head vigorously.

This is what Piers asked her to find out in exchange for the police report on Effie. Rags had figured he was being paranoid, that the council wouldn't seek to fire him without true probable cause. But this was worse than she'd imagined. Giving PHP Piper Madrigal *greater* authority, possibly even powers of arrest through the Medical Emergency Powers Act of 2024, would destroy Canary, in Rags's view. And traditional civil law enforcement would be weakened in the process. She couldn't imagine remaining in town under those circumstances and she didn't think Flint would, either. And she didn't have time to think about what a horrifying place the world would become if everybody went Terry's way.

"Look, Rags," Terry said, "we're at the start of something big, something good. Canary has a chance to be a leader, for once, not just a sleepy little town. We're going to show everybody how to do this right. Protect our health, preserve our future. Don't you see?"

Rags kept her face as neutral as possible. She already knew what was coming next.

"And when the time comes, I'm really hoping you'll back us," Terry said. "Even though nobody really reads the *Courant* anymore, it's still the only game in town. We should all speak with one voice on this, right?"

"I can't promise that, Terry," Rags said.

"I hope you'll come around. I really do. You're smart. You've been around. I'm sure you get it. But in any case," Terry said crisply, "rest assured we'll keep looking for ways to close any and all loopholes that threaten our safety. Canary will be run as a much tighter ship. No more of this loosey-goosey stuff. We can't have our children just disappearing on us, can we? And *no one* will be above the law."

Who is 'we'? Is this a cabal? A pact, like between Hitler and Mussolini?

And is she threatening me?

Rags had heard enough. She didn't want to get into an argument with Terry about the evils of authoritarian governments. That would get her nowhere. She stood and Terry joined her, leading her across the well-manicured back lawn and around the side of the glass-encased house toward the street. Rags was trying to decide how much to tell Piers, whether to tell Flint anything, and what might *actually* happen if she wrote an editorial strongly opposing the council's plans as soon as they were made public. She had no real allies in town and had no cue whether her mysterious publisher would swoop in with an edict of some kind.

I'm twisting in the wind. But so are Effie and Jaxson.

"So, I expect I'll see you at the fireworks tonight," Terry said brightly, as if the conversation they'd just finished hadn't even happened.

"Who pays for that?" Rags said as they stood on the curb in front of Terry's house. "Doesn't the fire station need a new roof?"

"What's that got to do with anything?" Terry said impatiently.

"It's obvious that Canary is flat broke. It's a fair question, Terry." The dig felt good. Terry explained curtly that she paid for the fireworks out of her own pocket—she and the Fallons and the owners of Mellonia, the only two money-making businesses in all of Canary. A different kind of cabal, Rags thought. Whoever holds the purse strings, holds the power. If they expected to get credit in the *Courant* for their gallant generosity, they'd wait an awfully long time.

Rags headed straight for Piers's office at the southern end of Main Street—an archaic, narrow white-stone building adjacent to the Victorian brick town hall, which was too antiquated, too dark, and too small to host the socially distanced township meetings, even though it was the nominal seat of government for the town of Canary. Rags had the impression that Terry conducted most of the town's business from her own airy home, not the tomb-like town hall, which was nothing more than a symbol of a vanished world.

The peacekeeper's office was a lot like the *Courant*'s office: unreasonably, laughably old-fashioned, both cluttered and gapingly empty at the same time. Rags thought again of old pictures from Disneyworld with its historic tableaus of yesteryear frozen in time—the old saloon, the blacksmith's shop. Except here, the pungent dry odor of weed was unmistakable. The office still had metal filing cabinets and stacks of manila file folders. Three empty desks sat pushed against a wall, as if the ghosts of past desk sergeants, deputies, and police officers were expected to step back in at any moment. At least Piers had a fairly recent digital screen on his own desk—alongside a slim pile of paper folders. Rags saw the folders and wondered if what she wanted—what she forced herself to want—lay right there. She imagined simply grabbing them and running out, thereby avoiding another wheedling conversation with Piers. But it wasn't going to be that easy. Nothing ever was.

"You know why I'm here," Rags began. Piers's belt and stun gun lay casually across his desk. She imagined grabbing the folders *and* the weapon, making a clean getaway. "When's the last time you used that?" she asked, pointing to the stun gun.

"I remember exactly," Piers said, leaning back in his chair. All he needed was a ten-gallon hat to look like an old-fashioned sleepy country sheriff. "Last months of The Big One. Though we didn't know it then—didn't know the thing was finally ending. Squatters in the bar. I wouldn't call them Luckies. More like crazies. Drinking up old gin. Setting fires for the fun of it. Maybe for warmth too." Rags vividly recalled the Fallons' description of the filth and remnants of chaos they'd found in the bar when they took over. "I had to knock 'em out, drag 'em out. It was a fuckin' mess."

"But they came back, some of them, didn't they?"

"Yeah, I could only be in one place at a time." Piers waved around the empty room. "They were all gone by then. It was just me. Lucky me." Rags wondered who he'd lost, personally, but that was still the unasked question. "We have an actual jail cell back there." He pointed. "Iron bars and everything. We put a digital lock on about five years ago, but otherwise, same as it ever was. I stuck the assholes in there, let them dry out for a coupla days. Some of 'em died, anyway, soon after that. Made my job that much easier, to tell you the truth."

"I expect you to keep your side of our bargain," Rags said.

"Then tell me," Piers said, sinking back even farther in his chair as if nothing she told him could matter.

"It's not good."

"I figured. Do you know when? They're giving me the axe, right?"

"She's still working on it."

"She's a real piece of work, huh? She's got it all figured out."

"She seems to think so," Rags said. "But anything could happen."

Piers took a hand-rolled joint out of his desk drawer and lit it up. He offered it to Rags. She said no.

"What do *you* think I should do?" Piers asked, closing his eyes as thick smoke curled in front of his face.

"You're not my problem, Piers," Rags said. She did not want to get sucked into this. "Now give me Effie's file. Jaxson's too. And don't forget they're a lot more fucked than you are at the moment."

Piers pushed two folders toward her. Each manila folder had a red tab along the long rim of the folder, which Rags assumed was some type of old-fashioned case coding system. The lower the tech, the greater the security—at least in this case.

"And the phones?" she asked. Piers disappeared briefly into a back room, presumably the evidence room, such as it was, and brought out two clear plastic bags, each one labeled with the victims' names. Rags could tell at a glance that Effie's dataphone was an older model than Jaxson's, which made sense, given their respective living situations. Evelyn Rutter appeared to be just hanging on, while the Fallons were obviously thriving.

"Who else will know all this is missing?" Rags asked.

"Well, that's the upside to being the only one enforcing the law in this town, at least for a little while longer," Piers said, running his hand through his hair. "It's nobody else's business unless I decide it is."

"Okay, then," Rags said, stuffing the material in her bag. She had no intention of saying a word to him about the encoded classified ads in the paper—if that were even true—and their connection to either or both cases. She'd let him know about that if and when the time was right. She thought about asking him what he planned to do, after they kicked him to the curb. But she didn't really want to know. And besides, he probably had no idea.

"Let me know if you hear anything else," he called after her, not particularly enthusiastically. Rags pretended she didn't hear him and let the door close behind her. She could tell that his hair and clothes reeked of weed.

Shortly before nine that evening, Rags was crouching on a well-worn footpath that led from the edge of the high school's Allen Athletic Field through a patch of woods and then out to Canary's neighborhood streets. Evelyn Rutter had said that during the school year, when the weather was decent, the cheerleaders practiced on a corner of the field nearest the bleachers, away from the football team. That night, the field was covered with spaced-apart blankets and picnic baskets. Rags could hear roman candles whistling skyward as people waited for the fireworks to officially begin. It might have been a Norman Rockwell kind of scene, except that Rags knew it wasn't. Not really. She knew Canary well enough to imagine people wandering from blanket to blanket, bartering corn for tomatoes, bread for pickles, cigarettes for whiskey. In small, quiet clusters, perhaps men and women also bartered sex for plumbing, sex for auto repair, sex or housecleaning for a week's worth of meat. All needs and wants seemed to have become interchangeable; whatever kept you afloat, kept you alive and kicking for another day, was fair game.

Rags aimed the light from her dataphone onto the path, which trees had enclosed in darkness as the summer night deepened. Mosquitoes, which knew nothing of the pandemic and would survive them all, swarmed ferociously. Rags angrily swatted at them, but it was pointless. Perhaps all of this was pointless: moving to Canary, limping along with Flint, getting caught up in a seemingly dead-end search for a girl who was loved and lost. She'd already lived through a version of that. Must she—she asked herself for the hundredth time since the day she arrived—do it all again? *I'm trying, Maya.*

The report on Effie Rutter's disappearance was not what she expected. She'd assumed there'd be more detail—that Piers had withheld a lot of information from her and from the town at large. But the incident file was not very robust. It included a few photos of the field and the footpath where Rags now crouched, her eyes scouring the ground. The most important photo, in all likelihood, showed a close-up of faintly visible tire tracks, which Rags was now looking for in vain, as if the tracks were holding on to secrets that only she could interpret. A photo of Effie's dataphone lying on the footpath was also in the file. Piers and the outside experts he'd consulted concluded that the unit's data had been wiped clean and then the kidnappers, whoever they were, had simply dropped it, considering it useless. Of course, these bad guys had never met Flint Sten.

The other piece of evidence in the file consisted of transcribed interviews with Effie's friends and teachers attesting to her character. Effie seemed to be chatty and friendly, much as her mother had described. She turned her homework in on time, and so forth. The last person to see her was a girl named Caroline, a fellow cheerleader, on the October afternoon she disappeared. Effie and Caroline had said goodbye and headed off in opposite directions, according to Caroline. So Effie must have set off on the footpath on her own. The only other detail Rags learned was that Effie's full name was Iphigenia. Rags hadn't figured that Evelyn was the type to choose such a fancy name. But it didn't matter now.

As Rags hunted along the ground, looking for anything at all that didn't seem to belong, she remembered that Evelyn had shown her only one pom-pom. Could the other one have been tossed somewhere in these thin woods? If so, might it contain fingerprints other than Effie's? Rags decided this was a distinct possibility. She didn't think that Piers or anyone else who may have searched for clues to Effie's disappearance would know about the pom-poms. Surely Piers would have brought it out from the evidence room if he'd had it. Why wouldn't he? Even Evelyn didn't seem to realize that a missing pom-pom could provide a key to the entire case.

Rags began shining her light in slow arcs, walking a few paces before shining it all around her again. She was trying to cover the area as methodically as possible. She didn't know how the police did this sort of thing, but this seemed logical. After months of rain, ice, and mud, there was no way Rags would find tire tracks. She knew that. So she tried to imagine what type of vehicle would have come back here. Not a small, compact ShareCar, surely? Something bigger, like a van, perhaps? Vans had no side windows. But this was just silly speculation. The report didn't include any information indicating any particular type of vehicle or that a tire's make and model had been matched to the tracks. And had Piers even pursued that tenuous bit of evidence? Maybe it was time for him to go—but not for the reasons Terry believed. Perhaps Piers, like so many other survivors in Canary, was simply at the end of his emotional and physical rope. Caring—about anything—required an awful lot of energy.

Despite feeling it was all pointless, Rags continued her search, slapping the mosquitoes away. Then the light from her dataphone caught a flash of something about fifteen feet off the path in the woods. She held the beam on the thing reflecting the light and walked toward it. Yes. It was unmistakable. Ripped, dirty, half-stomped into the earth by months of weather. But it was without doubt a red Mylar pom-pom. Rags picked up a narrow stick and carefully peeled the pom-pom from the ground. Evidence. Hard evidence. Piers really must have done a half-assed job out here. Her heart was racing, and she began shaking. She put the stick back down and searched through her bag for a plastic bag, or paper, anything that might be minimally contaminated with her own fingerprints that could serve as a receptacle for the pom-pom. The only thing she had was a folded copy of last Wednesday's *Courant.* She used her fingertips to pull the paper out of her bag, lay it on the ground, and open it to an inside page that she may not have touched. She picked up the pom-pom with the stick and slid it onto the paper, folded the pages in from the edges, and stuffed it into her bag.

Rags heard a loud explosion and nearly jumped out of her skin. The fireworks had begun. She didn't look up to see the starbursts of color. Instead, she walked quickly toward home, her bag pressed tightly to her side to keep the evidence stable. *I'm trying, Maya, see?*

17

!!!!!!!!

Because—Tiffany. She's here! One good thing. Finally.

They put her on deboning so I didn't see her until tonight. Somebody was coughing hard in the sleep shack. I looked over.

Light brown hair. Blue eyes. Tall with really broad shoulders, like a swimmer. Oh my God, I said. Tiffany, I called. She looked across. We'd never spoken. She was a senior when I was a freshman. But I knew her face and in here, that felt like knowing her forever.

Effie Rutter, I said. Canary High. You know me, I said. She had to recognize me. She had to.

She crossed over to me, coughing the whole way. Canary, she said, catching her breath. Is it still there? I told her I didn't know. It was there when I left. When was that? she asked. I couldn't remember.

Tiffany sat on my bunk until bed-check. She'd thought she'd been traveling for days. Tied down in the back of a van. Just like me. They transferred her from a textile factory, maybe in the Midwest? She was on a line making towels, socks, and shit like that. It gave her brown lung, she said. Something about all the loose fibers in the air. That's why they shipped her to chickens. To get rid of her. I told her they shipped me from crab island. What's that? she asked.

But then the sadist came in yelling about bed-check and we had to stop talking. I squeezed Tiffany's hand in my own red, scarred hand. The first human I'd touched on purpose in forever. She squeezed back.

Maybe chickens is where they send us to die, she said. We both laughed. You really should eat something, she said, wrapping her fingers around my bony wrist. Then she dragged herself back over to her bunk. In the morning, when the first light trickled in between the gap in the roof and the wall, I took out my dying Sharpie and found a blank space on my sheet to record this miracle meeting.

Yes, maybe chickens is where they send us to die.

I still feel Tiffany's hand squeezing mine. One good thing, finally.

18

Flint was trying to draft a white paper on integrating artificial intelligence in weapon systems. Drawing upon what he'd learned from this work so far, he knew the publication would burnish his credentials and likely snare him new contracts. The work entailed, in part, exploring the implications of increasingly capable AI in the kill chain. He had no intention of sharing this line of research with Rags. She didn't ask; he didn't want to tell. He did not expect her to understand that it was the pure research that excited him. AI applications in this realm were still in their infancy and he valued pushing the boundaries of data science. It's not like he was going to be responsible for actually killing anyone.

His enthusiasm for the work was marred by competing distractions. Flint distinctly recalled being immune to distractions nearly all his life. When he decided to concentrate on something, nothing could pull his focus. Even as a kid, he could easily spend hours building something sprawling and complex with Legos, forgetting to eat, breaking away only when his bladder was about to explode.

He had allowed Rags to become a distraction, to put it crudely, about four years ago. He hoped that loving someone, and being part of a couple, was important for self-improvement. That it would make him stronger, better, in some way. Now he wasn't so sure. He felt he was paying a price—beginning with his legendary powers of concentration, which he feared were eroding.

First, Rags had come to him asking for his help. It was the first time she'd ever done that. How could he say no? She'd given him a stack of newspapers to figure out what, if anything, the language in the advertisements was actually saying. Did they really contain encoded messages? Flint thought the idea was absurd, the product of overactive imaginations. Rags had told him that somebody on the town council, somebody who drank too much, apparently, had tipped her off. Flint felt stupid about wasting even a second on this, but he knew Rags was counting on him. And that touched him; he couldn't let her down, whatever he found. So this distraction wasn't even his choice. In which case, perhaps he could justifiably say it wasn't a distraction at all, but an obligation to help the only person with whom he'd ever truly been intimate. He wasn't even thinking about Effie Rutter.

Even so, the other thing *was* a distraction, and he couldn't explain it away: the small painting that Louisa Copperface had given them, which Flint kept propped up against a lamp on his desk. The swath of undisturbed forest that Louisa had described as a fragmentary image of the Potrero Complex. As he understood it, this six-inch-square painting represented a kind of camouflage, with layers of seasonal greenery masking centuries-old civilization. Human activities hiding beneath a veneer of topsoil, tree roots, and shifting rocks. Hiding in plain view, perhaps, if you knew where and how to look.

This moved him, unsettled him, in some profound way.

He'd always said, about life in general, *It is what it is.* The pandemic had proven his outlook to be true, in ways he could not have anticipated.

But wasn't his work, fundamentally, about proving things you couldn't really see or even anticipate? Training machine language to make connections where there had been none before? That was a form of exploration, wasn't it? A process entailing new discoveries?

Perhaps this was why he was drawn to this particular thing, which was so new to him. He could see that Rags valued Louisa as an artist, as a creator working in various media. Painting, sculpture, whatever. And that made sense. Rags, after all, puts words together to make something new, on a particular kind of canvas. She and Louisa were alike in that way. But he found himself responding to this specific little painting because of what it seemed to represent, to hint at, in the real world. He was no judge of art as art.

He forced his attention back to the screen, to the paper he was drafting. But his gaze kept wandering back to the painting. And then to the stack of newspapers sitting on the floor next to his desk. And then back to the painting.

This is unacceptable.

He felt as though he had an itch that he desperately needed to scratch.

He gave in. He wiped the draft paper off his screen and began gathering everything he could about the Potrero Complex. Archaeological surveys and studies. Classified aerial photographic records (using his secret clearance status). Federal tribal documents (sparse). Photos of artifacts discovered at the site—projectile points, ceramic pottery fragment, small patches of fibrous material. Two centuries of local maps. GIS data. The *Courant* had run a story in 1952 about local farmers giving permission for archaeological digs on their land, including a portion of the complex. Flint developed an algorithm to search for and analyze every potentially relevant scrap of information in every available form. He knew Louisa had said the site was private, but he wanted to find it anyway. He didn't see any harm in doing that.

After a few hours of research, collation, and analysis, Flint thought he had a pretty good idea of the boundaries of the Potrero Complex. He didn't yet know exactly where Louisa had made the painting, so he used topographical maps and botanical guides to identify the forested areas. He compared Louisa's meticulously painted leaves with specimens found in the area and figured out that the painting primarily showed stands of Northern red oak trees. That helped him to narrow down the location of her painting even further. He thought that with his GPS, he could come damn close.

What am I doing?

Flint wiped the maps, photos, and documents off his screen. He picked up the top newspaper off the floor and flipped rapidly through the pages until he reached the classifieds near the back, ripping a few pages along the way. Too bad. He used his dataphone to scan the relevant pages. He went through the entire stack of papers this way, working quickly, tearing more pages as he went. He didn't want to think, for once; he just wanted to get it done. He tossed each paper on the floor, until they lay in a scattered heap. He didn't care if Rags saw them like that. At least she'd know he was fulfilling his promise to do—whatever it was she thought he was going to do.

He used a software utility to convert the scanned OCR images into readable data, then exported all of it into a CSV file. His stomach growled loudly but he ignored it. He would concentrate; he would power through. He made a cursory scan of the data to see if any obvious patterns emerged. Nothing. Just random letters, digits, dollar signs, punctuation marks, and so forth. He re-sorted the images a couple different ways, but still nothing jumped out. He grew impatient, which wasn't like him. *Because it's a sideshow.* He made himself remember the point of this seemingly pointless exercise: Rags had said that the ads contained information for kidnappers. To be useful, that would have to include times, dates, and locations, at a minimum, if not also descriptions of the intended victims. Based on what he'd seen so far, none of it made sense. *I'm not a damn cryptographer.*

He wiped his screen again in disgust. He didn't want to think about any of this anymore. He remembered now the beaming image of blonde-haired Effie Rutter looking down at them as they drove into Canary months earlier. And he remembered feeling a finger of death when he looked up at her. He hadn't changed his mind. Based on what he'd seen so far, Canary teetered between life and death every day. He'd seen people bartering to stay alive, basically, just outside the farm stands and the half-provisioned grocery store. He hadn't told Rags that he'd been approached by sex workers more than once, willing to give him any pleasure he wanted in exchange for food, clothing, a ride out of town. He always declined the sex but gave them what he could. He vividly remembered the teens surrounding him in the city, lunging for his backpack filled with food. Rags hadn't noticed that his navy rain jacket was missing. Why would she? She had her own problems to deal with. He wondered what she had given away that had escaped his notice. Maybe they really should talk more.

Flint rose from his chair and circled the parlor. He hadn't noticed the bright, hot summer day outside the front window. The leaves on the cherry trees barely stirred. He had a plan. It had already taken shape in his mind. He didn't understand it but he knew he had to do it. He was going to find the oak forest in the Potrero Complex. Rags had nagged him for months to get out more. And now he would.

Later, that same night, Flint waited until he was sure Rags was asleep. They'd eaten a light supper together, chicken salad and a baguette. He told her he'd made a start on the newspaper ads. He didn't tell her he suspected the whole thing was pointless. She thanked him and asked him, when he had time, to see if he could retrieve anything from Effie's dataphone, which sat in the bag Piers had given her, which she'd placed in a half-empty cabinet in the kitchen. She had Jaxson's dataphone too, but she told Flint she wasn't ready to launch this investigation on both fronts together—and wasn't sure when she would be. One horror show at a time, she'd said. He was pretty sure she was only half-joking.

Flint had pre-arranged for a ShareCar to arrive out front at one a.m. He used a private account, which Rags would never see. He wasn't sure what he wanted to bring with him on this expedition, so he brought a variety of things, including a solar-cell flashlight to supplement his dataphone light, a large utility knife, a sleeve of crackers, and a bottle of water. He thought about bringing Louisa's painting but decided against it. Besides, in the dark, there'd be no way to match the trees exactly.

He quietly closed the front door behind him and stepped out into the summer night. He had been working through most of the night for months and had almost forgotten what a summer night smelled like. And in the city, there was no night sky to speak of. The sound of crickets reminded him of his boyhood, as did the fireflies flashing in the yard. He'd programmed the ShareCar to take him to the end of a rural county road, from which he'd have to walk on foot about two miles to access the land. He had chosen specific coordinates that would bring him to a sparse clump of forest filled with the oak trees like those shown in Louisa's painting. While the spot may not have been exactly where Louisa painted, it was on the complex's known land, and therefore was almost certainly ground where ancient Indigenous people had lived, loved, fought, ate, slept, and died.

The ride took about thirty-five minutes south and west of Canary. *Both near and far.* As the car made its way silently across stretches of old fields, the houses grew increasingly small, set back, widely spaced. Flint tried and failed to keep the obvious questions from fully occupying his mind. *Why? Why am I doing this? What is this for? What do I want?* But he refused to abort, which would make him feel like an idiot—or that he was coming unglued. When the car reached the designated coordinates, Flint exited the vehicle, hitched his bag on his shoulder, and walked across a wide expanse of fallow farmland which, he presumed, no one was left to cultivate. The land was reverting to meadow, the remnants of cultivated furrows made untidy by tufts of grass and weeds.

Shining his light ahead of him, he spotted a dirt road that seemed to parallel the farmland's edge. He guessed it was probably built to accommodate tractors or perhaps for cattle to make their way between the old grazing fields and the barns. He followed the dirt road for a mile or so, keeping his GPS coordinates heading west-northwest. Finally, the fields came to an end and the red oak forest began. Based on all the mapping he'd done, and with the GPS in hand, Flint was certain he was standing on the Potrero Complex, which spread out for miles all around him, nearly all of it classified as a protected archaeological site that only the descendants of Indigenous people should know about, at this point, along with a handful of discrete archaeologists. Flint guessed he was the only "civilian" alive with reasonably precise knowledge about where he stood. He looked up. The wide-open night sky was filled with stars, the same stars that Louisa's ancestors had stared at, as he did now. He wasn't interested in feeling closer to her—that much he knew. But feeling close to *them,* the ancestors, who had managed to perform their own rituals of humanity far removed from his own—that felt exciting.

He walked into the woods, into a silence even deeper than that of the fields. The air was absolutely still. There were no crickets or tree frogs or other summer night creatures that he could identify. The night was hot, and his T-shirt was glued to his chest with sweat. He didn't know what he was looking for. He just felt a deep need to experience this place for himself. Louisa had said the site's location—where her ancestors were thought to have settled for a period of time in the thirteenth century—needed to remain off-limits to outsiders because of nighthawks. Flint had looked up the word and discovered that a nighthawker was someone who took artifacts from protected archaeological sites like the very one he was standing on. In other words, they stole what did not belong to them. Flint wrestled with this concept. Didn't antiquities buried under layers of soil belong to everyone? In his circle, developers shared code for free all the time; they considered many aspects of the software-making process to be common intellectual property, part of a shared human experience, even.

Flint took out his knife and crouched down in the woods. He hacked randomly at the dirt beneath some grasses growing among the sparse oak trees—just like in Louisa's picture. The soil was dry and crumbly. He sifted it through his fingers. He wondered what it would feel like to discover something—a fragment of a buried tool, a bone, a pot. To reach across centuries and make a connection. Maybe another time.

He sat loosely cross-legged on the underbrush, taking slow, deep breaths. Taking in the night, the woody smells, the light crackle of dry twigs. He imagined himself in a parallel time and place, where he might pursue his interests, all of them, to the fullest without the encumbrances and distractions that were so tiring.

Foolishness.

He stood, wiped the dirt off his pants, put the knife back in his bag, and retraced his steps back to the car, which flickered to life when he pointed his dataphone. On the way back, he realized he had not once thought about Rags. That felt strange but also appropriate; this didn't belong to her, it was his alone. With the world shifting away from its old moorings, in the aftermath of The Big One, everybody needed something to call their own.

19

The only objects brighter than the hot glare of the morning sun beating down on Main Street were the digital faces of Effie Rutter and now the smiling, freckle-faced Jaxson Turner, whose image had joined hers on alternating corners. Rags refused to activate the AR on her dataphone just to watch Jaxson spring to life. What was the point? Why would anyone do that to themselves? Flint did it to Effie, Rags remembered, on their first day in Canary. He'd watched the vid of her smiling, dancing, time-frozen ghost. It didn't seem to phase him. Rags imagined how she'd feel if it were Maya's face up there, the face of a teen who no longer existed in the flesh, captured forever—trapped—in a collection of pixels that's supposed to approximate a state of perpetual happiness or joy.

What a lie.

If it were Maya's face on display, she'd tear it down. Maya belonged in Rags's memory. She wasn't for public consumption. She wasn't to be paraded on Main Street like a rare commodity or perhaps more aptly, as a constant reminder of what can go wrong, even when you think you're already bracing for the worst.

Yet there was Jaxson looking down on Main Street right outside the bar run by his guardians, the Fallons. MISSING. How could they stand it?

Rags was on her way to Piers's office, the pom-pom tucked inside the old newspaper. She had told Flint about her Fourth of July discovery but she did not take it out to show him; the less she touched the object, the better chance of recovering fingerprints that might finally provide a necessary clue to the teen's abduction—assuming that's what it was. Flint said encouraging words, but she could tell he was more distracted than usual. Perhaps he would tell her why, perhaps he wouldn't. She didn't have the energy to play psychological cat-and-mouse with him. She'd seen the messy pile of newspapers on the floor by his desk—the papers she'd brought home for him to analyze.

"Any progress there?" she'd asked late in the evening, after he failed to mention anything.

"Not yet," he said, "but I'm working on it. I am."

"And the phone?"

"One thing at a time, okay?" he said. "I do have other stuff to do. Paying work. You know."

"If you don't want to help me—"

"No, I do," he said. "But believe it or not, I'm not a machine. I can't just spit out answers for you."

This had turned into another one of their kitchen-sink conversations, where they did not need to make eye contact, their hands busy with washing and drying. Rags made a point of thanking him for the help before heading upstairs to bed, leaving him behind to do…well…whatever it was he did most of the night.

Rags found Piers staring closely at his screen. His eyes were hooded and his jaw was slack, but his gaze seemed fixed nonetheless. She took the bag off her shoulder and settled it carefully on the floor.

"Huh," he said. She waited. He seemed indifferent most of the time, but now, he appeared borderline serious. "So, you know how there are motion sensors inside the crematorium?" She didn't know, but she supposed it had to do with protecting a space that Canary considered sacred, or near to it. "I got pinged about an hour ago. Like something, or someone, is moving inside there. Or was."

"It's probably just rats, don't you think?" Rags had pictured them getting right down to business with the pom-pom, but clearly she'd need to get him to switch focus.

"There's nothing in there but an ice-cold furnace and a whole lot of empty. The rats are much better off in town."

"What, then?" Rags asked, just to keep him moving along.

This didn't seem interesting or relevant. Not compared to the news she was about to drop on him.

"Look," he said, pointing to the screen. "Shadows, human shadows. You see that, right? It's not my imagination?" He played a clip of black-and-white vid footage. "They're smart, keeping just out of camera range, but they forgot about the shadows."

"Could be," she said. "But why would anybody go in there? And how would they get in? I assume it's locked."

"It's locked all right. I've got a digi-key." He pointed to his dataphone. "There's only one other person who has the code to the crematorium. Guess who?"

Rags knew as soon as he asked the question: it had to be Piper Madrigal. Who else?

"Oh, shit," she said. "What are you going to do?"

"I have to go out there, I guess," Piers said, sounding as if he'd rather have his teeth extracted. "Do you want to come?"

"Why would I do that? It's police business, Piers."

"Um, you'd have a story, no matter what we found, wouldn't you?"

Rags was not ready to assume this was a story that should find its way into the *Courant*, at least, not yet. She almost felt sorry for Piers. He really didn't like this job, did he? It struck her that he was inviting her not because he was afraid—she didn't think that was his problem—but because bringing another person along would force him to follow through. With her in tow, he'd have to go through all the motions and tick all the boxes. He'd have to walk the perimeter, look for signs of forced entry, and, of course, enter the crematorium itself.

"Okay," she said, "but there's something else first."

Rags put on a rubber glove, which she'd brought with her, and pulled the pom-pom out from the crevices of the newspaper. It was still a mess, caked with dried mud and bits of grass and pebbles. The Mylar was shredded. But it was still unmistakably a pom-pom.

"What is it?" Piers asked.

"You really don't know?" He shook his head. "It belonged to Effie Rutter. It's her cheerleader pom-pom. Evelyn has the other one. She showed it to me. They come in pairs, you know. You gave one back to her in October."

Piers took a thick plastic bag from a desk drawer, identical to the kind of bag containing the kids' dataphones, and held it open by the edges. Rags dropped the pom-pom into the bag and peeled off the rubber glove.

"How did you find it?" he asked.

"Searching the woods not far off the trail where Effie was last seen. I can't imagine how you missed it. It wasn't hard. Even for an amateur."

Piers looked down. "I was really fucked up that night, Rags. I called off the search pretty early. I just…I just didn't want to be there." She did not ask him why; she did not want his back story—yet another back story—of loss, pain, guilt, or some combination of all three.

"Why are you telling me this, Piers?"

"Because the council is going to fire me anyway. It doesn't matter." He looked at her with reddened eyes. He slumped in his chair as though his body were filled with cement, almost too heavy to move. She saw no reason to let him off the hook.

"Do you remember Evelyn, Tim, and Roger telling you about the phone calls they received from a stranger right after the kids disappeared?" Piers nodded. "Did you trace those calls? It's not in the reports."

"I tried," he said. "They were untraceable. The data packets just vanished, like the kids. These cases… I'm hitting nothing but brick walls. I don't know what else to do, where else to turn." Rags knew that the date and approximate time of those phone calls was noted in the reports; she'd have to ask Flint to take on a bit more of the investigation. She didn't really believe the calls were untraceable just because Piers couldn't figure it out or find someone who could. No one would have to know about Flint's involvement. If he got results, then she'd take things from there.

Piers sat there with a hangdog look. No wonder he wanted

her to go with him to the crematorium. She guessed that, left to his own devices, he might not even bother to check it out. She felt like she was supposed to be his coach now, give him a good pep talk, rally him back out to the field. Maybe he even expected it.

Bullshit.

"How long will it take to get fingerprints back on the pompom?" she asked. He told her he thought they could have results in three days. He didn't thank her, but she didn't expect he would, as she was so obviously highlighting his failures. Nor did he ask her anything else about her independent investigation at the site where Effie disappeared. She figured he wasn't eager to hear any more about what a shitty job he'd done. Hopefully, with Flint's help, plus the fingerprint evidence, she'd finally have enough to break a news story about Effie Rutter that went way beyond useless platitudes.

Rags did not want to ride with Piers in his official peacekeeper vehicle. It just didn't feel right. She summoned a ShareCar and agreed to meet him at the crematorium in thirty minutes. On her way out of town, she passed a pack of wild dogs scrounging for garbage, Camilla negotiating on her usual corner with a man wearing shorts and flip-flops, and of course those damn digital billboards, practically chasing her out of Canary.

The crematorium was an ugly rectangle of a building. It looked like an oversized shoebox dropped onto what might have been a cornfield at some point. The exterior walls were an expanse of cinderblock painted battleship gray. There were no windows, only a plain door. Nothing on the outside gave away the building's purpose; there was no lettering, not even a street number. It was deliberately, almost aggressively anonymous—and why not, Rags thought. Everybody knew what it was and what it was for. Nobody wanted to notice it, so why draw attention to it? The ShareCar dropped her off near Piers's squad car. He was walking slowly in parallel along the building's long wall facing the street. He was looking down at the ground and appeared to be talking to himself. Rags had the uncomfortable feeling that she was witnessing something that was meant to be private. *I shouldn't have come. This was a mistake.*

She was irritated as hell and it took her a moment to figure out why. It seemed as though Piers was giving Terry, along with Missy and Piper, the excuse they needed to fire him. Perhaps he was not only incompetent but also crazy. She hated the idea that they were going to win and Piers was going to make it easy for them. But how could she prevent it?

"Can we just go inside?" she asked loudly, disrupting his walk and his secret train of thought. He could finish inspecting the outside later, on his own. Piers unlocked the door with the code in his dataphone and they entered. The room was pitch black and cold. Rags was about to turn on her dataphone light but Piers had an actual flashlight that cast a wider light. The room was enormous with high metal rafters. Their footsteps echoed. It was empty but for a couple of long metal tables and, at the far end, the hulking furnace itself, which looked like a sleeping beast in the arc of Piers's flashlight.

"Can you find some light, for God's sake?" Rags asked. "How long is this going to take?"

Piers passed his light around the room until he saw a switch plate on the wall. He footsteps echoed loudly as he went over to switch it on. Industrial lights mounted high up against the ceiling threw a harsh white light across the room.

Why, why, why did I let him drag me out here?

The contours of the furnace came alive in the light: a great beast with an enormous squared-off mouth, open and waiting for another meal of bone. Rags couldn't look at it for more than a few seconds. Nearly a century ago, her relations in Eastern Europe had perished during the Holocaust in a devouring machine that she imagined was not so different from this one. They were as helpless then, as much the victims of being in the wrong place at the wrong time, as were all her contemporaries who'd perished in The Big One. Including Maya.

This was not a good place to be. She had a newspaper to edit.

"Well?" she said. "What are you looking for?"

"How should I know?" Piers said.

"Have you even been in here?"

"No," he said. He paused. "I mean yes."

He pointed to the security cameras mounted high above them at several points in the room. "The cameras captured shadows, which means that whoever was here must have been hugging the wall." He pointed. "*That* wall, just outside of the camera's range, which is mainly aimed at the floor." Well, Rags thought, he hasn't completely lost his mind. Not yet anyway. She followed his gaze toward a metal door set into the wall, which she hadn't noticed before. If Piers was right, that may have been where the intruders were heading.

"What's behind there?" Rags asked.

"No clue," Piers said. They approached the door and he entered the code to unlock it. The door didn't budge. "I thought it was just one code for the whole building. It's all I've got."

Another fucking brick wall, Rags thought. Nothing in Canary was straightforward. So much for the idea that this was some kind of ye-oldey, sleepy, quaint village. Far from it.

"I'm done," Rags said and she headed for the exit.

"Will you write about this in the paper?"

"No," she snorted. "What would I say?" She mimed a headline. "'Canary peacekeeper discovers a locked door.' No, Piers. This was a waste of time. *My* time, anyway." She continued toward the main door while he stayed behind.

"We're gonna find them, Rags!" he called after her. She wasn't sure who he thought they were going to find. The intruders in the crematorium? Effie? Jaxson? The strangers on the phone? Piper Madrigal committing a crime?

Yeah, right.

For the first time in weeks, there it was: Rags's left eye began twitching rapidly. She put her palm over her eye as if that could not only stop it but uproot all the triggers, past and present, that came with it. She held her palm there all the way back into town. But the twitching continued for hours.

20

"Mmmphh!" Rags was screaming so intensely in her dream that her sleep-strangled vocalization was loud enough to bring Flint upstairs, away from the blue glow of his screens. But she didn't know that, wrapped up in a nightmare that did not seem to end: Maya strapped to a conveyor belt that was sliding her into the red-hot maw of a furnace—an immense version of the one in the crematorium, which Rags had tried and failed not to think about during her waking hours. Her ancestors who perished in the crematoria of the Holocaust—her long-lost great-great-great aunts, uncles, distant cousins—were standing by, doing nothing, while Maya edged closer to the incinerator. Some of them cried out as they held Rags back, their arms crossed around her chest. Someone tugged on her collar: *This is what happens! This is the world! You can't save her, so don't even try!*

Rags woke, gasping. She gasped again when she registered Flint sitting beside her on the bed.

"What?" she said, her lips still thick with sleep. "What happened?"

"Nothing happened," Flint said. "You had another bad dream. The same dream?" She shook her head.

"Something happened. Is happening," she mumbled.

"What are you talking about?" Flint put his arm around her and pulled her close. "Is editing a newspaper really all that terrifying?"

She couldn't blame him for being flippant. She hadn't told him yet about the trip to the crematorium earlier in the day. She hadn't wanted to relive it at supper. Instead, she'd pointed out they were living in a crazy town, where the only peacekeeper on the payroll was perpetually stoned and had begun mumbling to himself, and what was that about, she'd asked Flint rhetorically.

"Thanks for checking on me," she said. "You can go back to...whatever."

"Lie down," he said, softly. He molded himself around her. She couldn't remember the last time they had spooned—both awake. "How's your eye? Your magical, mysterious eye?"

"It's...under control."

"That's good," he said. "A good sign."

He didn't know about the flare-up she'd had earlier in the day. He didn't know a lot of things, and she felt badly about that, but all that *dredging*...it always seemed so hard and never the right time. Was he perhaps thinking the same? Holding back because it was easier than speaking out? Not exactly what you'd call *a healthy relationship*. But she didn't want to think about that. She wanted to fall into a deep, dreamless sleep, to check out for a while and not have to contend with all the liars and broken people around her in Canary and the disconnections in her relationship with Flint. Maybe she wanted to live like Louisa Copperface, in a bright room surrounded by beautiful things, with no apparent entanglements. Rags's last thought before falling back asleep was a half-baked question to herself: Did she need Flint's love just as much as his help?

In the morning, she tiptoed around the house quietly, letting Flint sleep. She brought coffee into the parlor and sat looking out at the leafy cherry trees with their rough brown bark, steeling herself to face the day. What had happened to the fearless reporter she used to be? She looked back on all the years during The Big One when she ran from one crisis to the next, never shying away from the horrors she'd witnessed up close. Even the bodies in the vestibule: she'd been horrified but not terrified. It would never have occurred to her, back then, to turn away or worse, simply run away. She'd had nightmares from time to time—who didn't?—but they didn't stop her or break her rhythm. In the light of day, she'd always managed to put one foot briskly in front of the other and get the story told.

Yet now that she was tucked away in little old Canary, she

was ashamed of herself for yearning to avoid the tough stuff. *Who hides out in an art gallery? No one who calls herself an investigative reporter. I'm going soft. Losing my edge.* Visiting a shuttered crematorium is not the scariest place you can be, she reminded herself. So why make it such a big deal? Why refuse to disclose the visit to Flint? *Why am I hiding from myself?*

She thought about all the stories she could be covering for the paper and wasn't. What about Camilla? Why not do a deep dive into the life of a sex worker? Who was she? Why and how had she made the choices that had brought her to this point? And how many others like her were there in town (men too)? What about Porter, the seemingly all-purpose handyman with the dilapidated truck and the weak-looking son—if he even was his son? Why not learn about him? And Keller, a half-crazed alcoholic keeping a bench warm on the council: What was his deal? What did he know about Effie Rutter, or perhaps Merry herself, and how did he know it? How about the wild dogs roaming around the town; were all their owners dead and gone?

Rags continued this train of thought for several more minutes, until she felt truly shitty—a complete failure and a fraud as a newspaper editor. She wasn't doing jack-shit in this place. She wasn't putting her stamp on the ancient *Canary Courant*; she was barely its caretaker.

Maybe I was already broken when I got here. But nobody likes excuses.

She consoled herself with one little outpost of bravery: she still wasn't doing daily temp checks. Once in a while, when Flint nagged her and stood there watching, she would do it just to get him off her case. Otherwise, she refused to do it just because the fascist PHP insisted that she should. Some laws were meant to be broken. But beyond that, she felt like a complete milquetoast.

She pulled herself together, finally, because she had to and headed to the office. The July morning was hot and humid, and a morning rain shower soaked her to the bone. She had paid no attention to the weather since they'd arrived in Canary. The seasons unfolded, taking her by surprise each step of the way.

It was high summer now; she and Flint were closing in on six months in Canary, and what did she have to show for it?

She sat down at her desk, dripping wet. Merry was already there, staring down at her hands.

"Hey, do you have a towel or something I can use?" Rags asked. Merry looked up and seemed not to realize Rags was there. Silently, she opened a drawer and tossed Rags a roll of paper towels. Rags didn't think it necessary to say thanks, so she just nodded instead and patted herself dry.

She opened the digital news folder to see which stories the freelancers had submitted for the coming issue. She was surprised to see that Brent had finally submitted a piece about Louisa's gallery. She read that first. It was workmanlike; Brent clearly had no intuitive feel for abstract art, or any art, as far as she could tell. He lacked a vocabulary to bring Louisa's vibrant work to life for a reader, falling back on generic words like "pretty" and "colorful" and "interesting." He quoted her as saying that the gallery was open to the public from eleven to three on Tuesdays and Fridays, and all were welcome. Rags was fairly certain she'd made that up on the spot; Louisa wasn't the type to create or enforce strict hours. Rags's unannounced visits were proof of that. But she made a note not to show up during the publicly announced visiting hours. At least Brent had taken a decent photo: Louisa in her painter's overalls, her hair loosely pinned up, smiling in front of a large work that looked to Rags like a two-dimensional version of her human-animal hybrid sculptures. She would give the story prominent play on page 2.

Dineen had filed the paper's first two obituaries in a long time, as they'd discussed. Both were men Rags had not met, both Luckies, both in their fifties. One had had a massive heart attack and died at home in bed. The other had fallen off his roof, landed on a hard stone patio, and died of a head wound. In Canary, falling off a roof could plausibly pass as a suicide attempt. But she'd let it go because there was no way to know, was there? Rags would place the obituaries just before the classified ads. As there were only two of them, the notices would be surrounded, incongruously, by the latest in a series of syndicated articles on summer gardening and, perhaps more appropriately, a column by a local pastor on forgiving one's neighbor for their trespasses. Rags was well aware that it was all a bit of a jumble, the discordant tones of various articles clashing with one another. But then again, Canary itself was also a bit of a jumble.

Ramona filed a story that reported on the effectiveness, according to health experts, of a new generation of respies that Canary residents would soon be able to order online or purchase from the pharmacy aisle of the grocery store on Canary's outskirts. The article discussed air filtration and air purity rates and other technical aspects as well as the sleeker, more comfortable design. She submitted manufacturers' product photos with the article. Rags hoped that Ramona was not accepting a kickback from any of them in exchange for writing the piece. And then she decided she didn't give a damn; let readers make up their own damn minds. It wasn't Rags's job to babysit them. She planned to bury the story as far down the paper as she could.

She pushed her chair away from her desk. It just seemed harder and harder to care. Or get it right. Or find a satisfying balance.

Rags's train of thought was interrupted by her dataphone, which issued an unfamiliar beeping tone, as did Merry's at the same moment. They read the same message simultaneously:

Effective immediately, under the Medical Emergency Powers Act of 2024, the township of Canary and all residents within its official borders are required to obey all posted laws as jointly drawn and enforced by the Public Health Police and the Town Council of Canary. All prior laws and rights will be superseded by this order. Such action is necessary to protect the health and safety of Canary, in accordance with the MEPA and other pertinent state and federal laws, which are publicly available online. Violators will be prosecuted to the fullest extent of the law.

Merry, for once, looked directly at Rags. "What's it mean?"

"Well, Merry, I think that your friend Piper and his partner-in-crime, Terry, have more or less stolen your town out from under you," Rags said.

"Something must have happened," Merry said. "They wouldn't do this without a good reason."

"Wouldn't they?" Rags asked.

"This is bad," Merry said. "Piper must have found new cases, here in town. I'm telling you, Rags, they wouldn't do this unless they had to—to protect us, whether you like it or not."

Rags's phone beeped again. It was Flint calling. He never called her during the day, so engrossed in his own world he forgot everyone and everything else. She guessed immediately that he'd gotten the same text. Everyone had. He asked her what it was about and without waiting for her to respond, he told her not to do anything rash. He said he thought she should let this play out and he urged her to hold back. Rags laughed. Acting rashly was entirely beside the point now, in her view.

"Hold back?" she said loudly into the phone. "Hold back? Is that the advice you would've given to the French and the Poles as the Nazis rolled their tanks into town? Holding back isn't an option, Flint." She hung up before he could argue further.

"What's *your* plan, Merry?" Rags asked. Merry was pale and slumped in her chair, practically sitting on her long gray hair. While Rags wasn't sure of her *own* course of action, she didn't want Merry doing anything stupid, anything that would harm the paper or the office. Rags wasn't sure *what* Merry was capable of, under pressure.

"I just…" Merry started. "I just don't want things to get worse. I can't. It's too much."

Rags didn't know what she was talking about, and didn't want to know, and besides, there was no time to worry about Merry any further. Rags took her bag and headed to the door.

"Where are you going?" Merry asked.

"Guess," Rags said, without stopping. She stepped outside

and despite the steady rain, there were more people than usual standing on the sidewalk up and down Main Street. People were reading their phones. Many had already put on respies. They clustered in socially distant circles, talking loudly to be heard through their masks. There was a general air of confusion and a slight sort of vibration—a vibration Rags felt in her own bones—that signaled the start of panic.

Getting soaked again, Rags dodged the loose crowds and the packs of dogs drinking from puddles on the street and made her way down Main Street to the peacekeeper's office. There was Piers, at his desk, also staring at his phone. The empty law enforcement office felt emptier than ever, as if the very notion of law enforcement itself was nearing obsolescence.

"I told you," he said as soon as she entered, running his hand through his hair more slowly than usual.

"You didn't know about *this*, Piers, did you?" Rags asked.

"No, not that. Me." He held out his dataphone, which Rags couldn't possibly read. "They already shut me out of all the official digi-locks, including all active case files and even the evidence room." Rags's first thought was that now he couldn't bring her back inside the crematorium, but she knew that was ridiculously irrelevant.

"Did they bother to give you a reason?" Rags was trying to figure out how best to report all this. Gathering facts, she reminded herself, was still essential. She couldn't spend all her time simply reacting to events as they unfolded. Piers read from his dataphone.

"'Failure to adequately and consistently protect the residents of Canary from any and all external threats.'"

"What the fuck is that supposed to mean?" Rags said. Pier shrugged and continued.

"'Failure to make adequate progress in the criminal disappearance of two minors'… There's a lot more."

"Oh shit," Rags said. "The fingerprints on Effie's pom-pom. If you're locked out of the system—"

"I knew they were out to get me, Rags. I'm not completely

crazy—not yet. I gave the processing center a private number." He held up another smaller dataphone. Rags was surprised he'd thought of this—which must have shown on her face. "Look, I know I fucked this up. They're not wrong. But I'm trying to… to do something right. I'll make sure you get the report."

Every time Rags thought she had Piers figured out, or was certain that he was about to completely lose his shit, he surprised her. Just then, Porter slipped in quietly. Rags saw his son—still pale, still so slender—peeking around the edge of the door.

"They sent me to help you collect your stuff," Porter said, stone-faced.

"Who is *they*?" Piers asked, though Rags assumed he knew it was Terry and Piper, if not the whole council. Porter shrugged. "Well, *they* wasted your time. I don't have fuck-all. Look around. Everybody leaves everything behind when they go." Piers gestured to all the empty desks and cabinets. He suddenly burst out laughing. "When they go, they're gone, aren't they?" He laughed some more. Rags couldn't tell if he was stoned or just on the edge of crazy, as she'd thought earlier. Or maybe both.

"They want me to collect your gun," Porter said. Piers removed his belt with the holstered stun gun and threw it down across his desk. He stretched his arms out, as if he were about to be frisked.

"You wanna check?" Piers asked.

"What for?" Porter asked.

"Forget it," Piers said, dropping his arms. Rags instantly guessed that Piers was gambling that Porter wouldn't actually frisk him and find the other phone. And even if he had, Piers was presumably allowed to keep his own property. How far will they go? Rags wondered.

Porter took the belt and headed for the door. Rags watched as his son reached out to finger the gun. Boys and their toys, she thought. She wondered if Porter would take his son out to the woods somewhere and use the stun gun to hunt for squirrel or maybe rabbit. Dinner. Porter stopped and turned around, looking back at Piers and Rags inside the office.

"I just do what they tell me. Go where they tell me," he said. "It's not personal." Porter and the boy got into his beat-up truck and drove away. Rags wished she had a quick way to follow them, but she was only on foot. Still, she already knew what her next stop would be.

"Good luck," she said to Piers. She didn't know what else there was to say. He stood in the doorway, watching her walk away. She knew that once he stepped outside and closed the office door, there was every chance he'd never be allowed to step back inside. Who knew when—or if—he'd be replaced, now that the PHP had accomplished such a blatant power grab? She was awfully glad she'd gotten the files for Effie and Jaxson from him, and the dataphones. That ball was now entirely in her court. Which meant, she realized with a lurch in her heart, that the fate of the two missing kids was entirely in her hands—especially once the fingerprints came back.

Rags jogged in the rain all the way to Terry's elegant house. Her dripping face showed up on the visi-cam at the front entrance, and, as on her last visit, Terry was instantly there to meet her, like a guard dog keenly picking up the scent of an intruder. Terry was wearing a respie—one of the new models that Ramona had written about. Maybe Terry was the one who'd bribed a manufacturer for early samples, not the guileless Ramona. In any case, Rags knew this was a blatant display of bullshit security theater—a ploy to frighten people so they'd do exactly what she and Piper told them to do. And there was the PHP. Of course. Piper stared at Rags over Terry's shoulder in the doorway as Rags stood in the pelting rain. The pair of them, masked and vaguely menacing, reminded Rags again of the bulldog PHPs in the city, waiting on street corners for innocent passersby to break a "rule"—or pretend they had—purely so they could stop them, or arrest them, like the girl with the polka dot umbrella. Any flimsy excuse to harass people and remind them who's in control.

"Who is it?" a voice called from inside the house. Rags recognized it as Missy's. "Get rid of them, Terry." But Terry didn't listen. She brought Rags into her modern, sunken living room. Rags stood dripping water on Terry's spotless white carpet. Keller was there, too, sitting far apart from Missy, holding what looked like a glass of whiskey. Keller was the only one among them who was not wearing a mask, perhaps because it interfered with his drinking.

"We may need her," Terry said. "She could be useful. And she knows what's at stake."

"She's a scofflaw, Terry," Piper said. "I don't see how she's our ally."

Rags took perverse pleasure in being discussed in the third person while she stood right there, moistening Terry's expensive carpet. The room was over-cooled, however, and she felt goosebumps rising on her wet flesh.

"What do you want?" Missy said sharply.

"She's prob'ly wondering what 'n the hell we're doing," Keller said quietly.

"Shut up, Keller," Missy said. "Here." She refilled his glass.

My God, they're trying to poison the poor man.

"I never doubted you'd trot over here, Rags," Terry said, "once we sent out the bulletin. Actually, I'm surprised it took you this long." Rags wouldn't tell them about her visit to Piers. "There's a reasonable explanation for everything we've done. And you'll recall, I did warn you there'd be changes. So I don't expect you're surprised."

"Surprised? No," Rags said. "But where is all this leading?"

"To a better Canary," Terry said. "As I told you before. Stronger, healthier, safer, and more resilient."

"A perfect headline," Rags said.

"It is, isn't it?" Missy said. "And you'll write up something for the paper along those lines?"

Rags laughed. Missy may have been a bully, but could she really be quite this naïve?

"It doesn't work that way," Rags said, still laughing.

"It does, though," Piper said, breathing hard and circling the living room. "It does when lives are at stake. When you have to tell people the truth. Isn't that your job, Rags?" Piper came up to her and put his sweaty, respie-covered face close to Rags's face, thinking, perhaps, this would actually intimidate her. She noticed that the ever-present kohl rings around his eyes had begun to run, giving her the impression that Piper was crying tiny black tears.

"And what is the truth, Piper?" Rags asked, looking straight into the PHP's masked face.

"The truth," Piper said, pacing again, "is that the virus is back among us. In all likelihood, a new strain."

"They say we should be worried. Very," Keller said. Rags wasn't sure who he meant by *they* and perhaps Keller wasn't sure, either.

"We're only doing what any governing body would do to protect the populace," Terry said.

"Prove it," Rags said. "Prove that the virus is back, that people are getting sick. Or dying. Prove it, and then I'll see what I can do."

"Keep in mind, Rags," Terry said, steering the conversation away from her request for proof, "the council's realignment of authority is completely legal. We've dotted all the i's and crossed all the t's. So it's no use getting all worked up about it."

"My readers, as you call them, are your constituents, your taxpayers, the people who live and work and barter here, the people just trying to figure out how to continue, one day at a time," Rags said. "Though from what I've seen, they're not doing a great job of it." She began to shiver in the cold room but worked to control it; it wouldn't do to let them think she was frightened of them or the situation in general. "And now you want to terrify them all over again."

"Protect them, Rags!" Piper said. "We want to protect them! If putting the fear of God into people, or the law, or both, is what it takes to keep them alive, then that's what we have to do!"

"Nobody wants to live in fear," Rags said. "Nobody wants to be ruled by Nazis."

"You're way out of line!" Missy said. "I don't know why you just want to make trouble, when all we're trying to do here is keep people safe and alive. That's the opposite of the Nazis. You should choose your words more carefully, Rags."

"You know, Rags," Terry said, "I'm really getting tired of your high-and-mighty act. As if you're right and we're wrong. This council has acted responsibly. And the changes we're making are necessary and essential."

"Well, where's the proof?" Rags asked.

"Proof of life!" Keller interjected. "Proof of life for Effie and Jaxson."

Terry looked over at Piper.

"Piper will get you proof," she said. "But we have to handle this delicately."

Rags shivered more deeply as she suddenly suspected that Terry didn't have any proof—any firsthand proof—that the virus, or any deadly contagion, new strain or not, had re-emerged in Canary. She was relying on Piper for that information, wasn't she? Rags thought that was quite a gamble for Terry to take. But it also stood to reason, as Terry didn't hide the fact that she was eager for more power over the council, which meant, power over the town at large. And this was the most plausible and convenient route to get it. Nothing like a terrifying emergency to help everybody fall in line. Rags remembered that Terry had said something about wanting Canary to lead the way forward, and now Rags felt she understood what that might really look like: fascism.

Without another word, Rags left the house and broke into a run, back to the *Courant*'s office. She felt an urgent need to move through time and space, as if she could somehow get ahead of what was happening. She sailed down Main Street, where scores of people were milling aimlessly, talking, practically walking in circles, at a loss for what to do or how to figure out what came next. The Canary Bar & Grill was unusually packed, given that it wasn't yet noon. And there was a line out the door at Mellonia, which Rags guessed had already reimposed social distancing measures (unlike the bar), allowing only a handful of customers inside at a time. Rags seemed to be the only one out in the open, not wearing a respie. Canary was fueled by rumors now, she supposed, and there was no way to control them. Her only means of persuasion, her only way to try to introduce a measure of sanity and rationality, was through the newspaper—if only people would actually read it.

Merry had left the office by the time Rags returned, but the freelancers were there waiting for her. She wanted to be rid of them; she wanted to take the reins and write the damn paper herself. But of course that flew in the face of her more democratic impulses. The three of them surrounded her desk.

"I don't think they've called a township meeting," Brent said. "That would seem logical, but I haven't seen any notice, have you?"

"They won't," Rags said. "They've done what they've done."

"I'm not sure what to write about," Dineen said. "People are scared."

"*I'm* scared," Ramona said.

Rags decided on the spot that they'd all pitch in together on a suite of related articles. She fired off assignments and had to hope for the best from all of them. She hoped they'd rise to the occasion. She told Brent to find out how many other PHPs had invoked the MEPA of 2024 to suspend local laws—and what happened when they did. Dineen was assigned to walk around town and interview people to find out how they were taking the news and what questions they had about what was going on, and also to learn what rumors were floating around. And Ramona would investigate whether any new outbreaks of the same virus that had allegedly attacked them had arisen anywhere else, and if so where, how widespread was it, and were there any actual documented cases in Canary. Rags told Ramona that she could not interview Piper Madrigal for the story; she'd have to independently verify as much information as she could through the non-PHP side of the state health department, the CDC, and wherever else she might turn to. Ordinarily, that would be an odd condition to impose, but Rags could not run the risk of turning the newspaper into a mouthpiece for the PHP. Rags told them all to gather as much as they could by the next day, so that she'd have time to pull a news package together for Sunday's edition. She said it was okay to turn in rough copy; she'd polish it up. They could always run follow-up articles in Wednesday's paper.

Rags stopped talking and the three of them looked at her, nodding.

"What's going to happen?" Ramona asked. She had deep worry lines between her eyes. "To us? To everyone?"

"And what about the missing kids?" Brent asked. "Do we just forget all about that now? Those poor kids. God knows where. Doing God knows what. Assuming they're still alive." Brent frowned and shook his head.

Rags was on the cusp of telling them she had Piers's evidence and that she was pursuing that independently. But she decided it was a bad idea to share any of that.

"Nobody's forgetting about Effie and Jaxson, Brent," she said. "But we don't have enough hard information yet to run a full story. We will, though. I'm sure we will. For now, I need you to focus on what the council and the PHP are doing right here in Canary. We can't let them operate in the dark. We must shine a light on everything they do. Agreed?"

The writers left and Rags spent the next six hours banging out two different articles. The first was a factual overview of what had just happened: the invocation of the MEPA, the transfer of law enforcement authority to the PHP, the firing of peacekeeper Piers Olsson, and the town council's decision to set all of it in motion on the *suspicion*, as yet unproven, that new cases of a deadly virus had surfaced in Canary. Rags felt that piece set the stage for what was to come, including the sidebar articles that the freelancers were writing. The article contained an implied challenge to the council—a public version of what she'd said in private at Terry's house: proof was needed, and soon.

The second piece she wrote took longer but mattered to her even more. She wrote a lengthy editorial that relied heavily on what history has taught us about fascist regimes, and about the undemocratic application of the rule of law. She pulled no punches in warning that without solid evidence to back up the claims made for imposing an emergency government, there would be a heavy price to pay—and a reckoning as well. The editorial was a bigger, sharper companion to her earlier piece: "A Town Bends Over." That was a mere shot across the bow from a safe distance; this new piece was more like aiming your rifle at the whites of the enemy's eyes. Rags realized that she was developing a consistent editorial voice for the *Canary Courant.* She was well aware that her positions were not uniformly popular. But she couldn't live with herself if she didn't say what needed saying, especially now.

Rags arrived back home in the humid summer twilight, exhausted. Flint fed them both. He asked how she was coping and she told him about the meetings with Piers and Terry, and shared her feeling that Canary was in real trouble. Flint agreed and tried to draw parallels with his own line of work: in the fog of war, it was hard to maintain, let alone discern, the path of ethical purity. Life was messy everywhere, he said. Maybe there really was no such thing as "normal," there was only action and reaction. Rags tried to listen but kept losing the thread of what he said.

Over the next few days, Rags lived and breathed the newspaper in a way she had not done in nearly six months as its editor. Now, suddenly, everything mattered: finding and telling the truth, and not relying on the narratives that the council was feeding to everyone. The freelancers turned in a jumble of rough drafts and raw notes, but she pulled enough from all of it to round out the news package for Sunday's paper. Her lead story, plus their sidebars, plus photos of townspeople milling around anxiously, took up the entire first page and the two inside spreads. Based on what they all knew so far, dozens of cities and towns around the country had invoked the MEPA, but only for short periods and mainly, it seemed, to impose crowd control measures—not to commandeer local government. And Ramona had not found any credible information on new outbreaks anywhere in the United States. There had been reported scares, to be sure, but no frightening, deathly contagions. And no signs of any new strain of virus for which there was no vaccine.

Rags's editorial took up another two-thirds of a page, leaving room for the usual quasi-irrelevant assortment of syndicated musings, religious thoughts, and of course, the bulging classifieds. Rags took the precaution of locking Merry out of the digital files so she could compose the paper herself. She didn't want Merry tampering at the last minute with any of the copy. She imagined Merry was fully capable of spiking a story she didn't like—making it disappear for her own reasons, which Rags found mystifying. Whether or not that was something Merry would actually do, Rags would take no chances.

Whatever else he might have been up to, Porter was as reliable as ever. The Sunday edition of the *Canary Courant* plopped onto front porches all around town between six-thirty and eight a.m., including Rags and Flint's.

On Sunday night, while Rags and Flint were both in the front parlor, they heard a bang, followed by a flash of light that lit up the cherry trees. They opened the front door to a column of flames. A thick bundle of *Courant* newspapers was on fire, just steps from their front door. Flint ran outside to turn on an old hose attached to the side of the house. It took him half an hour to put out the fire, by which point, one of the cherry trees had been badly burned, its trunk blackened and charred, the lower branches burned naked. Rags watched from the front steps, imagining the tree crying out in pain. She wept silent tears of rage.

21

Yesterday on the line the chickens were talking to me. Not only talking, but dancing, singing, clapping. I know the song, but I forget what it's called.

Somebody, maybe Debbie, poked me sharply in the ribs. Stand up straight, she said. Stop tipping into me.

I didn't know I was tipping.

I don't see too clearly now. And I get so dizzy.

But I'm winning. They're losing. I'm going to leave them and they'll have to scramble around. Hah.

Tiffany says she's worried about me. Am I eating? she asks. I say I'm worried about her.

Chickens: the last stop. We still laugh about that.

She whispers in my ear at night, coughing into her arm. I don't think it's a dream. I think it's real. She whispers that she has a plan. Rat poison. She found some. She's putting it in the big bottles of clear water only they drink from. She tells me to hang on. She'll take me home. I just have to wait a little while longer.

I say okay, but I don't really think so. Take this with you, I say. Take what? she asks. My sheet. See? Oh, she says. You bring it home yourself.

I have to stay here to beat the sadists. But I don't tell Tiffany. She can win her game and I can win mine. So we both win. Yeah.

The Sharpie is drying out.

Remember me.

Iphigenia Penelope Rutter

22

Flint made his third trip out to the Potrero Complex the week of the fire. He had almost decided he would not go back. He was on the brink of allowing himself to get sucked into something he didn't understand and he did not want that feeling to develop further. *Better the devil you know.* But the fire unsettled him. It made him long for the quiet mystery of the ancient, wooded place, which was the very opposite of the seething, rippling despair that enveloped Canary, now compounded with the fear he could feel rising up around him.

The night of the fire, Rags used a broom and dustpan to sweep up the ashes as best she could, while Flint held open a compostable garbage bag. He had a small folding shovel, which he kept packed in his 'go' bag, but he didn't bring it out. They returned to the parlor and poured themselves large whiskeys.

"What's this about, Rags?"

"Isn't it obvious? They don't like what I wrote."

"Seems like it's more than that."

"I've made enemies here, Flint. It's good. It means I'm doing my job."

"All those years you were reporting in the city, nothing like this ever happened."

"Everything's a bigger deal in a small town. In the city, people are better at rolling with the punches."

Flint didn't like her answers. She was either flipping him off or she wasn't taking it all seriously enough. First, a porch fire. Next, what? Shots fired through the window? He pictured himself sitting at his computer as a bullet whizzed by, barely missing him. Or worse, somebody planting a bomb at the *Courant* office when Rags was there. That suddenly seemed entirely plausible. He wasn't scared, exactly. He just hated living in an environment where everything was beginning to feel out of control. That day he'd stepped over the dead body in the street and kept going: That day, things were out of control and he'd felt shitty about it for a long time. That memory contributed to his willingness to agree to move with Rags to Canary, though he had no particular longing to live in a small town. Maybe there was no such thing as "normal," but there had to be equilibrium, somewhere, and he wanted to find it more than ever.

He went to the woods in the middle of the night, as usual, after Rags had fallen into an exhausted, dream-haunted sleep. She still had no idea that he had left her on those nights, and he hadn't decided when, or if, to tell her about his excursions. If he couldn't explain to himself what he was doing, or why, how could he explain it to her? He knew the way by now. He walked briskly across the fields, along the path, and then into the woods. He had continued searching for a cluster of trees that matched the ones in Louisa's painting. But it was a foolish waste of time. Perhaps Louisa hadn't copied exactly from nature; she might have changed the number and arrangement of the trees in her painting. And the underbrush would not look the same now as it did when she painted it. So on this third trip, he settled for a spot deeper in the woods than he'd gone before. He found what looked to him like a bit of a rounded clearing, where the underbrush, and the feel of rocky soil beneath it, was encircled by trees. There was nothing really special about this spot; he just decided it felt right.

He slid his bag to the ground and stood a moment, listening for any human sounds. There was only a light rustle of wind in the leaves and the buzz of mosquitoes darting around his ears. He took out a headlamp, which he'd ordered online, as no such thing was to be found in Canary. He took out his folding shovel too, and a small cloth bag. He aimed the light toward a spot near the center of the imagined clearing and dug his shovel into the dirt. He remembered Louisa's warning about digging on the sacred land of her ancestors. But that seemed less real to him than the desire to find ancient treasure. He had done enough research to learn that this area had been occupied by a Late

Woodland horticultural and hunting-based society. These people had lived and died over half a millennium ago and could not hurt him now—nor he them. Their strife would not become his strife. Yet they had left behind a record of their industry, their livelihood, their artistry. Flint felt that to have even just a small piece of that would help to remind him that life may be hard, but it flows on. *What feels like a massive storm today is barely a single ripple on a still pond across time.* He knew he'd never say something like that out loud. But he felt it nonetheless.

Flint began making a series of holes with his shovel, each one about six inches wide and ten inches deep. He wasn't looking for anything in particular. He assumed he'd know an artifact when he saw one. And then he felt something. In the fourth hole, a tiny pair of triangular projectile points made, he knew, from either rhyolite or quartz. Each one was no more than three centimeters wide but feeling his way in the dirt, he could tell they were not formless pebbles. They were symmetrical triangles, their planes beaten with other handmade tools, he'd learn later. He ran his thumb over the tip of each point. He put the objects into the cloth bag. He loosely backfilled the holes he'd dug—out of respect, not because he thought they'd be found.

The discovery made him feel light, which is what he'd hoped for. He felt a little less attached to the present, and more in touch with the past. This was a kind of equilibrium, as close as he'd hoped to come. He packed up his shovel and his headlamp and headed back toward the road, blinking hard in the darkness after the glare of the lamp, which he did not want to risk using out in the open.

An hour or so later, he entered the house and was met with reassuring silence but for the hum of the refrigerator motor. After stashing his bag, he gently wiped off the arrow tips with a moistened paper towel and put both on his desk, propped up against Louisa's little painting. He thought they seemed right at home there. He did not feel guilty for having liberated them. Louisa would never know. And he didn't think Rags prowled around his desk.

Too wired to sleep, he turned on his screens and let their blue glow settle him. He needed to turn his mind to something logical, mundane even. Perhaps owing to a twinge of guilt for sneaking out on Rags, he remembered he still owed her an explanation for the classified ad language. He assumed that despite the fire and everything else going on in town, she still cared about Effie Rutter. He pulled up the spreadsheet he'd made, sorting the data in different ways. It had not made any sense up to this point. But now, with fresh eyes, he saw new possibilities. He'd need to run multiple sorts to test out several permutations. But suppose that phone numbers and other numbers, such as street addresses, represented map coordinates as well as times of day. And what if certain letters, perhaps capitals, or letters followed by punctuation marks, such as exclamation points and question marks, could be translated into dates. Still wide awake, he wrote a software routine that would run multiple combinations of potential correlations. It would take a few hours to generate results, despite his fairly robust computer.

A wave of exhaustion hit him hard. He moved to one of the worn armchairs, unable to drag himself up to bed, and fell asleep instantly while his computer whirred and the screen flickered, doing its work.

Flint dreamed he was riding a horse across a wide-open plain. The sky was vast and blue, and his horse was fast. He felt free.

"Hey…Hey." Rags was shaking him awake. For a split second, he didn't recall where he was. Oh. The armchair. In the house in Canary. After his "venture." She thrust a mug of hot coffee at him and the scent of it brought him more fully awake.

"Thank you," he said, sipping the coffee.

"What's going on?" Rags asked. She was dressed. He asked her the time and she said it was nearly eight and she was heading to the office, but what the fuck?

He scrambled for an explanation and then he remembered: the software program, the data. It must have found something. He went to look at his screens.

"My God, you stink, Flint. Take a fucking shower, maybe, huh? You smell like a lumberjack after a long shift."

Flint flipped across several screens and there it was, all neat and tidy: a list of dates, times, places. He had no idea what the information actually meant, but at least it made sense intrinsically. Rags would have to take it from here.

"Look, look, look," he said, drinking coffee to restore his senses fully.

"What?" Rags said. "I gotta go."

"But this is what you asked me to figure out. The ads in the newspaper. What they meant. Or what they might mean. Look!"

Rags looked at the screen and saw the neatly ordered list.

"Wait," she said. "I need to understand. You fed in all the ads, from all the papers I gave you."

"Yes," Flint said.

"And you somehow decoded—I don't pretend to understand this—but you somehow figured out what the ads are really saying. And it's dates, times, places."

"Yes," he said again. He had begun to feel itchy all over, and he did want to shower.

"This is…this is huge," Rags said quietly. "Keller was right."

"Really?" Flint asked. He looked again at the generically intelligible information and still had no idea what it conveyed.

"Send it to me right away," she said. He clicked a few keys. Her dataphone beeped.

"Thank you so much," Rags said. She kissed him. "Did you stay up all night doing this for me?" He smiled at her but said nothing. "I really, really appreciate it. Honestly. And I appreciate you, even if I don't always show it."

Flint did not want any more adulation. He did not think he'd earned it, not with all he was hiding from her.

"Go," he said. "You have stuff to do. I'm glad this is helpful, though I have no idea what it does for Effie Rutter."

"I got it from here," she said, smiling a rare smile. "I hope you'll tackle the phone next—but I'm not going to press my luck right away. I know you also have things to do. Like showering. And maybe getting some more sleep."

After Rags left, Flint returned to his desk and fingered the precisely carved little objects he'd excavated during the night. He looked at them on and off throughout the day, his thoughts pinging back and forth through time and two forms of warfare—the direct piercing of deer flesh, for example, on one end of the time band, and the intellectual precision of remote target acquisition on the other.

Several days later, after trying and failing to resist, a third object joined the projectile points. Flint had returned to the small clearing yet again. He dug new, slightly deeper holes and put his hands into the dirt, sifting it carefully. He felt something slim and hard. It appeared to be a tiny shaft of bone, tapered at one end. He put the bone into his cloth bag and began researching what it might be as soon as he returned home in the night. He concluded it was an awl, possibly made from deer bone, and it may have been used to punch holes in leather or to etch markings on animal skin. He propped up the slender bone awl alongside the projectile points. He knew he had officially become a nighthawker, and while others may have judged him harshly for this, condemned him, even, he could not deny that he loved it more than anything he'd ever done away from a computer. The questions he put to himself, at that point, were how much more of this he was going to do, and when—if?—he would confess to Rags.

23

Gripping her dataphone as though it might decide to fly away on its own, Rags walked quickly to the office, determined to make sense of the data Flint had detangled during the night. The side streets in her neighborhood were eerily quiet as usual, but as soon as she turned onto Main Street, it appeared that Canary was creating a new new-normal for itself. Yellow circles had been freshly painted along the sidewalks to indicate how far apart people were required to stand or distance themselves while walking. Digital paper had been affixed to every window, every commercial front door, with bright letters sliding across the screens like modern ticker tape. KEEP YOUR DISTANCE...RESPIRATORS REQUIRED AT ALL TIMES...REPORT SUSPICIOUS ACTIVITY IMMEDIATELY...SAFETY VIOLATORS WILL BE PROSECUTED.

Rags knew this had to be Piper's work, and he'd worked very quickly. Overnight, Canary had begun transforming into a place that felt *occupied*. Perhaps *invaded* is more accurate, Rags thought. A band of six men and women in black coveralls, similar in style to the ones the PHP wore, were walking up and down the sidewalks—in blackjack-boots, no less—clipping collars and leashes on roaming terriers, collies, retrievers, and assorted mutts. Rags watched as they kicked some of the dogs into submission, yanking tightly on the leashes as the animals squealed and barked in protest. An awful image arose in Rags's mind: the dogs all being thrust into the crematorium at once, yelping as they were consumed by the white-hot flames. Surely not, she thought. Surely not even Piper... People milled around watching the small sea of black coveralls at work. None of the bystanders spoke up or sought to stop them.

"What are you doing with them?" Rags said loudly, approaching the band of uniformed men and women.

"Step back!" one of the men said. Rags ignored him. As they were all masked and gloved, and identically dressed, it was impossible to recognize any of them. Rags had no way to know whether they'd been recruited from the local population or imported from outside. Given Piper's paranoia, she suspected they were all local citizens, perhaps including many who'd shuffled innocently into the township meetings she'd attended.

"Health hazard," one of the women said, yanking three dogs at once. "They've all got to be removed." Rags didn't believe a word of that. In all her time in Canary, she'd never seen any of the wild dogs foaming at the mouth, let alone attacking people. What sort of health hazard could the animals possibly pose? What information did these brainwashed uniformed recruits have that she didn't have? *They don't know a thing.* Rags noted that everyone in the crew wore black lanyards with blinking green discs hanging from their necks—a sign, she assumed, that they'd personally been scrubbed clean, all traced, cleared, and purified. Perhaps, in their own eyes, they'd been sanctified to do whatever it was they'd been assigned to do. The dogs would just be the beginning, certainly.

"I said, step back into the circle," the same man said. "Now."

"Who's in charge? Who ordered you to do this?" Rags persisted.

"Leave them alone!" one of the bystanders shouted at Rags. "Let them do their job!"

"That's right!" shouted another. Like nearly everyone in Canary, they were all dressed casually, even haphazardly, in varying shades of browns and grays. They were generally pale, despite weeks of bright sun, and no one carried an ounce of extra body fat. And they too were impossible to tell apart, thanks to the respies covering two-thirds of their faces. The bystanders were spaced out among several of the yellow circles on the sidewalk—symmetrically arrayed as if they were lining up in formation. Lining up like a marching band, a band of soldiers, a band of prisoners about to march to their deaths. *Is this what Canary will become?*

"Are any of you feeling sick? Or know anyone who is?" Rags shouted to the shrouded onlookers. All of them reflexively looked to the dogcatchers, as if they needed that group's permission to speak. But the dogcatchers had by now taken a dozen barking dogs in hand and were heading in the direction of the high school. "*Are* you?" she repeated, hoping they'd feel they could speak freely now.

"None of your damn business," said a woman standing in one of the yellow circles. She reminded Rags of Merry because she had long gray hair. And because of her attitude, as if she couldn't see where her own best interests might lie.

"You're with the newspaper, aren't you?" asked a man from another circle. "We don't have to talk to you. You can't make us."

"Where the hell is your mask?" came another voice from another circle. "You're putting all of us in danger, you know!"

"And breaking the law!" someone shouted.

"I'm just trying to tell the truth about what's going on," Rags said to as many bystanders as she could reach with her voice. "Don't you want that? To know the truth?" She was standing in the middle of Main Street now, facing the people standing in their circles. This felt like a tribunal.

"What *I* know is that we can't be too careful," said one of the men from his circle. "We won't beat this thing if we don't follow the rules."

"Beat *what* thing?" Rags said.

"If you have to ask, you're already in trouble," said someone loudly from farther down the sidewalk. "And we don't want any trouble, do we? Things're bad enough."

Rags saw nods of assent ripple across the circles.

"I should report you!" shouted one of the women. Everyone nodded again.

Rags wondered if any of these people had been responsible for setting the newspapers on fire on her front porch. *Such a chicken-shit thing to do.* She gave up on them and continued walking toward her office, glancing behind her once or twice to make sure the mob had not decided to follow. She walked straight down the middle of Main Street to avoid the circles, which she considered an artificial and unnecessary imposition given that there was zero evidence to support that they were needed. She walked past the peacekeeper's office, which also had the digital ticker with its warning message affixed to the old front door. She knew Piers would hate that, even if he might try to laugh it off. She wondered where he'd gone, and when she'd hear from him, but had no time to deal with that now. She walked past the alley that led to Louisa's hidden gallery oasis. She longed for a day when she could shut out the shit-show swirling around her and just hang out with Louisa, studying her artwork.

Before reaching the *Courant* office, Rags heard gunshots ring out, one after another, leaving behind a series of echoes. The shots seemed to go on forever, though they probably only lasted fifteen seconds. *The dogs,* she thought. It had to be the dogs. Killed on the high school athletic field, no doubt. Execution-style. That's where the black-clothed brigade seemed to be heading and where the shots were coming from. Killed just yards from where Effie Rutter had tossed her red pom-poms in the air and Jaxson Turner had spiraled a football. To Rags, it was another sign that Canary was in serious trouble.

As soon as Rags reached her desk, she flipped on a screen and called up the file Flint had given her. She couldn't dwell on the dogs now. Instead, she sent a message to Dineen, who was the best among the freelancers at wheedling information out of people. Rags asked her to head over to the field right away and begin investigating. And to get pictures of any incriminating evidence if at all possible. Like blood on the field. A lost collar. Anything. She told her to start asking questions of everyone who seemed to be within earshot of the shootings. She warned Dineen it wouldn't be pretty, but she was trusting her with an important job and was counting on her. Merry was not in the office. Rags had no idea where she went or what she did when she wasn't there during normal working hours, but she couldn't dwell on that, either. It was for the best, anyway, given the chore ahead.

She opened the spreadsheet Flint had created. It contained multiple tabs, one tab each for dates, times, places, and proper names. The data within each tab was further divided. For example, dates were broken into columns for days, months, and years; the time tab included hours of the day and times of day (morning, afternoon, evening) and so forth. Each cell within each table was populated by elements Flint had found in the ads, covering all the numerals, forms of measurement, and proper names that had appeared in print. Rags was never more grateful for Flint's anally retentive habits and steel-trap mind.

She decided to test whether any of this meant anything at all—whether Keller had steered her in the right direction—by beginning with what she knew, or as close to it as possible. She knew that Effie Rutter had disappeared from the Allen Athletic Field on October 9, 2029, at around six p.m., based on what Evelyn had reported to her about Effie's habits. Jaxson had disappeared on May 14; she didn't know what time.

Less than fifteen minutes later, Rags sat back in astonishment. Combing through each of the tabs Flint had sorted based on the ads, she found the date (October 9), the time (six p.m.) and separate references to a Mr. Allen and an athletic field.

What did all this really mean?

Perhaps within any given issue, these clues—instructions?—were scattered across multiple ads. If someone gave you a key in advance, so you knew what to look for, you could pull the hidden information from the ads and then…what? Were these kids really kidnapped, and if so, to where and for what purpose? And then she wondered: Was she working for, and getting paid by, someone so evil, twisted, and corrupt that he or she would steal children for profit? Obviously, it wasn't for ransom, as neither Evelyn nor the Fallons had been contacted to pay up, as far as she knew, and Evelyn Rutter was the last person one would try to extort for money, as she had none. Rags thought again about all the mystery surrounding the arms-length publisher of the *Courant*, Merry's inexplicable dedication to taking in the advertising information, and her secretive employment contract. Where did Merry fit into all this, exactly?

Rags decided she had to do two things, sooner rather than later. She needed to go through the newspapers at home that Flint had analyzed, to see if she could confirm her theory. If she could find even just one page of classifieds containing multiple clues that corresponded to the times, dates, and places she already knew, then she'd have doubly confirmed her working theory.

The second thing she needed to do was to call Merry to confirm a suspicion. She had to hope she'd get the answer she was looking for—if Merry answered her at all.

Merry answered her phone only after several rings.

"It's me," Rags said.

"What do you want?" Merry said. "Why on earth are you calling me?"

Rags heard noise in the background. It sounded like a bar, and there was only one bar in town. So is that where Merry spent her so-called free time? Was she with Keller, perhaps?

"I'm going to ask you a question, Merry, and I need you to give me a straight answer," Rags said firmly. "Don't give me any bullshit about your special contract and all that. I don't care about that right now. I need to know one thing."

"What?" Merry said

Rags was worried she was about to hang up on her. "The thing I'm going to ask you might help us find Effie Rutter."

"Oh fuck," Merry said. Rags didn't know how to take that. Was Merry really worried about Effie or was she afraid of being dragged into something she wanted no part of? After nearly six months of working in the same office, Rags did not understand a thing about this woman.

"When you get the weekly advertising info, do they—whoever they are, and I'm not asking you to divulge that now—do they tell you specifically how they want each ad placed? Like, vertical upper left, horizontal lower right? That kind of thing?"

There was a long pause on the phone. Rags could hear Merry

breathing. Then the sound grew muffled. She thought Merry might have cupped her hand over her phone, perhaps to talk to someone else with her in the bar, if that's where she was. Rags didn't care. She just wanted an honest answer.

"Yes," Merry said.

"I'm sorry, will you repeat that?" Rags said. She had to be sure.

"I said, yes, Rags. They care a lot about placement, and I make damn sure it goes the way they want it."

"Thank you, Merry." Rags heard the line click off. *And why do you care so damn much, Merry?*

This was the answer Rags was hoping for. If the ad placements were known in advance, it was that much easier for a mastermind to provide a key to the actual kidnappers, the ones tasked with the dirty work, so they knew what to hunt for in specific ads. This way, you had only to turn to the classifieds on, say, page 12A a week ahead of your operation, search for a date in an ad in the upper left-hand side of the page, a place in an ad in the middle, and a time in an ad at the bottom. Simple as that. And poof: a kid could be made to disappear.

It was almost foolproof, Rags thought. But not quite.

Rags was so lost in thought, she jumped when the door opened and Dineen came in, white as a sheet, tears streaming down her face. Rags's first thought was that another child had been taken or worse, found dead. Dineen stood there, crying silently, breathing heavily. Rags wondered if she was in shock. She had nothing to offer her, not even a cup of water. So she slid over a chair and signaled for Dineen to sit.

"Tell me what happened," Rags began, hoping to coax Dineen to begin speaking.

"It was…it was…awful," Dineen said, between sobs. She handed her dataphone to Rags, who flipped through several photos. She was taken aback. The dogs—dead, bloody, all shot through the head—were splayed on the athletic field. It really did look like an execution. Which, of course, it was. "They were…just lying there… There was…so much blood."

"Did you see anybody? Any of the people who did it? You can't miss them. They're all wearing black coveralls and black boots." Dineen shook her head. The killers must have disbanded quickly. Perhaps they'd been instructed to split up and disappear as fast as possible. "Dineen, I know this is hard, but I need you to ask around. There are houses a block away from the field. Surely the people living there heard something, saw something. I heard the shots all the way from Main Street."

"I can't," Dineen said softly.

"Yes, you can," Rags said. "This is the most important story you'll ever write. You care about Canary, right?" Dineen nodded. "You want the newspaper to report the truth, don't you?" She nodded again. "You can do this. You can find somebody who's willing to talk. And when you do, I want you to write about exactly what you saw, and what any witnesses saw. And send all the pictures to me now."

"Why?" Dineen said, her eyes still filled with tears. "Why would anybody…what's this about?"

Rags had a pretty good idea what it was about. She decided it was important for Dineen to get some perspective on what she'd witnessed. So she shared her theory.

"Look," she said. "The PHP, I mean, Piper Madrigal, personally ordered this to make a point."

"What? No. That's not—"

"Listen to me, Dineen. Just listen. Piper wants to show everyone who's in charge now. He wants everybody to fall in line. To become obedient. And the way to do that is to scare the shit out of people. There was nothing wrong with those dogs—I'm sure of it. Animals don't spread the virus. They never have, right? Plus, we don't even have any evidence there's an infection to spread, or any trace of any virus whatsoever."

"But the Emergency Powers Act. Doesn't that mean something?"

"Don't you see, Dineen? Doesn't anybody see what's really going on here?"

"What if you're wrong, Rags? How do you know?"

"Oh, for God's sake!" Rags said. "Those thugs were told to kill those dogs in public, and leave their dead bodies on the field, as a warning to everyone in Canary. Piper is sending a message. And it's working, isn't it? Look at you!"

"I don't think—"

"Dineen, go back out there. Write the damn story. Write it fast. Or you'll never write for this newspaper again, and I'll see to it, somehow, that you never publish anything, anywhere, ever. Got it?"

Dineen, still pale, nodded. She turned away from Rags and left, her head down. Rags wasn't entirely confident that Dineen would follow through, but she felt the dose of tough love was needed and wouldn't hurt Dineen in the long run. In any case, Rags had the pictures of the dogs on the field, and she'd publish them with or without a story. She hoped the freelancers would not all back out—to prefer writing nothing to writing the ugly truth. The world, let alone Canary, could not survive on a glut of stories about prize roses, cats stuck in trees, and high school football victories. She herself could not imagine living in a place, or a world, where the superficial blind eye won out to the exclusion of everything else there was to say about what was really going on right in front of them. Nobody should be allowed to ignore history, especially when they were in the middle of making it. Somebody needed to testify to reality.

She distinctly remembered something she'd heard about another small town years ago, as The Big One was ramping up. The town had had its first wave of viral illness and bloody deaths. But the front page of the local newspaper, the story above the fold, was about a family's pet lemur and how they cared for it. The paper's editors had blinked—and the truth that mattered had lost out. Rags would never let that happen on her watch at the *Canary Courant*. She made a fresh list of stories and angles that she could assign to Brent and Ramona. She herself wanted to stay focused on Effie Rutter, in particular, no matter what Piper and Terry did. The promise she'd made to Maya—to herself, really—had to be honored. The editorial page, however, would still be the outlet for her skeptical wrath.

Rags was taken aback when Louisa Copperface walked into the *Courant* office. She wore a long summer dress that looked like a watercolor painting and a straw hat. She looked like someone who had just wandered in from a fancy beach town. Apart from Louisa's one visit for dinner, Rags had only ever seen her at the gallery, never even on the street. In Rags's mind, Louisa was almost an apparition, a classy ghost who haunted Canary at will. But now she was crying.

"What's wrong?" Rags asked. Louisa took off her hat and sat in a chair next to Rags's desk. She looked worried.

"Something's happened," Louisa said. "Something terrible."

At first, Rags thought she meant the canine murders and she was surprised that Louisa had taken such an interest, but then again, Louisa was tenderhearted.

"Our land has been desecrated," Louisa said, twisting her hat in her lap. "It's so ugly, I can't imagine who would do that. Why?"

I'm sorry," Rags said. "I'm not following."

"Remember I told you about the Potrero Complex? It's where my ancestors lived centuries ago, after migrating up from North Carolina. They settled on several dozen acres near Little Bear River. They built villages, trading posts, a real community. These were real people, Rags. And I share their blood."

"What happened, exactly?"

"Somebody, or maybe more than one person, I don't know, has been digging holes on the land. They're scattered all over. They tried to fill some of them in, but it's obvious where they've been digging."

"Digging for what?" Rags still felt at sea, and she felt that Louisa was wrenching her away from the real business at hand. What did this have to do with anything that really mattered, given everything that was going on in Canary?

"Well, digging for artifacts, I assume," Louisa said. "Antiquities."

"How do you know?" Rags forced herself not to glance over at her screen or her dataphone, where she had messages waiting.

"Because a bunch of us routinely inspect the property, Rags," Louisa said, as if she were stating an obvious fact. "We walk it to ensure it's undisturbed. And up to now, it has been. But those holes. Someone is stealing from us! Stealing things that do not belong to them, that should remain in their resting place, unmolested. It's disgusting."

Rags had never seen her like this.

"How can I help you, Louisa?"

"Isn't this a front-page news story, Rags? Don't you write about this sort of thing?"

"You mean, a mysterious theft."

"It's not mysterious. It's called nighthawking. And these awful people must be stopped. Please. You have to help me." Louisa went on to say she didn't trust the local peacekeeper to care; that the police never saw this sort of thing as actual theft. A victimless crime, they always called it. Rags acknowledged that Canary was between peacekeepers, anyway, at the moment, so there wasn't really anyone to report this to.

"That's why you have to use the newspaper to expose them!" Louisa said.

"I'm really sorry this happened," Rags said. "I will try. But you do know, don't you, that Canary has been taken over by fascists." As soon as she said it she realized it sounded overly dramatic. But she also knew it was true. "I have to use the paper to fight that—to make sure everybody knows what's going on. So all our reporters are committed to covering that, right now. And then there's the case of the kidnapped kids. We've got some new evidence, and I have to deal with that too."

Louisa stood, gripping her hat. "You don't care," she said coldly. "You don't think this is important."

"That's not true, Louisa."

"Indian affairs. Who cares, right?"

"Look, under normal circumstances, we'd be all over this," Rags said. "I do get it. It's an awful violation. I understand why you're upset. It's just that we're spread really thin, right now. I can't fight all the battles at once."

"Try." Louisa glared at her, then turned to walk out. Rags felt their friendship slipping away, painfully. *I shouldn't have made excuses. I have to help her fix this.*

Louisa opened the door and was met by a crowd of people, talking loudly. She slipped out and Piper Madrigal, gloved and masked, in thick black boots like his henchmen, stomped into the office, ignoring Louisa as if she really was a ghost. Just behind Piper was a crowd of people in black coveralls, their green discs blinking around their necks as if they were a herd of robots awaiting orders. And behind *them,* several Canary residents. They all came through the door, until more than a dozen people stood before Rags, who was by now standing behind her desk. She knew she was being mobbed. But she stood her ground.

"Three strikes, Rags Goldner!" Piper said, playing to the crowd rather obviously, Rags thought. And they ate it up. "Three strikes and you are out!"

"What've I done now?" Rags asked calmly.

"One. Refusing to provide temperature data as required by law."

"You already punished me for that one. Ever heard of double jeopardy?"

"Two," continued the PHP without a trace of humor, "interfering with sworn deputies performing a public duty."

"What the fuck are you talking about?"

"You got in the way of the dogcatchers," said a woman who Rags recognized by her voice as one of the people standing inside a yellow circle on the sidewalk earlier that morning. So one of them had told on her, like a third grader. She wondered if a small clique of them had gone running to Piper, or Terry, or both, when she'd left them earlier that morning. Of course, she hadn't "gotten in the way" of anyone, least of all a band of thugs hauling off innocent dogs to be slaughtered.

"And three," Piper continued, "you refuse to wear a mask,

in direct violation of Canary public ordinance and section 2.4 of the MEPA."

"Tell her!" the woman shouted.

Piper pulled out of a pair of digi-locking aluminum handcuffs.

"Rags Goldner, I hereby place you under arrest for endangering the welfare of the citizens of Canary."

Rags burst out in angry laughter. The old-fashioned language, the drama—this was just too ridiculous to be believed, though she knew perfectly well they meant every word of it and the sycophants were enjoying the show.

Piper roughly grabbed Rags's wrists and clipped on the handcuffs; she didn't bother to resist. She wouldn't give the crowd the satisfaction. A familiar orange light blinked between her wrists.

"This is really fucked up, Piper," she said. "You're a disgrace *and* you're on the wrong side of history."

"You don't know what you're talking about," said one of the men in black coveralls. She pictured him shooting the defenseless dogs. "If it were up to me, I'd run you out of town."

Rags laughed again, harshly, at the absurd scenario she found herself in the middle of. *The star of security theater! Take your seats, please, the show is about to begin!*

"You're wrong, Rags," Piper said, leading her to the door. She didn't have time to grab her bag or her dataphone, which was sitting on her desk. She'd have to find a way to get word to Flint. "You're selfish, thoughtless, arrogant, and putting everyone in Canary at risk."

"Prove it, Piper!" Rags said. Piper ignored her. She turned to face the crowd as they trailed behind her. "The PHP is lying to you. The town council is lying to you. And if you don't figure that out soon, you'll all begin to wonder why you survived in the first place."

As Piper paraded her out to the street, a woman spat on her. Then a man in black overalls came up behind Rags and roughly put a respie over her nose and mouth, eager to muzzle her. She felt almost overcome by white-hot anger, especially as she was helpless to react. The only weapon she possessed to fight back, the only thing still in her control, was the newspaper. And by God, she would use it. She felt badly for Louisa, but that was a mere sideshow compared to this.

Piper led her up the steps into the peacekeeper's office. The crowd was told not to follow them inside and they began to disperse. The show was over, for now. Terry was standing inside Piers's old office like the owner of a bed-and-breakfast—albeit masked—waiting to greet her guest.

"I'm sorry, Rags," Terry said, "but I did warn you. You knew the risks."

Rags glared at her. She suspected Terry wanted her to push back, to argue, perhaps even to plead. But she wouldn't do that—especially not the pleading part.

"In any case," Terry said, "you have broken the law and we can't let that slide, not now. I'm sorry it's come to this, but you brought it on yourself."

And you need to make an example of me, Rags thought.

"What's next?" Rags said. "Will you take me out and shoot me in the street? The dogs really made an impact. Great job."

"We're not barbarians, Rags," Terry said. "We're citizens who care about the public's welfare. We take that responsibility seriously."

Rags laughed through her mask. *Spoken like a tone-deaf autocrat.*

"In you go," Piper said, leading Rags to one of the cells. The iron bars on each cell had once been painted white, but all the paint was flecking off. Once she was inside the cell, Piper unlocked her cuffs, then locked the cell door. Rags rubbed her wrists. There was an awful odor coming from inside the cell or nearby; it was strong enough to penetrate the respie. She hoped she'd go nose-blind in a couple of minutes.

"How long?" she asked.

"Two days, two nights," Piper said.

"I suppose you'll tell me you're just following the law."

"That's right," Piper said.

"You'll be fed and given bathroom breaks," Terry said through the bars. "As I keep trying to explain, we're not the enemy. The enemy is out there, in microscopic droplets. But you're an enabler, Rags, if not a vector, and we can't allow that." Piper nodded.

What a pair.

Terry and Piper left her. She immediately took off the respie and slumped to the floor, a million thoughts running through her head. The newspaper: how would she get it out on time? Flint: how would she get word to him? Effie Rutter: how could she keep the investigation on track? And Louisa: Could she win her back? Find a way to help her? She didn't see how, even once she'd been freed. What a fucking mess. And so pointless.

Rags heard a noise—a scraping or shuffling. She'd hoped it wasn't rats. That would send her around the bend in a way that Terry and Piper never would.

"Rags?"

Rags gasped, hearing her voice spoken from somewhere. Then she knew. "Piers? What the fuck are you doing here?"

Piers appeared from an area back behind the last of the three jail cells. He looked like shit. Unshaven. Dirty, wrinkled clothes. He was dressed like a civilian, in worn jeans and a T-shirt the color of dirty dishwater. And he was, she realized, the source of the terrible smell: sweat, old weed, and she didn't know what else.

"Somebody has to keep an eye on them," Piers said. "That's what I'm doing. Can't trust 'em."

"You mean, you're living here?" Rags asked, trying to understand his situation.

"Yup. Never left really. Or barely. Just long enough to grab some clothes. There's a small storage room at the back that nobody knows about. I can duck in and out without being seen. Grab some food at the café. That sort of thing. It's the only room without a digi-lock."

"What happens when they replace you?" she asked. "They

will, you know. They'll hand-pick somebody to do their dirty work. Maybe their wet work, you know?"

Piers shrugged. "I'll cross that bridge when we come to it."

"Can you get me out of here?"

"I lost the keys to the kingdom, y'know. But I have something for you. I called you earlier, but you didn't pick up."

Piers opened a file on his dataphone and held it up to her at eye level, so she could read it through the bars.

"Holy fucking shit," she said.

"Yup," Piers said.

"Merry? You're absolutely positive?"

"A hundred percent sure. It's a match."

"So Merry's fingerprints are on Effie's pom-pom. Why? Was Merry there when Effie was taken?" Rags gripped the cell bars as a wave of dizziness ran through her. White paint chips stuck to her damp palms.

"Seems so," Piers said. "Unless she handled the pom-pom before all that happened."

"Why on earth would Merry be anywhere near Effie, or the field, or cheerleading practice, or the pom-pom itself? It doesn't make any sense."

"There has to be a reason."

"She has to be brought in for questioning, doesn't she, Piers? Isn't that how this works?"

"Technically, that means I have to turn this report over to Piper and convince him I received it officially before I was canned. Piper *is* the law in Canary, until I'm officially replaced. And even then…"

"Shit," Rags said. "I don't think this is a high priority for Piper. I think he'll sit on it. And anyway, there's one more piece of the puzzle—Effie's dataphone, which I have."

"Wish I could help you, but, you know, I'm no use to anybody now."

Rags suddenly noticed how tired he looked—sad and washed-out. "We'll figure this out," she said, feeling genuinely sorry for him, even if he'd been something of a fuck-up. "Can I borrow your phone?"

The next two days passed by in an uneasy blur. She'd let Flint know she was safe, but he wasn't allowed to visit. Piers could have opened the door from the inside, to let Flint in, but Rags wouldn't put Piers in that position. She'd been able to check with Dineen about the article on the dogs. Dineen told her she had interviewed two people who'd watched the whole thing from their front porches, since their street faced the edge of the athletic field. Rags refused to coddle her; she simply asked her to file the story as soon as possible. Dineen may not have signed up to be a war reporter, but this was the hand she'd been dealt. She called Brent and Ramona and asked them to assess the impact of martial law, as she called it, on Canary's small business community as well as the barter economy. She also asked Brent to find out what the council's plans were for hiring a new peacekeeper. She didn't tell any of them where she was or why.

Piper instructed one of the women in black coveralls to bring her food twice a day and let her out of the cell long enough to go to the toilet and splash water on her face. On the first visit, Rags caught a familiar look in the woman's eyes—like the eyes of a dead fish.

"Camilla?"

"Yeah, so?" Camilla responded, opening the cell just wide enough to give Rags a very stingy bag of food and a small water bottle.

"Why are you on *their* side?" Rags asked her. "Do you really believe all this shit?"

Camilla locked the cell and stepped back. "I didn't really have a fucking choice. They were gonna stone me. I'm a super-spreader, remember?" Her voice was deep with bitterness. "You know what they say, right? If you can't beat 'em, join 'em."

Rags wondered how many more of the jack-booted thugs had been given a "choice" like Camilla, to join up or face some kind of punishment that might barely seem plausible enough to be legally deserved. Not that Camilla was spreading the virus; that was clearly a bald-faced lie. Rags thought perhaps she should feel sorry for all the "recruits," but she couldn't bring herself. There was always a choice, wasn't there?

The jail cell had no cot or mattress. It hadn't been furnished because it had so rarely been used in the last few years. So Rags was forced to sleep sitting up, her back against the wall, her knees drawn up, her head resting on her arms. It was either that or lying down on a filthy cement floor. She dozed uneasily.

The first night, she dreamed she had put on black judge's robes and was sitting high up on a judge's bench, looking down at a sea of masked faces, all of whom were waiting for her to pass judgment. Piper and Terry were below her, in the front row. Flint sat next to them. The three of them chatted so loudly she had to bang the gavel to call the courtroom to order. She was about to issue her sentence when a bomb went off, human limbs flew through the air, and Rags searched frantically for a way out, as bloody arms and legs came at her.

On her second full day of incarceration, she mentally composed an editorial about the implications of imposing martial law in a small town, consolidating law enforcement power in the hands of so few, and the vulnerable position the town was in without a new, and fully independent, peacekeeper. She'd mix in any dire economic news that the freelancers uncovered. She knew she was continuing to beat the same drum over and over, and that was the point. As for exploiting her own situation, there was no payoff; she was not well known in Canary, and those who knew of her, disliked and distrusted her. She'd find no sympathy by talking about her time in jail. She expected many residents, beyond those who actually walked alongside her when she was arrested, would approve of Piper's actions toward her, if they knew.

Rags was relieved that Piers made himself scarce most of the time. He only visited her once after sharing the fingerprint report. She thought she heard him coming and going out the back, but she wasn't sure. She couldn't imagine what he did with his time. She pictured him lying on a dirty cot in the old storage room, smoking dope until the room was thick with it. Did he ponder his future? Think about ways of avenging his dismissal? She didn't know and didn't want to ask.

She was not released until noon on the third day. She'd paced the cell all morning, waiting to be sprung and absolutely helpless to learn when that might be. Piper didn't bother to come but sent Camilla, who did not speak to Rags. She seemed in a rush to unlock the cell and leave the building. Rags wasn't sure why until she herself stepped outside into the summer rain. A convoy of driverless pick-up trucks, all of them black, were snaking along Main Street like a funeral procession, or, Rags thought, like a convoy of tanks ready for battle. The truck beds were filled with men and women in black coveralls, their green discs glowing around their necks. The trucks displayed digital tickers, each one sharing a different message: MASKS SAVE LIVES…KEEP YOUR DISTANCE…CARELESSNESS SPREADS DISEASE…OBEY ALL LAWS. Camilla hopped up into one of the trucks as it passed by. Clearly, she'd come to embrace her new profession. Rags did not spot Terry, Missy, or Keller on the trucks. She thought Terry, in particular, was being very canny about this: she was perhaps picking and choosing when to associate herself publicly with this whole effort. Should Piper fall away from her control, or sphere of influence, she might have plausible deniability and be able to separate herself from him and whatever was happening.

The very last truck in line held just one person: Piper Madrigal, standing out from the others in his green uniform. Piper held an old-fashioned bullhorn and was shouting into it as the truck passed.

"Canary is under attack," Piper blared. "We will keep you safe. Respect authority. Obedience is your best option."

The digital icons of Effie and Jaxson, still affixed to their posts, could not hope to compete with this new, and seemingly more urgent, spectacle.

Rags imagined others coming to the conclusion that those kids were far away from here; perhaps they were safe. And meanwhile, *we* are here, under threat, under siege. First things first. That thinking seemed very much in line with what she'd learned about Canary.

Rags stood on the steps of the peacekeeper's office, next to the old city town hall, and watched the somber parade of black trucks crawling in the gray drizzle. The sidewalks were lined with onlookers, standing apart in their separate yellow circles. For several minutes, the horrifying display of history nearly, and eerily, repeating itself held her spellbound. She felt her left eye begin to twitch and knew she would not be able to get it under control for many hours, if at all.

24

Rags arrived back home wet, filthy, tired, and cramped from sitting in the cell. She wanted a long shower and a nap. But she worried that if she closed her eyes and drifted away, she'd wake up and find the world an even darker place. Flint met her with a hug, wrapping his arms around her tightly, his beard pressing against her cheek.

"Are you okay?" he asked. "Not hurt?" She knew he was watching her eye twitch. She nodded. "Come on." He led her into the kitchen and poured her a tall glass of iced coffee, which she gulped down. "More?" She nodded again and tried to smile as he refilled her glass.

"Isn't it funny," she said. "I was so sure that if we left the city, we'd escape the tentacles of creeping fascism and find ourselves free again. Great plan, huh?"

"Do you want to leave?" Flint asked. "Do you want to go back?"

"Do you?"

"I asked you first." Rags took this to mean that Flint, in his roundabout way, secretly wanted to return to the city, but didn't want to make her choose, or at least, not right away. She couldn't face that conversation. "Canary is not—"

"Easy?" she said.

"Right. It's not easy… But, Rags, you have to admit, you brought this on yourself. All of it. Both arrests. You knew—you had to know—this might happen."

"Oh, like the Jews in Vienna or Lodz knew the Gestapo would round them up and ship them off to the gas chambers?"

"Oh, c'mon," he said. "That's not—that's not the same thing and you know it."

She felt too raw to argue, but how could he not see this the same way she did?

"So it's my fault that the local PHP made a power grab and the head of the town council is a collaborator? It's my fault that they're making shit up so everyone falls in line and does whatever they're told?" She felt her voice rising, penetrating her exhaustion.

"You'd have to be an idiot not to see the risks you took, and the consequences that were staring you in the face," Flint said, "and I know you're not an idiot." He swept her glass off the table and banged it into the sink. "Just be honest."

"You want me to admit that I was asking for it, that I went looking for trouble. That I have a martyr complex."

"Well," Flint said quietly. "You do. Sort of."

"Oh, in that case, all the Jews and Gentiles who fought in the Resistance in World War II, everybody who's ever fought back against fascists, dictators, racists, they're all unnecessary martyrs too? So nobody can honestly fight against injustice without being accused of, like you said, 'asking for it'? Is this what you really, really think, Flint?"

"You're exaggerating."

"I don't think so," Rags said, standing. Every bone in her body ached. "I think you said exactly what you meant." She paused, then looked straight at him, her eye still twitching. "It's so easy for you, isn't it? You've made your own world. And it's small. Very small. And you don't have to play by anybody's rules but your own. Which makes it possible for you to pass judgment on all the mess out there, which never touches you. You want me to be honest? I don't know how you can stand to live like that."

"Rags," Flint said. She could tell from his tone that they were both heading to a place they could not come back from. "I'm sorry. You're exhausted. That wasn't fair."

"I'm sorry too," she said. She felt a stab of dishonesty twisting in her gut. She needed Flint's help. She could not afford to alienate him. She meant what she'd said, and she believed he did too, but she could not walk away from him now, even if she really wanted to, and she didn't know whether she really wanted to. She sank into the ratty armchair in the parlor, seeking a few minutes to herself while he stayed back in the kitchen, burying himself in a recipe. Then she saw the messy pile of *Courant* newspapers stacked on the floor and everything she had to do came flooding back to her. She pushed herself out of the chair and went over to the stack. Kneeling by Flint's desk, she pulled the first issue off the pile and opened it up to the classifieds. She remembered what to look for: three separate ads, each carrying one of three clues to a date, a time, or a place. She ran a dirty index finger along the page. And sure enough, she found something that seemed to make sense. An ad for chartered fishing trips included September 10 in the ad copy. An ad for a vineyard wine-tasting listed five p.m. The third clue, a place name, stumped her until she realized that an ad for a blow-out sale on shoes listed, in small print, the corporate address of the shoe manufacturer. Fresno, California.

Rags sat on the floor, puzzled. Fresno had nothing to do with Canary. This could not logically be an instruction for kidnapping a local child. But what if—Rags almost stopped herself from thinking this through—what if, for some reason, the *Canary Courant* was being used as a conduit for kidnappings, or other horrific acts, not just locally but all over the country? Suddenly, this made sense. The endless ads for expensive charter trips, champagne hot-air balloon rides, and so forth, didn't have anything to do with Canary or its environs. The paper was merely the carrier for secret messages. And the readers of the *Courant* didn't think to question the contents of an advertisement; who would? The scheme was brilliant: ads carry a lot of compact information to which few people actually pay attention, and even fewer would ever think to question or criticize.

I can't handle this. But what if I'm the only one who knows? What then?

Rags felt pinned to the floor, unable to move, weighed down by lack of sleep and this newfound knowledge—assuming she was right. And she was pretty damn sure she was right. It just made sense, suddenly, all of it. She needed now, more than ever, to understand Merry's role in all this and to find out what might be on Effie's dataphone. She figured that whatever she found out about Effie's disappearance would apply to Jaxson's too. Same people, same modus operandi. The other outstanding question was *why*.

As she forced herself up slowly from the floor, something on Flint's desk caught her eye. Louisa's little painting was there, but Flint had propped something up in front of it. She knew he loved that painting, so why would he obscure the view? She leaned in for a closer look. Two small, rough-hewn arrow tips and something that looked like an ivory-colored needle. She glanced toward the kitchen to make sure Flint was still in there, out of sight. She needed to get a closer view of these objects, without touching them. She didn't want to disturb his arrangement because she knew he'd notice any change. The needle, she saw, was made of bone. The tiny arrows were some kind of stone, clearly hand-beaten. These looked like…

Rags gripped the back of Flint's chair. Her heart was pounding. What was the term Louisa had used? *Nighthawker.* Thief. She thought there had to be an explanation. Perhaps Flint had bartered something—a casserole?—for these artifacts. That made perfect sense. He met people when he went food shopping. Of course. Rags began to feel shaky, lightheaded. Too much coffee on an empty stomach. She needed to walk away from this, all of this. She decided to run a cool bath in the old clawfoot tub and soak in it until she found a way to shut out everything and everyone, at least for a little while. The darkening world would still be there, waiting for her, she knew.

25

Flint sat at his desk, staring at his screens but seeing nothing. He had no idea how long he'd sat there, nearly motionless. From time to time, his eyes shifted to the artifacts and the painting. He forced himself to remember what they made him feel. The feelings were still inside him, he knew. Good feelings. Exciting feelings. A way of feeling enlarged in the world. But now these feelings were buried beneath layers of numbing anxiety—an oxymoronic set of feelings that nonetheless seemed accurate. He'd spent most of the last thirty-three years perfecting ways to avoid feeling worried; he found work to be the most reliable coping mechanism, a no-fail way to soothe his nerves, bring down his heart rate, and give him a steady feeling. A feeling that the world was an okay place, and he was okay in it, mostly. This is how he got through most of the years of The Big One.

But for weeks now, this method had been failing him, little by little. It wasn't Rags's fault—not exactly—yet he could not stop himself from blaming her. The crumbling did not begin until he'd met her, until they'd been together a while. And now it was accelerating.

Everything is going wrong.

Flint picked up one of the arrowheads and scraped the tip against his thumb. He did the same thing with the bone awl. They were not sharp. Time and weather had dulled them. But he wanted to connect with a simple feeling, something easy and superficial, like stone and bone on flesh. It was real, anyway. He could name it.

He had expected Rags to give him the silent treatment that morning, after their blow-up the day before, for which he felt sorry and not-sorry. He had slept uncomfortably on the old sofa in the parlor. They each needed space, and they knew it.

He'd heard Rags running her bath, and then an hour or so later, draining it. He'd heard her sink onto the creaking bedframe. She tossed for a while. He imagined going upstairs and making tender love to her, as they did before they moved to Canary. But he was afraid he'd be partly faking it, and he was also afraid she might push him away. He couldn't face either outcome, so he remained downstairs, working a little on a machine learning logic problem, but mainly not working, until even he couldn't hold his eyes open.

She woke him when she found him on the couch in the morning. His right arm had gone numb, pressed beneath his body in the wedge of the sofa. She held out a glass of iced coffee. A peace offering. Perhaps they would speak, after all. Then he saw she held a dataphone in her hand. Not hers. *Oh. We are transacting business.* He sat up and took the coffee. He did not look her in the eye.

"Look," she said. "What I'm asking—it's not about me. It's not about my so-called martyr complex. It really is for Effie. And," she added, turning away from him, "for Maya."

"I get that," he said. "And I get that you want to do the right thing."

"Yes," she said.

He followed her gaze over to his desk. He thought she was looking at the painting, at the things leaning against it. He felt a wave of panic rising in his chest but remained still, gripping the cold coffee. He was imagining that she had noticed the objects and that she knew what he'd done. She hadn't. She couldn't. She had her own shit to deal with. She never thought much about his, that was for sure.

"So I'm asking if you can hack this phone and find the last call Effie made, or the last call made to her. This would be last October. We know the phone was tampered with, when they took her, so it probably won't be easy."

"You know how I feel about this sort of thing. Hacking."

"I do," she said, "but I'm asking you to look past that, for once. Can you?"

Flint sighed and got up off the couch. Rags put the phone on the edge of his desk, where she knew he could not ignore it. And then she left, taking the stack of newspapers with her.

He put the artifacts down after he'd rubbed them a few times. He picked up the phone and disassembled it, popping out the chip, the microphone, and the camera. He logged online to find the factory settings for the phone's make, model, and the serial number etched on the chip, which he was able to view through the magnifying lens built into his own dataphone. He already knew—but had no interest in telling Rags—that the data randomizing security feature on this phone left gaping holes that could be exploited if you knew what to look for. He set up a side communications channel to interact with the device and used the phone's receipts feature to execute a remote code that routed information directly to his computer.

After several minutes of fiddling around with various components and settings, a short audio file popped up on Flint's screen. The file was corrupted—damaged, probably, by the incompetent people that tried to wipe the phone in the first place. But he found a date embedded with the file 10/09/29. He had no idea precisely when Effie was taken, but Rags had said October. He tried cleaning up the message by running the audio file through an AI program that could fill in missing phonemes. He played the file.

Hello? It sounded like a girl's voice. There was a short pause. Flint thought he could actually hear the girl breathing. *Hello?* she said again. Several seconds passed and she hung up. That was the entire message. Flint assumed Rags would be disappointed. Despite everything that had passed between them, he still did not want to let her down. He knew she'd want to know where the call originated. That might be more important than the content of the message itself. He knew this part would take longer. He had to download phone-tracing software to find the caller's number, which he guessed would be anonymous. Then things got much more complicated. He needed to hack into the network management system used by the caller and then triangulate the satellite navigation antennae that would have carried the signal. He could not stop himself from taking perverse pleasure in figuring all this out. Solving problems always made him happy, or near to it, and while he had deeply ambivalent feelings about why he was doing this, it was, he had to admit, fun.

After a few hours had passed, he had an address for where the phone call to Effie originated. He plugged the address into GoogleSoft. When he saw the result, he double-checked to see that he'd entered the street address correctly. It appeared he had. The call came from the crematorium on the outskirts of Canary.

What the fuck?

Flint swept the pieces of the dataphone into a paper bag and removed them from his field of sight. He left the bag on the kitchen table. Rags could do whatever she wanted with it. He didn't care. He didn't understand what she was getting involved in—or what she was involving *him* in, mainly against his will. He would call her and tell her everything he discovered. He didn't want to hold on to that information—to be its sole keeper. Once he dumped it on her, it was going to be her problem.

He felt an irresistible urge to go nighthawking later. To get lost in something that was only his, something that felt clean and apart, and which fed his soul in a way nothing else could.

26

On her way to the office in the morning, Rags sent a message to Porter, asking him to meet her there as soon as he could. Main Street was ominously quietly. The bar and Mellonia were closed, as it was still early. The café, Eat Clean, was glowing neon inside but had no customers. Every two blocks, a sentinel in black coveralls stood inside a yellow circle on the sidewalk, on alternating sides of the street. Each of them was masked and gloved, their green sanitation lights blinking brightly in the morning light. Rags, keeping to the middle of the street, saw that they were armed with stun guns, like the one Piers used to carry. She wondered what orders Piper, and perhaps Terry, had issued to them about when they could, and should, fire their weapons. She wondered how much they were being paid to stand there—time that might otherwise have been spent bartering or hustling a more innocent gig. What would she herself need to do to provoke them? What if she were to hurl a stone at Effie Rutter's digital face? Would that set them off? Probably not. What if she were to spit on their shoes? Get back a little of her own. That might work. She was still unmasked, yet none of the sentinels seemed interested in speaking to her or re-arresting her. They really were behaving like programmed robots. She was tempted to provoke them, but she knew she could not take such a risk.

The street was even more quiet without the ever-present packs of wild dogs sniffing for garbage and drinking street puddles. She wondered what had become of the dead dogs; whether they had been hauled away and dumped into a big hole somewhere, or perhaps fed into a woodchipper for fertilizer. They did not end up at the crematorium, as there had been no smoke coming out of there. Everyone would have seen the smoke.

A sentinel had been posted just outside the *Courant* office. *Shit.* Rags was determined not to let this person inside the building. She would fight, if necessary, to keep this *thug* out of her domain.

"What the fuck do you want?" Rags asked, stepping into the sentinel's personal space. Rags could tell by the shoulder-length light brown hair and slight build that this was a woman behind the face-covering respie. The woman took a step back, putting more air between the two of them. She could have been anyone: a hairdresser, an accountant, a mom.

"I'm here to protect you," the sentinel replied.

"Bullshit. You're here to spy on me."

"Obey the law and you'll be fine."

"And if I don't?"

"Do you want to go back to jail?" the sentinel asked. Clearly, then, everyone knew about her recent stay. Rags still had no intention of wearing a respie and it appeared that the sentinel had been instructed not to make that an issue. Perhaps they were all waiting for her to make a bigger mistake, something showy, something Piper could use to make an even more public example of the punishment in store for rule-breakers.

"Are you sick?" Rags asked. The sentinel shook her head. "Know anyone who is? I mean, really sick, like before?" She shook her head again. "Then what the fuck are you so afraid of?" The sentinel looked away without further comment. "Thought so," Rags said.

She walked into the office, telling herself to ignore the unwanted guard and get on with business. She returned the old newspapers to the archive, and before she'd even had time to turn on her screen, she heard Porter pull up in his pick-up. She hoped the sentinel would not interfere; she certainly had no grounds to do so. Porter knocked before entering. He was the only one who ever did that. She called for him to come in. He looked the same as always, like a sad reed blowing in the wind. For once, the boy was not with him. Perhaps Porter had someone he could count on to look after the kid, after all. Or perhaps he left the child to fend for himself. She asked him to sit by her desk, which he seemed to do reluctantly.

"What do you make of that *creature* out there?" she asked.

"They're gonna do what they're gonna do," he said, shrugging. "Can't stop 'em."

"Doesn't it bother you, even a little? Do you have any idea what it's all *for*?" She wanted to shake him loose from his apathy. But he remained a cipher. "Is your boy doing okay?"

"What do you need, Ms. Goldner?"

Rags gave up. Porter seemed to be an empty vessel into which anyone could pour their own needs and desires, which he would fulfill, and once discharged, he would be ready for a refill. He was nearly inert, like a bottle. She knew, without dwelling on it, that this was a disrespectful way to think about someone. But she'd reached a point where every action was a means to an end, and the morality could be debated later. And he wasn't going to yield, anyway. At least he hadn't joined up with *them*. She was counting on his neutrality, or apathy, or both.

"Two things," she said. "The easy one first. When you pick up the papers at the printing press, are there extra copies printed that you don't bring back to Canary? Bundles that you leave behind?"

"Yeah," he said. "So?"

"Every time? All the time?"

"For the last couple years, I'd say."

"Do you have any idea where these extra papers go? Did you ever see anybody pick them up?"

"I don't have any reason to hang around at the press. I just get the bundles for the subscribers, and I leave. The rest isn't my business."

"So you know there are extra copies printed—you've seen them," she said. "But you don't know why, what they're for, or who picks them up."

"Nope."

Rags believed him. Porter's apathy was his best defense. He just didn't seem to give a shit in general. Why would he involve himself in something messy? He wasn't the type. At least he'd confirmed her suspicion: the *Canary Courant* was distributed to places outside Canary, presumably so that the people involved could track the advertisements and follow their hidden instructions.

"Okay. Now the second thing." Rags took a deep breath. Tears stung her eyes—taking her completely by surprise. She couldn't stand the idea that Porter was seeing her this way. She walked away from him. "The second thing," she repeated. Her breathing did not feel normal. "I want you to follow my partner, Flint Sten. At night. When he goes out. Can you do that?" She still did not turn to face him.

"When?" Porter asked.

"I don't know, exactly. Maybe you could try tonight. He won't leave before midnight. And if he doesn't go tonight, then maybe tomorrow night. I can't be more specific." She knew that he trusted her to pay him fairly, and that he'd accept whatever amount she'd offer. "This is important," she said, finally turning back to face Porter. "It could affect a lot of people."

"Okay," he said. "I'll let you know what I find out. That it?" Porter was already heading for the door. Rags nodded and he slipped out quickly. Rags wondered if the sentinel was keeping track of everyone coming and going to the office so she could report back to Piper. She hated having eyes on her, but what could she do?

Later that morning, Flint called to tell her what he'd learned from hacking Effie's dataphone. Rags had trouble concentrating because of the sick feeling in the pit of her stomach triggered by her own guilty conscience. She had to remind herself that Flint had put her in this position—sort of—forcing her to find out if he was doing something he shouldn't. Something that might be hurting the only other person she truly cared about in Canary—Louisa. She was well aware of the cold irony of the situation: the sentinel spying on her, as she turned around to spy on her one and only lover. But none of this was her doing.

Little by little, what Flint told her sank in. The brief call to

Effie came from the crematorium. Someone hiding out there? Did this have anything to do with what Piers had caught on the building's security camera? And the call to Effie: It seemed the only logical reason for the call was to confirm her location for the kidnappers. That call must have taken place moments before she was taken away. She told Flint she really appreciated what he had done, and she acknowledged it could not have been easy for him.

"But just one more thing. Just one," she said to him on the phone.

"I'm done, Rags. I really don't want to take this any further. I don't think you understand that I could lose all of my clients over something like this. I don't think you've thought about that, even once."

"No, you're right. But—"

"There is no 'but,' Rags."

"But you're no saint, Flint."

"What's that supposed to mean?" he said. She pictured him at his desk, staring at Louisa's picture, probably.

"Oh, well, you know," she said, rushing on. She thought she'd said just enough. "I have to get back inside the crematorium. Which means, I need you to hack the digi-locks—all of them, inside and out—and send me the codes."

"Is that all?" he said, his voice rough with sarcasm. "Just hack the codes and give them to you? Jesus, Rags, you really are stepping in a steaming pile of shit, aren't you?"

"That's beside the point. And *you're* beside the point too. This isn't about either of us crossing lines. There's nobody out for justice here. We have to do something. *I* have to do something—and like or not, I can't do it without your help."

There was a long pause. She gave him time to process.

"This really is the very last time," he said. "That's not negotiable."

"I know," she said. "Just do it now and be done with it. Okay?"

Flint mumbled something and hung up. She knew he was

furious but so was she—not just at him, and his potential betrayal, but at the entire situation. She really did think this was shaping up as a battle between good and evil, and good seemed to be losing.

Dineen's story about the killing of the dogs had come in. Rags spent the next hour cleaning it up, writing a headline ("Canine Killing Field Shocks Residents"), and choosing which photos to run with it. The two people Dineen had interviewed were indeed shocked and frightened by what they'd witnessed. Yet neither of them had tried to interfere, either. And that was Canary in a nutshell, she thought. Dineen had also dutifully obtained a statement from Piper ostensibly explaining why the slaughter had been necessary. The statement said something vague about "animal-borne disease vectors." Rags edited the piece to subtly raise doubts and questions about the PHP's perspective. Once she'd finished that, she drafted the editorial she'd sketched out in her head when she was in jail. *You're right, Flint: I am asking for trouble.*

Her phone pinged and she picked it up immediately. Flint had come through with the codes. She left the office and headed for the peacekeeper's office. She looked over her shoulder to see if the sentinel would follow her. Fortunately not. By now, there were more people out on the street. There was a long line out the door to Mellonia, and no wonder. If a new pandemic was brewing—as people seemed to believe, despite the lack of any credible evidence—many of them would want to get through it as numbed out as possible. Two sentinels monitored the line of customers, which hardly seemed necessary, as everyone was behaving like sheep, standing patiently within their spaced-out circles. The Canary Bar & Grill was also lively. Rags wondered if both Merry and Keller were inside, but she wouldn't stop to find out. Why hadn't the PHP, or Terry, shut down the bar if they wanted to play into people's fears about a new virus? No sooner did she pose the question to herself than she realized how deeply cynical these fascists really were. They knew the town would more easily fall in line with their wishes if they left a couple of loopholes open. Preserving people's strong desire for social drinking and flirtation helped ensure that they would cooperate in other ways—even if they didn't realize they'd struck that bargain.

When she arrived at the old office building, she walked around back, looking for the door she thought Piers must use to get in and out of the storage room. The back of the building was pure nineteenth century: rotting wood eaves, peeling paint, and a door with an old, tarnished brass knob—no digi-lock attached. She banged hard on the door with the heel of her hand and flecks of white paint fell to the ground, just as they had from the iron bars of her cell. She hoped that Piers was still holding it together. She banged a few more times, keeping her eyes peeled for anyone in black coveralls. Finally, Piers cracked the door open a few inches. When he realized it was Rags, he motioned for her to come inside. The back of the building was dark, and the stench was almost unbearable. Perhaps a rat or a raccoon had died inside somewhere. Perhaps Piers had stopped practicing any personal hygiene. He looked worse than ever and older than she remembered. Most of his remaining black hair was gone. He stank, as always, of weed.

"We're going back to the crematorium," she said.

"Why? What for?"

"I'll explain on the way. Meet me at the far end of Haymarket in fifteen minutes." They both knew that Haymarket Street was at the southeastern edge of town, as far from prying eyes as they could get on foot. That's where Rags would send the ShareCar.

"I'm no use to you, Rags. Go without me."

"No," she said, grabbing his wrist. "You're coming. Don't be a wuss." Piers brushed his hand over his non-existent hair. She knew he'd be there.

Once inside the ShareCar, Rags suggested they both sit on the floor as a precaution so that no one would spot them. Piers awkwardly folded his bulky frame. She explained what Flint had discovered on Effie's dataphone. When they got to the crematorium, Rags instructed the car to pull around back and tuck into the alcove at the loading dock. That way, the vehicle could not possibly be spotted from the street. She didn't think they'd been followed but she wasn't taking any chances. She used the hacked codes to get them inside.

"Now what?" Piers asked. "It's your show."

"The side door—the one we couldn't open before," she said. "Let's try that."

Their footsteps echoed softly as they crossed the cavernous room. Rags made a point of not looking directly at the cold furnace. Instead, she kept her eyes fixed on the metal door ahead. The digi-lock obeyed her command, blinking from red to green. Piers used both hands to pull the heavy door open. The room was pitch black, so Rags turned on her dataphone light. She swung it back and forth several times, giving them both time to process what they were looking at. Weapons. Real ones, on racks filling the entire room, which was the size of a generous walk-in closet. Assault rifles, Rags guessed. She didn't know one gun from another.

"AS50s, SA80s," Piers began, taking inventory. "AK-74s."

This is why I brought you along.

"Holy shit," she said.

"Holy shit is right," Piers said.

"Any guesses?"

"Do you think the shadows put them here?" he asked. "The shadows from the security camera?"

"Who else?" she said. "You ever seen anything like this in Canary?"

"Never. There's nothing in the files, either."

"What would you do now, if you were still…you know," Rags said.

"Take pictures. Lift prints. Look for serial numbers. But I can tell you now, we can take the pictures, but even if we could check for prints, we wouldn't find any. I'm betting the serial numbers are illegible too." Piers tugged the bottom of his shirt and used it in place of gloves to lift a rifle off the rack and inspect it. "See here? The serial number's been filed off. Low-tech, but effective."

"So they're not traceable."

"Right."

Rags took several pictures and sent them to Porter with a note that he should not delete them. Then she erased the photos from her dataphone.

"Let's go," she said. "We're done here."

Piers set the rifle carefully back on the rack. He didn't bother to tuck his shirt in. He pulled the door behind them and Rags reset the lock, waiting to see the red light blinking before turning away.

"What are you going to do?" Piers asked her as they crouched in the ShareCar.

"Aren't you awfully cramped in that shitty storage room?" she asked him. "Wouldn't you like to spread out more?"

"What are you talking about, Rags?"

"I think you should move into the crematorium. Think of it as a stake-out. You already know how to avoid the cameras so they capture nothing but shadows. You explained it to me, remember? There are other rooms you can get into. I'll give you the codes."

"You're kidding," he said.

"No, not at all. You're still really useful, see? The minute something happens, you call me."

"And then?"

"I have no idea," she said. "We'll just have to see."

27

After his phone call with Rags, Flint threw himself into work. Ten hours straight, no break, like the old days. He centered himself by probing for vulnerabilities and contradictions in a complex army logistics supply chain that involved a dozen countries and scores of ports and depots. He still loved the work but was well-aware that his motivation had changed—at least temporarily. He told himself that if he completed two sprints, he could return to the Potrero Complex that night. *For the last time. Because this isn't me.*

Rags came home and they looked at one another from a distance. Flint had not cooked. He remained at his desk while she foraged in the kitchen. He heard the distinctive *plomp* of the cork being pulled from the whiskey bottle. After a while, he came in and sat with her. He poured himself a whiskey. They sat together, still not talking.

He wanted to say: *Part of me still loves you.*

He wanted to say: *I don't think I can keep doing this.*

He wanted Rags to give him a sign that she was still holding on to something that belonged to both of them. But all she said was that she had editing and writing to do, and she'd do it on her laptop in bed. He nodded and watched her bring a full glass of whiskey with her as she headed upstairs.

It is what it is.

He sat in the worn armchair in the parlor for a long time, watching the late summer night sky deepen from dark blue to blue-black. It was a clear night, less humid than it had been. He took that as a sign: he would go out. *To say goodbye. To deny this thing its hold on me.*

He thought he saw headlights trailing the ShareCar once he was out on the two-lane country road. But the lights disappeared, and he did not think about it again. He thought, instead, about what he might find that night on his dig. He felt a surge of excitement, like a kid going on a scavenger hunt, confident the treasure is out there somewhere, waiting to be discovered. He walked to the far side of the clearing, pacing back and forth, shining his head lamp as though it were some sort of divining rod guiding him to a special patch of earth. He stopped once, then twice, when he thought he heard faint crackles, like footsteps crunching dry branches. He held his breath for several seconds before resuming his search. The woods were in constant motion, he reminded himself, never still, always evolving.

Finally, he picked his spot, though he could not have said what made it special. He took out his folding shovel and began carefully turning over the earth beneath the wild grasses. The head lamp provided a concentrated circle of white light, blinding him to everything outside his peripheral vision. Someone might have stood ten feet from him while he was kneeling on the ground, digging, and he would never see them. He dug a number of holes at close range, more than usual, as he was determined not to leave empty-handed. Once a hole was made, he used his hands to sift through clumps of dirt. Finally, about ten inches down from the surface of a hole, he grasped something that felt both hard and delicate. He carefully wiped the dirt off the piece, which was curved and fit easily in the palm of his hand. He studied the material—mottled brown and yellow squares, not geometrically aligned, but close enough to form a pattern. The pattern was familiar, but he couldn't place it. He felt a delicious sense of anticipation, looking forward to figuring out what his latest find had been, or what it represented. He put the object in the cloth bag and refilled all the holes. He retreated to the edge of the clearing, where the woods were slightly denser, and turned off the head lamp. The moon was bright, and he knew the way by heart.

"Thank you," he said out loud to the woods, feeling foolish and yet compelled. "I'll say goodbye now."

Back in the ShareCar, he took the object from the cloth bag and inspected it again. Of course. It looked like a turtle shell; the pattern was unmistakable. The curvature suggested it belonged to a small cup or bowl. He put it back into the bag. This one would not join the others alongside Louisa's picture. This one would remain hidden, for his eyes only.

Back out on the road, Flint again thought he caught a flash of headlights about half a mile behind him. But so what? There was no reason to think he would be the only one traveling on a summer night. The ShareCar pulled up to the curb in front of his house and he was hugely startled to see Rags coming toward him. She was never awake at this hour. She held something large and roundish in her hand and for a moment he was confused, as if she too had gone digging for artifacts and wanted to show him her own treasure. But no.

"Too bad you missed all the excitement," she said in that way she had when things were happening, not good things, and she spoke as matter-of-factly as possible. While underneath, he knew, lay a deep, unquenchable rage. "Somebody sent this rock," she held it out to him, "flying through the window." She pointed to the front window, the one that looked out onto the damaged cherry trees from the parlor. Flint could just make out the shattered glass and the hole the rock had made as it sailed into the house.

"My God," he said. "Are you all right? You weren't hit?" He reached out for the rock, but she held onto it. "Rags, I'm so sorry. I'm so, so sorry I wasn't here to—"

"The best part is, a note was wrapped around the rock," she continued. "So low-tech and yet so effective."

"What did the note say?" Flint stood on the walkway, his bag on his shoulder. He had not even had a chance to dismiss the ShareCar.

"Back off."

"That's all? Just 'back off'?"

"Isn't that enough?" She bounced the rock in her hand. "It was for me, not you."

"I should have been here," he said.

"It doesn't matter. You're not a barking watchdog scaring

away burglars. They're gonna do what they're gonna do, whether you're here or not."

"But still." He felt all wrong and helpless with her. He had no idea what to say.

"You may as well come inside," she said, as though that was just one option. Flint sent the ShareCar away and followed Rags back into the house.

"Tomorrow, I'll figure out how to fix the window," he said, carefully picking up shards of glass off the floor. "I might have to barter for it. I'm not sure." Rags got the broom and dustpan and they cleaned up together. They left the hole alone.

"I know where you were tonight," Rags said. "What you've been doing."

Flint got the feeling she wanted him to feel dirty. He fought against that. He wanted to hold on to the pure feeling he had about the Potrero Complex. He wanted to explain it to her, but he couldn't find the right words fast enough. All he could manage to ask her was how she knew. She told him she'd had him followed, and she'd already been given a full report of the night's activities. He remembered the headlights behind him, in both directions. The thought of someone getting that close *did* make him feel dirty and shameful. As if someone had spied on him masturbating to a raunchy porn vid.

How did this get so twisted?

He was relieved when Rags did not seem interested in probing him further. She didn't pummel him with questions as to why he did what he did. And he knew, as well as she, what came next. She picked up the artifacts on his desk—the arrow tips and the bone awl.

"These are going home," she told him. "I'm taking them myself, tomorrow."

Flint nodded. It was all he could manage. He was relieved that the cloth bag containing the fragment of the turtle shell bowl was still in his pocket. Something, after all, still belonged to him. After Rags went upstairs, he sat in the armchair, staring at the broken window. If that rock had hit Rags, everything would have turned out differently. She would have needed him. They might have gotten past this and let the emergency carry them to a new place. But that was wishful thinking. He felt something inside him begin to close up, like a collapsing black hole that pulls all the light into it. He felt an ending. And for the first time in his adult life, he cried.

28

Flint had slept on the couch again, Rags supposed, though she couldn't say for sure whether he slept much at all. His eyes were closed, at least, when she came down in the morning. One leg was on the floor, the other dangled over the worn upholstered arm of the furniture. His hair was long and his beard unkempt. There was a lost quality to him that reminded her, for a split second, of Piers Olsson. She made coffee in the kitchen and sat at the table drinking it alone. She did not intend to bring Flint a cup and wake him up. Not today.

Moments from their life together flickered: Their first time making love; eating pizza on the floor of their city apartment; the way he gently laid his thumb to still her wildly twitching eye. Who was he now? Who was she? What was happening? She drained her cup and left it on the table. She picked up the paper bag holding the artifacts he had stolen. *Yes, my partner is a thief. A thief in the night.* She went out the backdoor because she didn't trust herself to look at him again, lying there. She felt on the verge of either bursting into tears or screaming at him.

Main Street was as quiet as the crematorium. The black-clothed sentinels—*Call them thugs, call them collaborators, because that's what they are*—were stationed inside the circles on both sides of the street. Rags walked down the center of Main Street, as before, thinking up all the ways she might provoke them. She wanted to shake them out of their blind complacency. She wanted to yell to each of them: *Don't you see how you're being used? Don't you see you are protecting nothing but fascist authority? Don't you see you are betraying your own neighbors?* But rattling these idiots would have to wait. She noted that she still was not wearing a respie and they still were letting her get away with it. She was convinced, now, that Piper must have given them specific instructions where she was concerned. She had a target on her back, and *fuck them.*

Rags turned down the alley to Louisa Copperface's gallery. It was still early, not yet eight in the morning, but she didn't care. This couldn't wait. She got an eyeful of the glowing pink wall, but this time, it did not fill her with anything like joy or relief. It seemed out of place, like it belonged in some other town, far from Canary. Rags gently tried the handle. Classic Louisa: Never mind that the world was falling to pieces, she didn't bother to lock the door to her white kingdom, as if nothing, and no one, could ever spoil it. Rags thought Louisa was a fool to be so trusting, or else so cavalier, but she also admired her for it. As if Louisa, too, were saying *fuck you* to all the insanity. As if it couldn't touch her.

Rags crept in quietly. The gallery was lit only by the morning light filtering down through the skylights. The space felt, as always, clean and beautiful. That had not changed, and Rags was still moved by it. She studied the work hung on the walls. Acrylic abstracts with thick cross-hatches of primary colors that looked as though they'd been slashed across the canvas in a blinding hurry, and as if they were still racing to the edges of the frame. On the far wall, something completely different: a huge version of the miniature Louisa had given to her and Flint. A realistically painted forest, the trees slim and spaced apart, allowing sunlight to penetrate the forest floor, where wild green underbrush grew in a tangle of grassy spears. This must be the sacred land, Rags thought, where Louisa's ancestors had made a home over half a millennium ago. She wondered how they had coped with crisis and betrayal in their midst—and all the flawed human impulses that transcended time, place, and culture. She peered into the bag, making sure none of the artifacts had been damaged on the way over.

The lights flickered on, and Rags turned around, startled. Louisa came out from the far side of the gallery, beyond the partition separating her studio. Rags guessed she must live in an apartment above the gallery. Rags had never bothered to ask and she'd never been invited up. Louisa wore silky pink pajama bottoms and a cropped T-shirt. Her thick black hair hung loosely down her back. Her feet were bare.

"What are you doing here, Rags?" Louisa did not sound happy. "It's one thing to drop in casually during the day, but this is—this feels intrusive. You tripped the security system. Scared the shit out of me."

Rags noticed for the first time very small blinking lights set way up in the recessed corners of the gallery's ceiling. So Louisa was not nearly as cavalier as Rags had thought. Of course. She had a right to protect her work.

"I'm sorry, Louisa. But this couldn't wait." Rags held out the paper bag.

"What?" Louisa said, sounding more inhospitable than ever. She was still clearly angry with Rags for seeming to ignore her request to find time to write and publish an article about the desecration at the Potrero Complex.

"I have something that belongs to you," Rags said. "To you and others, I suppose." Rags lifted out the arrow tips and the bone awl and held them in the flat of her palm. Louisa came closer. When she saw them, she let out a small cry.

"How did you—?" Louisa's dark eyes flashed with anger. Rags could tell that Louisa knew exactly what these objects were and where they had come from.

"I didn't," Rags said quickly. "I didn't know anything about this, Louisa."

"You'd better tell me the truth, or we are done," Louisa said, taking the objects from Rags. "I mean, really done."

The two of them stood in the center of the gallery while Rags explained that once she'd seen the artifacts on Flint's desk, propped up against Louisa's picture, she didn't want to believe he'd been responsible for trespassing on sacred turf—especially after Louisa had been so generous to them both. She explained about hiring Porter to follow him, to confirm her suspicion. There was no doubt, Rags told her, that Flint was the nighthawker. He was digging all the holes at the Potrero Complex.

"Flint?" Louisa said. "Your Flint? But *why*?"

"I don't know."

"He didn't tell you?"

"He won't," Rags said. "Maybe he can't. I'm not sure."

"I'm not letting him get away with this, Rags. He needs to be punished. We have to discourage other nighthawkers. But…my God…how did he figure out where to dig? That information is incredibly private. It's not published anywhere."

"He's very resourceful, Louisa," Rags said. "When he wants to learn about something, nothing can stop him."

"You can't stand in my way, Rags. I'm telling you now. I'm warning you. And I want the painting back. I can't let it sit with him, with either of you. It's not right. It's hugely disrespectful."

"Louisa, I came here to apologize to you. To tell you how incredibly sorry I am that I failed you. That I couldn't find a way to tell your story. It's not because I don't care. It's because…" She didn't want to give Louisa a sob story about being in jail, about trying to face down Piper and find Effie Rutter. She didn't want to seem like she was making excuses—and minimizing Louisa's concerns. "Well, Flint and I, we're not… I'm leaving him. Or he's leaving me."

Saying this out loud, Rags felt as if she'd been gut-punched.

"Over this?" Louisa asked.

"It's complicated." The two stood in silence. "Louisa," Rags said quietly. "I don't want this to come between us. I want…I want us to be friends. Is that possible?"

Louisa put her arm around Rags's shoulder. "You look exhausted," she said. "Come upstairs and I'll make coffee." Rags was ready to cry. But she wouldn't. She just couldn't. So she simply nodded and followed Louisa. Her apartment above and behind the gallery was small and filled with a jumble of paintings, drawings, and sculptures—her own and others. Louisa volunteered that the artifacts, which she carefully wrapped in a soft cloth, would be returned to the Potrero Complex in a private ceremony involving only tribal members who lived in the area. And she told Rags that she did not ever want to discuss this land with her again, and that whatever she and others she consulted decided to do about Flint, would be none of Rags's business. Rags assured her she would not speak about it again. Then Louisa changed the subject.

"I want to paint you for my persons in crisis series," she said. Rags conjured an image of the portraits of Effie and Jaxson that she had seen months ago in Louisa's studio. She thought they must still be back there, awaiting some kind of parallel fate. "I think you sort of owe me."

"But I'm not in crisis," Rags said.

"Oh no?" Louisa said. "Then you're doing a damn fine imitation."

"Really, I'm fine. There's a lot going on but…nothing I can't handle."

"Still, I'm asking." Rags shrugged. She gave Louisa a noncommittal 'yes' and hoped she could put her off as long as possible, maybe forever. They parted on good terms. And while Rags felt relieved, she didn't feel better.

An hour after walking into the gallery uninvited, Rags was back out on the street. The daily line outside Mellonia was already forming. The township meetings that had been held over the spring were somber but certainly not silent, she recalled. But now, it seemed no one was talking. They just stood there waiting, silent as upright corpses, shuffling forward a few feet every several minutes. She could practically smell the waves of defeat, of hopelessness, radiating from them. The thugs were at their posts with nothing to do. Of course. What was there for them to do except tacitly and silently terrorize people? Or at least remind them that they were under threat—though the threat had yet to actually materialize. But the people of Canary, Rags realized, were already primed to expect the worst and therefore were already preparing themselves physically and mentally. Piper had lit a match—and the tinder was already parched and ready to receive the flame. These people were burning up, turning to ash, right in front of her.

She would go to the office and do the only concrete thing

she could do while staying out of jail. She would try to put together a newspaper, lining up the facts as best she could and blasting the truth—on the editorial page—as straightforwardly as possible. Her job felt somehow inadequate, too small for the task at hand. But it was the only thing more or less in her control. Her dataphone made a specific beeping sound and she knew right away that it must be another broadcast message, which meant more bad news was on the way. She stopped to read it and saw everyone in line at Mellonia doing the same thing.

From: The Town Council of Canary
To: All Canary Residents

In keeping with our efforts to safeguard all residents, we are implementing all possible measures to forestall and, if necessary, contain new virus outbreaks. To this end, we are announcing that, effective immediately, all bartering will be subject to regulation. Everyone participating in barter systems must register for a permit and submit all trade data to the Council's database. A transaction fee of 3 percent will be levied on all trades. There is a one-time fee of 15 e-credits to register for a bartering license. All revenues will support our efforts to implement the MEPA and protect community health.

Rags's first thought on reading it was a strong hunch, probably unprovable in the short run: Terry intended to control all the revenues that would be generated by regulated bartering and this would constitute a de facto slush fund with no oversight. After all, there was hardly any governmental infrastructure in town at this point, so who, or what, would oversee this money trail? She also believed that the minute Canary's bartering trade was forced out into the open, much of it would dry up. This would put a lot of people in jeopardy, to the point where people could actually get very, very hungry. She thought of Porter and wondered how he'd feel about turning his private economic system inside out. She couldn't imagine he'd want to comply.

What would that do to his ability to earn a livelihood and feed his son? And then there was the question of compliance: who was going to make sure that trades were recorded and reported? Rags thought the answer was obvious: Piper's army, or whatever you want to call it. What was to stop them from prowling people's backyards? Looking in their garbage cans? Peering into windows and sheds?

Wasn't it obvious now? Rags wondered. Piper and Terry were tightening a noose around the neck of the town—around her neck—and she sensed that she could be arrested or swept up in a raid at any point, for any reason. For all she knew, she had only hours of freedom left before new charges were levied against her and she was thrown back in jail. The paper would have to wait. Writing the truth would have to take a back seat to actually living it. Rags knew she had to act now on what she knew about the Effie Rutter case, or she might never get the chance again. She sent out a broadcast text of her own to Evelyn Rutter, Tim and Roger Fallon, Keller, Merry, and Piers. She told them all to meet her at the far end of the athletic field, where the footpath left the field toward the woods. She said she had urgent new information about the missing children. She had to hope this would be enough to convince all of them—especially Merry—to show up.

Rags headed to the footpath, keeping an eye on the sentinels to make sure they were not interested in following her. She still seemed to have freedom of movement, but she remained convinced that would not last much longer. She thought about what she would say once they were all assembled. Merry's fingerprints on the pom-pom: that was the bomb she needed to explode in their midst and see how it landed. She reached the meeting spot first and began pacing rapidly back and forth, kicking up small rocks and dried leaves to release the nervous energy rocketing through her. She vividly remembered finding the pom-pom just three weeks ago. So much had happened since then. Once everyone fell even further in line with the clamp-down under way, life in Canary would become more intolerable than it already was. Rags worried that within a few days, pursuing justice for Effie Rutter, let alone Jaxson Turner, would be impossible. There would be no one to turn to and no avenue of recourse.

And then they came. First Roger and Tim Fallon, looking angry and tense with worry. Then Evelyn Rutter, walking slowly from the far side of the footpath—the very path that Effie used to walk every day through the woods when she left the field after cheerleading practice. Surely Evelyn was thinking about how she was retracing her daughter's steps, placing her own feet where Effie's had been. Then Keller, limping slowly, with Merry by his side.

Rags realized, with a pang, that they were all wearing respies. On some level, they must have believed all the unfounded rumors about a fresh disease outbreak. Between the dog killings, the warning slogans, the first street convoy, and the posted sentinels, they'd been persuaded to take precautions. Their respies proclaimed their feelings of defenselessness against an enemy that had yet to materialize. Yet there was no point in challenging them now.

"I told her she had to," Keller spoke up first, in a rusty voice, glancing at Merry. "I told her she couldn't stay silent any longer." Merry's eyes were dark and hollow with distress. Her long gray hair appeared tangled and unwashed.

Rags said nothing, waiting for Piers to show. She wanted him there to corroborate her, to back her up. She didn't have the pom-pom or any of the paperwork with her. She'd have to persuade everyone she was telling the truth. And that's why she needed Piers. He was the only other person who knew.

But Roger and Tim would not stay silent.

"Why are *you* the one calling us out here?" Tim said. "What's this got to do with you?"

"You better not be jerking us around," Roger added. "Or asking us a bunch of questions. We've already told you everything we know. We're not the villains here."

"Nobody's blaming you for anything," Rags said. "Just be patient a little while—"

"Rags!" Piers came loping across the field. Thank God he

was *not* wearing a respie. He was holding up his hand as if he wanted to halt their proceedings before they'd begun. But Rags was ready to begin now that he was here, and she couldn't afford to hold off any longer. "Wait!" he said before Rags could speak.

"Piers, we may not have much time. I need to—"

"You already know, then?" he asked, looking startled.

"Know what?" Rags said.

"What's going on?" Roger said, looking back across the field, ready to bolt.

"I saw the whole thing," Piers said, breathing hard. "Piper has put together some kind of…army…I don't know what else to call it. They loaded weapons, real weapons, rifles, into their black pick-ups and they're heading down Main Street in a convoy."

"Now?" Rags asked. "Right now?"

"How many people are sick?" Roger asked. "Should we even be here?"

"Roger's right," Tim said. "It's not safe."

"It's not safe anywhere in Canary, but not for the reason you think," Rags said sharply.

"They've been storing weapons in the crematorium," Piers said.

"The crematorium?" Evelyn said faintly. "What's this got to do with Effie?"

"It's got nothing to do with Effie," Rags said. "Or Jaxson. That's why I need you here, now, because time is running out."

"Where are they headed?" Keller asked. Merry remained stonily silent.

"I'm guessing they're headed…here…to the field…to muster," Rags said.

"This is where they shot the dogs, remember?" Piers said. "It's the only wide-open space in town. Perfect for putting on a show of force."

"For sending a message," Rags added. "So listen to me. I found one of Effie's pom-poms in the woods a few weeks ago, right over there." She pointed. Evelyn let out a little cry. "It had Merry's fingerprints on it." Merry immediately looked down at the ground.

"It's true," Piers said. "I handled the report myself."

"What really happened here, Merry?" Rags asked. Everyone looked at Merry.

"It's time to tell," Keller said to her softly. "You must hope for the best."

"Shame on you, Merry, if you know something about Effie and didn't come forward!" Evelyn said. "Shame on you!" Evelyn took a step toward Merry and looked ready to assault her.

All eyes were on Merry as she began to speak, but Rags grew concerned as she saw another person making their way very slowly across the field, coming toward them. She didn't think it was one of Piper's thugs, given the way this person stopped and started on the field, but she couldn't be certain. As the stranger approached, Rags thought it was a young woman, carrying something balled up under her arm.

"My daughter, Tiffany," Merry began, her voice shaking. "I told everyone she moved to Pittsburgh to become a massage therapist. But that was a lie." She took a ragged breath. "I got a call from a stranger. He said they took her, they were putting her in service. I didn't understand. But he told me if I told anyone else, they'd kill her. And he told me if I didn't help them take more kids, younger kids, they'd kill her. What could I do?" Merry began to sob. "Evelyn, you're a mother. You have to understand."

"What did you do to Effie, Merry?"

"And to Jaxson?" Roger said, gripping Tim's hand.

"I was here when the van took Effie," Merry said. "They made me come. If I didn't, Tiffany would be dead. I picked up Effie's pom-pom. I wanted to get rid of it. I threw it into the woods. I couldn't bear to hold it."

"I should have found it—the pom-pom," Piers said, "but I didn't. If I had, we wouldn't be standing here now."

"Yes, I'm ashamed of myself for doing that," Merry said.

"But I didn't have a choice, see? And I still don't know what's become of her. For all I know, she's dead or dying, and I still have to live with what I've done."

"Did they hurt her?" Evelyn asked, grabbing the much larger Merry by the arm. "Did *you* hurt her?"

Merry shook her head. "They drugged her, I think, and put her in the van," she said. "I don't think she felt a thing." She glanced at Tim and Roger. "I don't know anything about Jaxson, but it must've happened the same way."

"Liar!" Evelyn screamed and slapped Merry's face. Merry didn't move. She simply put her hand to her cheek and stood there.

"Tell them about the ads, Merry," Rags said. By now, the strange woman was halfway across the field. And right behind her came the convoy of black pick-up trucks. The riders in their black coveralls jumped out onto the field, a rifle strapped across every chest. Everyone turned around when they heard the trucks, except Merry, who appeared numb.

"I told you," Piers said.

"We have to move," Rags said. "Evelyn, your house is the closest."

"But I don't want—" Evelyn looked sharply at Merry. "She's not welcome."

The sound of someone barking orders to the armed group floated across the field. It had to be Piper, Rags thought, though she could not make out the words. Meanwhile, the woman continued weaving her way slowly toward them across the field, like a wraith. She cut through the armed men and women as they began lining up in formation. For what? There was no time to dwell on this. Everyone's dataphone beeped simultaneously—another bulletin.

> Effective 11:00 a.m. today, all residents are asked to remain indoors while the town perimeter is secured and a house-by-house inspection is conducted to identify and isolate active virus infections. Your cooperation is appreciated. All violators will be apprehended immediately.

Piper Madrigal
Public Health Police Magistrate
MEPA Administrator
Township of Canary, Maryland

Rags thought fleetingly of Flint, but she knew he'd be fine. He had all the data they could want, and he was in full compliance—for now. If he ventured back out late at night, that was on him.

"Shit," Roger said. "We should get back."

"No," Rags said sharply. "If you want to learn how they got to Jaxson, you'll come with us." Roger and Tim exchanged a look. The group stayed together, backtracking with Evelyn along the footpath that led out to the street, and then two blocks over to her house. They were silent the whole way. There was too much to think about.

They entered Evelyn's dark, barren parlor and stood there expectantly. Evelyn made no move to act hospitably.

"Hurry up, Merry," Rags said.

Merry stood apart from the others, trembling. "They told me the only way to keep Tiffany safe was to run the ads in the paper. They told me exactly what to write and how to lay them out."

"This makes no sense," Tim said.

"The ads gave the kidnappers instructions," Rags said. "They contained hidden clues about dates, times, and places. Not just here in Canary, but in towns all over." Merry nodded. At last, Rags had a full picture to explain Merry's odd behavior since the day she first walked into the office of the *Courant* and Merry had radiated a defensive wariness. "And they gave you all the copy about Effie, didn't they? So it looked like the paper was covering the story, when actually it was just a cover-up. What a fucking nightmare."

"You said it's not just Canary—the ads," Keller said, his voice shaky. "So this is happening in other places? More kids are being taken? Merry didn't know that. Did you?" He put a hand on her shoulder. She shook her head, tears running down her cheeks.

"All I know is," Merry said, looking directly at Evelyn, with a hint of the old fierceness in her voice, "I would do anything to keep my child safe. Anything. And so would you," she looked at Tim and Roger now, "given the chance."

"Hello?" The young woman who had followed them from the athletic field walked in through the open front door and into the parlor, her voice weak and breathy. She was tall and dangerously thin and coughed almost continuously. She held a white cloth balled up under her arm. Merry looked at the young woman and then crumpled to the floor in a heavy heap. "Mom!" The young woman kneeled by Merry. "Could you get her some water, please?" No one moved until finally Tim muttered under his breath and went into Evelyn's kitchen to find a cup. When he returned, Merry was trying to sit up, staring at her daughter.

"Tiffany," Merry said, reaching out to touch her daughter's cheek to make sure she was real.

"Mom, what are you doing here?" Tiffany spoke in a whispered rush. "Are those people with guns coming to take everybody away? I thought I escaped. I thought I was home. I thought it was over. But it isn't over, is it? It's not safe here. It's not safe anywhere. We have to go. Where can we go?"

Tiffany was wracked by a coughing fit. Afterward, she sat on the floor, flushed and spent, her eyes closed. Rags, along with everyone else, simply stared at her. Merry stared too, gripping Tiffany's hand tightly, as if to keep her with her always. After a long silence, Tiffany spoke again, barely above a whisper. "Effie called them the sadists."

"Effie?" Evelyn cried out. "Did you see Effie? Where is she?" Evelyn tugged on Tiffany's thin arm. "Why isn't she with you? Why didn't you bring her?"

"Don't you fucking touch her!" Merry roared, practically throwing her body across her daughter's.

"What about Effie?" Evelyn said.

"Iphigenia," Tiffany said, smiling, her eyes still closed. She held the white cloth in her lap. Rags saw that the cloth had black writing all over it. "I poisoned them," she said. "The ones with the guns. No, I mean the sadists. You should poison the others. Out there. I can teach you." Rags thought the girl, who looked to be about nineteen or twenty, was probably feverish, as her thoughts seemed to be wandering.

"What...about...Effie?" Evelyn repeated in a shaky voice.

"She needs rest!" Merry said. "I have to get her home." Merry struggled to her feet and gently tried to get Tiffany on her feet too. But she was too weak.

"I'll help you," Rags said. "But we need to hear the truth, Merry. We all need to hear what Tiffany has to say. We may never get another chance. We don't know what's going to happen...tomorrow, or the next day."

"We need to know how to help Jaxson. How to find him," Roger said.

Tiffany shook her head. "Don't know about Jaxson."

"What can you tell us?" Rags said.

"Go easy!" Merry said, flashing the anger Rags expected from her.

Tiffany lay Effie's bedsheet diary (her second, and the only one to survive) on the floor and unfolded some of it. She ran her hand across the dirty, ragged-edged sheet, covered in smeared black Sharpie pen, the lines running across the width of the sheet and vertically along its edges.

"Effie gave it to me," Tiffany said. "The night before she—"

"Before what?" Evelyn said.

"She made me promise that if I made it back, I'd give it to you." Tiffany held up the sheet toward Evelyn, who took it from her, crumpling it against her chest. Evelyn pushed her mask up and buried her nose in the sheet, as if to capture Effie's scent.

"What happened?" Roger asked. "Where were you? Where do you think they took Jaxson?"

"She doesn't know, Rog," Tim said. "She can't tell us. Nobody can."

"They put us in the factories," Tiffany said, only managing

short bursts between bouts of coughing. "To work. All the time. Nobody else left. That's why. The fibers got in my lungs. At the textile factory. They move us around. Effie gutted chickens. That's where we met. Before that, she gutted crabs."

"My God," Rags said. "They used you as slaves. They trafficked you." Tiffany nodded. "That's what they did to you. Effie and Jaxson too. And who knows how many others."

"A network? A ring? A syndicate?" Piers asked, looking at Rags.

"Jaxson could be anywhere," Roger said. "Doing anything. Any dirty job."

"Our poor, bright boy." The two men leaned into one another, full of sorrow.

"They work us until…until we can't," Tiffany said. "Then they bring in others. So many. Just like me."

"Effie," Evelyn said.

"She didn't make it," Tiffany said. "I'm sorry. That's when I knew. I had to go. Or I'd be next. I said to her, hang on, but—"

Evelyn released a high-pitched keening sound and fell to her knees. No one tried to silence her. Nor did they comfort her. Her grief was too big to be contained. Tiffany didn't explain how she'd found her mother, but Rags supposed she'd used Merry's dataphone account to summon a ShareCar once she got near Canary, which also provided GPS coordinates to Merry's location, or close to it. As to where she'd actually been, and how far she'd traveled, that would have to wait.

Evelyn cried into the sheet.

"My baby," Merry said, cradling. "You're home. I can't believe you're home." Rags could not get used to seeing Merry this way. But she had to admit that this might actually be a rare bright spot, something good amid all the shit going down.

"It doesn't feel like home," Tiffany said, tears sliding down her cheeks. "Not anymore."

29

Rags left them all behind and went straight to the *Courant* office. She knew what was coming and it infuriated her that no one else seemed to see it too—or maybe they just didn't care. New quarantine orders. Door knocks. Jackboots patrolling the streets. Curfews. Followed, quite possibly, by the rise of a ruthless black market, as everyone who did not want a light to shine on their bartering business, or to pay for the privilege of trading, would head underground. Piper would rule the streets and Terry would control the purse strings, with an able assist from Missy. Rags guessed that Keller had probably had enough of them—and they of him.

Meanwhile, there was still not even a whiff of proof that the old virus had re-emerged or worse, that a new strain was spreading, for which there was no vaccine. The mere *idea* that this was possible was so powerful it could be wielded to manipulate people, just as Piper was doing. Rags refused to concede that Piper was acting on principle, that he truly put community health ahead of everything else. No. Piper needed to feel important, as did most PHPs. It was an intrinsic flaw in the position and the people it attracted. Dictators were not motivated by altruism, quite the opposite. And they did not spring up into positions of power—legitimate or not—when things were going well. And things in Canary were not going well. The Luckies were drifting, numbly, unsure of what or who to believe in.

By the time Rags reached the office, she knew what she had to do.

First, the *Canary Courant* had to be destroyed. She was going to put out one more issue, all by herself, with no advertising. In it, she would share everything she knew about Effie Rutter, and about Tiffany and her reports on the labor camps. And she would try to connect the dots between Piper and the council, and what it all meant. She would point out that they fired Piers Olsson in order to bring in someone they could control, giving ordinary citizens no recourse to seek justice or legislative changes outside the new triumvirate taking shape. Whether or not any of this persuaded anyone in Canary to form some kind of resistance movement was beyond her control.

Once the final issue was sent to the press, she would destroy all of the newspaper's templates and digital files, the phone numbers and instructions for transmitting the composed paper for printing, and even the historic masthead itself. This century-old instrument of democracy had been weaponized by people beyond her reach. At least she could destroy the weapon itself. Canary would survive without a newspaper, especially one that was a vehicle for information that endangered children. It was too late for Effie Rutter, but maybe not too late for Jaxson Turner. Tiffany's return suggested that it was possible, at least sometimes, to escape the clutches of occupational slavery.

And that led Rags to the second thing she was going to do—or at least, try to do. She would become a freelance journalist with one assignment: to find and expose the people who were trafficking children. She would go out to the presses and watch who picked up the extra copies of the *Courant* on its last run. She would begin hunting for news stories all over the country about missing teenagers, and then pounce as quickly as possible on the evidence, such as strange phone calls to distraught parents, florid ads in other local newspapers. None of this would be easy. She'd need to find allies along the way. And find a way to eat too. But she couldn't imagine doing nothing. Or doing anything else.

She didn't see how she could do this and stay with Flint. They were already coming apart at the seams, and now she felt that seam ripping wide open. They had come together at the height of an extraordinary crisis. Now that it had passed, the stakes had shifted for each of them. They looked out on different horizons. She sensed an ending, and she thought that Flint did too. But she also sensed a beginning. The post-pandemic world would continue to unfold in many directions at once—many of them troubling and disheartening, she imagined. She had to counteract even just a fraction of that negative energy.

Over the next few days, Rags and Flint finished saying all that they had to say to one another. Flint told her he was returning to the city. She made him promise he would not revert to his old ways, that he would seek out others, and continue looking for people he could trust and hopefully, to love. He wished the same for her. At night, in bed together, they held one another, memorizing the feel and smell of skin, the angles and curves, the way their bodies still fit together, after everything.

Rags had three stops to make on her way out of town. She was traveling more lightly than ever, not quite sure where she was heading or what she might need. She carried nothing but a backpack with some clothes, a tablet and dataphone, and a couple of notebooks. She stopped first at Louisa's, to say goodbye and to return the painting of the Potrero Complex. She knew Flint hated to let it go, but in the end, he did.

"Stay," Louisa said. "We'll get through it."

"Come with me," Rags said. "You can paint portraits of all the missing children I find. And their parents. So many people in crisis."

Louisa smiled. "Sorry. I belong here. I have to stay. Maybe I'll even find a way to be useful."

"You mean, like, joining the Resistance—if there is one?"

"Yes," Louisa said. "Probably."

Rags was encouraged by this and almost wished she could stick around to see Louisa become a bad-ass. But she couldn't. They hugged and Rags left the Louisa Copperface gallery empty-handed, with nothing to remember Louisa by except her memories of vivid abstract paintings, entangled sculptures, and the immortal faces of Effie and Jaxson.

She went to find Piers. He came to the backdoor of the peacekeeper's building, clean-shaven, his eyes looking much clearer than she'd seen them. Even his jeans and T-shirt appeared clean.

"Well, look at you," she said.

"For Effie's funeral," he said. "I figured I'd make an effort."

Rags was about to head to Evelyn Rutter's herself. She hadn't expected Piers to bother. They walked over together, cutting back and forth across as many side streets as possible to avoid getting stopped by Piper's thugs, who were now officially called MEPA officers. On the way over, he told her that he had resolved to find a way to make a stand.

"I grew up here. Canary is better than this. It has to be."

"What will you do?" Rags asked.

"I don't know yet, Rags. But I'm going to watch them, all the time, and wait for my chance. And…I'm gonna stay clean too."

"You mean, you have a reason."

"Yeah, now I do. A new reason."

When they arrived at Evelyn's, a very small group of people were in the small backyard. Without a body, the funeral was symbolic. And Evelyn had clearly decided she didn't need consecrated ground to say goodbye. Merry and Tiffany were both there, surprisingly. Tiffany leaned against her mother. She looked awful. Rags didn't think she would make it, but she was here now, and clearly that's all Merry could have wished for.

Evelyn said a few words, crying as she spoke. She hammered a small white cross into the ground and tied a yellow ribbon around it. She laid both of Effie's pom-poms near the cross, one pristine, the other battered.

Rags felt Maya's presence next to her. "Ragamuffin," Maya said. Rags could hear her so clearly, her high-pitched sixteen-year-old voice. "You don't make the rules you know," Maya said, "who lives, who dies. It's not up to you. Bossy-pants." *I know, but there are always exceptions that prove the rule. You should've been an exception.* Rags pictured Maya shrugging in her yellow sweatshirt. "Now go do what you have to do," Maya told her. "And cut yourself some slack."

Rags felt an urgent need to be gone, to put Canary behind

her and start doing something that mattered. She lifted a hand to Piers and turned out of Evelyn's yard. She hoped that someone had had the good sense to finally switch off Effie's digitally beaming face with the sunburst tattoo, so the girl could finally get some peace.

ACKNOWLEDGEMENTS

I am deeply grateful to Philip Feldman for sharing insights about the software developer's mindset and work habits, and for providing the basis for Flint Sten's ideas about machine learning. I am also grateful to Kelley Berliner with The Archaeological Conservancy in Frederick, Maryland, for invaluable information and photographs pertaining to protected Indigenous sites. I have taken liberties with the information they provided, including fabricating some details. Any factual errors or distortions are entirely my own.